PRAISE FOR *Gus in Bronze*

"In a clear, often poetic, and even authoritarian style, Miss Marshall explores the intricate feelings, the small but essential epiphanies of trust and care, which constitute and sustain love and therefore life itself . . . Above all, this is a story about the small, strange, and important ways people have of expressing love."
— *Christian Science Monitor*

"It reduced me to tears at least once every ten pages. Miss Marshall has the essential novelist's gift . . . the creation of vivid characters . . . *Gus in Bronze* is a *Love Story* about grownups, written by someone with a grownup mind."
— **Katha Pollitt,** *New York Times Book Review*

"A poem of a book. A perceptive, ineffably touching, heartwarming story . . . What surprises most is the humor that arises out of the knowingness of marriage and family life. I loved it!"
— **Martine Latour,** *Mademoiselle*

"Moving . . . written with insight and sensitivity."
— *Columbus Dispatch*

"A book you will read with wonder and respect."
— *The Real Paper*

"Very touching, always straight-to-the-gut . . . a novel that cannot help but move readers."
— *Publishers Weekly*

"A lesson about living-in-dying patinaed in gold leaf . . . often catching a little sweetness, a little light."
— *Kirkus*

"This is a most moving book, spare and taut, peopled with characters one cares about, dramatic and understated."
— *Chicago Daily News*

"Rather beautifully done . . . successful in portraying the impact of death on the living."

— *Houston Post*

"A tearjerker, but there is no mawkish sentimentality here."

— *Booklist*

"Perhaps Alexandra Marshall, in her first novel, has done too good a job of telling the story of Gus, her husband and children, who lose so much so unfairly, but with grace."

— *Detroit Free Press*

"Alexandra Marshall has written a beautiful, tender novel."

— *News & Leader*

"This one will make you cry. Not from any maudlin, soap-opera quality — that, which so easily could have been the tone of the novel, is missing. Instead there's a real sense of real tragedy and pain experienced in the way honest people act."

— *Sunday Oklahoman*

GUS IN BRONZE

Alexandra Marshall

Gus in Bronze

A Mariner Book
HOUGHTON MIFFLIN COMPANY
BOSTON · NEW YORK

First Mariner Books edition 1999

For information about permission to reproduce
selections from this book, write to
Permissions, Houghton Mifflin Company,
215 Park Avenue South,
New York, New York 10003.

Grateful acknowledgment is made to the following
for permission to reprint previously published
material: Harcourt Brace Jovanovich, Inc., and
The Hogarth Press Ltd.: Excerpts from Between
the Acts, Three Guineas, and The Years by
Virginia Woolf are reprinted by permission of the
publishers and the Author's Literary Estate.
Copyright 1937, 1938, 1941 by Harcourt Brace
Jovanovich, Inc. Copyright renewed 1965, 1966,
1969 by Leonard Woolf. Macmillan London
and Basingstoke Ltd.: Excerpts from Poetical
Works of Matthew Arnold, 1822–1888.

Library of Congress Cataloging-in-Publication
Data is available.
ISBN 0-395-92490-1

Printed in the United States of America

QUM 10 9 8 7 6 5 4 3 2 1

For Elizabeth McDowell Marshall

*And with grateful acknowledgments
to Nancy Nicholas*

Splendor! Immensity! Eternity! Grand words! Great things!
A little definite happiness would be more to the purpose.

— *Madame de Gasparin*

GUS IN BRONZE

Chapter One

D aphni insisted to her mother that Nicky would need the head when he got lonely, growing up. She said nobody was thinking of poor Nicky, or of what it would be like for him to grow up without a bronze head of his mother to stroke and consult. "You have no idea," Daphni pressed, "the way I do. I mean Nicky just has to have somebody, Mum, when you come right down to it. And well, as I said yesterday, think it over a lot. I just would hate for you to have regrets about poor little Nicky, even though of course I'll be doing all I can for him, which you can bet on, to provide sort of a normal childhood and all. Won't we all, I mean. Have you thought it over?"

"Not yet."

"Well I mentioned it to the nurses, which I hope was okay, and they say it's not too unsanitary or anything to bring clay into your room. I believe it's sterilized clay too, in a way, that Jackson uses. At least I know it's not just mud or pure earth."

"I don't think it's a question of germs."

"Well me neither, but I thought I'd bring it up."

Gus lowered the top third of her electric hospital bed and tucked a pillow under the small of her back while she spelled l-o-n-e-l-y, b-r-o-n-z-e, and s-t-e-r-i-l-i-z-e-d, spelling the pain's duration with held breath and behind closed eyes. "Please don't sit on the bed just now, Daphni," she said gently, "and see if I can have more ice."

"I understand, and gladly for the ice." Into the breast pocket of her jacket went the pen she had been fooling with in imitation of the doctor who fooled with pens between cigarettes. "Too bad my jacket's only beige," Daphni muttered, "but be right back." She picked up the milky plastic cylinder and briskly left her mother's room, the door hissing shut on her cheerful greeting to an ambulatory patient, her favorite, called Mr. Baum.

Gus let her legs fall from bent to straight and turned out as if unhinged from the hip, as if her legs were shutters being opened to let in light and air. That turnout was left from when Gus had danced for Martha Graham something more than fifteen years earlier, before Daphni was born, when turnout meant working at the barre in plié sequences, rather than the voter turnout it meant that day, Election Day, on which she lay ruined in a private room, her midsection from stern to sternum a complete loss. The trouble was, Gus admitted to herself, that Daphni was selfish but might be correct.

Nicky was only a baby, and though younger than her cancer was, he was growing of course just as furiously. One moment Gus wept with love for him, and the next with grief over her ambivalence. Did she owe Nicky her head in bronze by way of atoning for having given birth to him? But then did she dare leave her head behind for him to curse? Or love him enough to be glad he would have other mothers?

The hospital white was made pearly by the queer low-beam

neon fixture whose string switch Gus held by the tin Chinese hat on its very end, the kind of pearly that is greenish, and her legs hardly had form under the sheets. Wasn't there such a thing as an amputee from the breastbone down? They could balance her on a pedestal they could cover up with bishop's robes and cardinal's cloaks, and who would know? They could nail all her organs to the base and roll her around like an I.V. pole, life on wheels, and she could smile and wave and give a proper benediction. Then they could stick the bronze in her place, and who would know? On her day off they'd stick the bronze in her place for Nicky to consult, growing up, Nicky who would prefer the bronze to her because it wouldn't be malignant. Gus pulled the string twice, and it went bright and then went off. The light from the bathroom, coming feet first, was a sunnier color and showed up her legs turned out in that creditable first position. It was only that now if she pointed her toes, her legs would cramp first in the arch and then in the calf and then in the turned-out tops of her thighs.

When Daphni returned, Gus asked her to see where Maya was to find out if Maya wanted to take a homework break. "But don't make it dramatic," Gus instructed, "just ask her if she feels like it, and sweetie, I'd like you please to get started on your homework too."

Daphni didn't like reminders that she wasn't on the hospital staff but was only a visiting ninth-grader. "Must you be so condescending, Mummy? I'm able to care for myself, you know."

"I know."

"I'm sorry." Daphni put her hands on her mother's feet. "Papa told me this morning when I made Nicky cry that I am a brat."

"I'm sure he meant to say only sometimes."

"No, I've been bad all day, and I'm sorry, but can't you tell me something that I can tell Jackson?"

"Daphni, all you can tell him is that I haven't decided yet."

"But couldn't you meet him? Could I tell him that?"

"Not yet, and there's nothing more to say."

"Dammit! Everything in this place takes so long!" Daphni pressed the top of her ball-point pen to make the writing tip move in and out continuously, the clicking ticking fractions of seconds off. "Dammit, Mummy!"

"A better use for that pen would be homework."

"I'm going." Daphni stuck the pen, and it held, in her hair, a trick only she and her father could do with their Byzantine waves and a skill Gus had coveted, she who had received from her mother and handed down to her own second daughter, Maya, a long thin braid. "Okay, I'll tell her."

Maya brought in the Aperture Monograph whose black tones she'd been studying in the solarium's vinyl-covered aluminum bamboo furniture that was too deep for children. What she admired, she guessed, was the pain, Eugene Smith's pain and the purest blacks ever reproduced as symbols for the pain he knew and saw and caught; no grays. Smith's subject was grief.

"Daphni said to tell you she's gone to look at those poor emergency victims all bloody."

"I wanted to ask you something, Maya. Whether or not you think I'd like Jackson."

Maya sat in the padded reclining chair and raised the foot end to bring her boots three feet off the ground. The boots were fashionable Frye's but scuffed and wrinkled. "I guess," said Maya. "Though I can't say his class is great or anything, not like Daphni does. Jackson's okay, and he shows us his heads, which are okay too. Which are good, I should say. If you don't like the clay, you could always tell him don't bother in bronze."

Gus deliberated admitting to Maya how boring the mornings were. "Would the project be a waste of my time?" she asked instead, and then, seeing how she'd turned it around, added, "Not that this whole time isn't a waste."

"Well his classes do go fast, I must say, and he tells corny jokes that speed things up."

"Do you think you'd like to have a head?"

"I have all these pictures I took of you, Mom, but I'd like it if he got you right." Tears were boiling up and over. "Can I get you something?"

Gus extended her arm, and Maya stood to be in its circle. She bent for her mother to kiss her hot face, and Gus whispered, "Perhaps I ought to sleep. If you like, stay and read."

Maya stayed and read the photographs in the room in which everything was white, except for the busy chintz curtains behind her. except for the vinylette easy chair in which she sat, except for the flowers. She looked up from Smith's black to her mother's white, and back and up until it was certain that grief is white sheets and bedframe and wall and ceiling and hospital nightgown and arms and face, and that still-life is Gus's mouth framing words that don't have voices anymore. Grief isn't in black, standing up, but a woman who mutters inaudibly, lying down in white. Pain is white, it is black, it is thirteen years old. Maya thought she would boil and freeze to death if something didn't happen fast.

What happened was that Andreas arrived and brought violets, and that Gus whirred her bed to an up position.

"Hello, Gussie." He kissed her mouth. "How do you feel?"

"Oh, stable, as always."

"Quote unquote, right, Mom?" Maya smiled shyly at having a joke with the adults and reached with her arms for her father's hug.

"That's right." Gus sighed. "Derby hasn't been in today, and no one's told me how my blood was this morning."

Andreas sat on the bed and stroked her arm. "Did you go to treatment?"

"All morning. The attendant was a Filipino just arrived who, if in fact he could speak English, refused to admit we were lost. He wheeled me all over the place trying to get from up here to underground on the Broadway side, and then when we finally made it there and back, the nurse screamed at him that it was eleven in the morning and the patient had missed lunch. She told me in this furious hiss, 'And that's why there's unemployment, all those damn foreigners getting jobs. You must be furious.' No, I wasn't, I said, only tired. I work with foreign students, I told her, and I'm married to one. She said, 'But he's sweet and speaks English your husband. It's those others that are wrecking things here if you want my opinion. Now I'll get the medication you missed, my dear, and the lunch I saved you. First up we go, that's right, feel better?' "

"Gosh," Maya said sadly.

Gus smiled. "And then I had one of those quick unsedated dreams, of beautiful horses with silky blond tails arching up from glittery buttocks. And the steaming hay-flecked stones dropping down on me as I lay on my back on our living-room rug. Then the nurse brought in the medication."

"What a bad dream, Mom."

"It was." She stopped. "But what's it like outside?"

"Election Day," Andreas answered, "leaflets all over and me thinking how if I'd gone back to Greece I'd not have been able to vote in all these years. So I voted early, had no lines, and then we had a partners' lunch to vote on the associates for partnership. The only one I know for sure got in was my favorite at the firm, that young man who helped on the oil spill this year."

"Frank? How nice."

"Frank. He's working with me on the Boston collision. The trial date's been set for a week from today."

"Will you win, Daddy?"

"We have to meet so the damages can be assessed and responsibility allocated. My client was probably more responsible for the collision."

"Your client's guilty? How awful."

"No, sweetie, it's somewhat more complicated." He looked to Gus.

"Go ahead," she said.

"Briefly: one of the ships of one of our clients collided with another one which happened to be Greek."

"Your father would love it"—Gus laughed—"your representing Americans."

"The Americans did it on purpose?"

Andreas wished he'd not mentioned the trial, or that Maya'd gone to fetch ice. "No, they simply collided off Boston, and the Greek interests are suing, and the trial is in Boston, and the Greek company wants to collect for its damages. They were at fault too to a certain extent, so it's a question of how much and then how much money."

"I'm always sorry when there are collisions. I guess it's very sad being a boat lawyer, isn't it? Let me get ice for our drink, okay?" Maya patted her father on the shoulder.

"Actually," Andreas explained, "it's routine in admiralty law."

"Oh good." Maya left.

"It could have been one of your father's ships if this were years ago, so be grateful for not having to explain conflict of interest to Maya."

"Is she interested?"

"I think she wants to believe that what you do is romantic. She wants to know and doesn't yet want to. Perhaps you should tell about crimes at sea: theft, murder, hijacking, abduction, assault and battery." Gus kissed his hand. "I'm not sure towage fee controversies are what interest someone who's thirteen."

"Perhaps a stowaway case?"

"Better. How are things at home?"

"Could be better." He'd taken off his jacket and was rolling up his sleeves. "Is Daphni pressing you?"

"Hard. It's Jackson and Nicky, and what should I do?"

"It's a schoolgirl crush on the art teacher, and don't think about Nicky either because Daphni surely isn't."

"How is he?"

"On one verge or another every minute: fever, tears, hysteria, laughter. He sleeps in our bed now, talks in his sleep, and hates being alone. He wants you to know he seldom wets, and he wants to know if you'll color with him."

"What's he saying in his sleep?"

"I don't think it's English he's saying it in. I wish they'd allow him to visit just once so he knows where you are. Maya's pictures don't help, since all he can see is that you are in bed. When he's sick, he says, he stays home in bed."

"And colors."

"And colors." Andreas sighed. "You're right, Gus, a patient shouldn't be thirty-nine but ninety-three, so all your children are in their sixties, which make your grandchildren in their thirties, so that only the youngest great-grandchildren are too young to visit. By then who cares? Is that his postcard?"

Gus had a collection from all the places she'd ever been, and she sent one to Nicky every day she wasn't home. That day's was of a flamenco dancer from Seville, flouncing her tulle underskirts knee-high and arching impossibly. "*¡Hola* Nicky!" she'd written. Andreas slid it into his shirt pocket.

"Here comes the ice!" Daphni announced, barging past Maya. "Martinis? Hi, Papa."

The ritual was one drink together and then Gus and Andreas alone for time to congratulate each other on the day's having passed. The girls, after one ginger ale's worth of chat, would go pick out their dinner from under the infrared lights in the hospital's basement cafeteria: grilled cheese and apple pie for Maya, a salad for Daphni, who, though she hated ice-

berg lettuce, despised whatever else there was and especially
that which was infrared-warmed.

But Dr. Derby, it seemed, always came just as Gus and
Andreas got going, arriving with the metal clipboard labeled
KALIGAS, AUGUSTA, written in Magic Marker on masking tape.
He'd give Andreas an "If you don't mind" nod and sit in a
heap in Andreas's chair. Andreas gone, he'd pass the time by
saying what a day it had been and looking crumpled, and
then by pressing around Gus's middle to see if anything didn't
hurt. Sometimes he'd interpret her blood for her, and sometimes he wouldn't. He'd always say her food intake was good
and never ask if the pain medication they had her on was still
sufficient.

"Good evening, Augusta," he said, nodding over his glasses
to Andreas, who rose to shake hands, shook, and was nodded
out. "Your dark-haired daughter accosted me with a good idea,
and how are you feeling?"

"Fair. Which idea?"

"Of spending your mornings as a model, which never oc-
curred to me, frankly, as therapy, but it's a darn fine idea I
agree. Occupational therapy picks up the spirits. She has my
full approval, I said. Who's the artist?"

"Just Daphni's art teacher, who does bronze on the side."

"Well, I fully agree."

"I have not yet decided to do it or not."

"Let's just see how you're doing." The doctor's hands ex-
plored the masses, but he said nothing.

"Why am I swelling?"

He concentrated. "Do you feel pain here?" He was high on
the right side.

"Yes," she gasped.

"Here?"

"Yes."

"Or here?"

"Yes!" The only part that didn't hurt was the left side around the plastic bag she'd voided into since the colostomy. She guessed there wasn't a tumor there, only plastic and excrement. Anyway, the heavy, black, greasy lines told her that. They marked off the areas being beamed in on back- and frontside, and she who'd been onstage a lot surely knew how to read them.

Andreas intercepted Derby in the hall to ask how Gus was, but the answer was only "Stable," as always, after which the doctor wished Andreas a pleasant evening, again as always. Andreas, who was sucking on a butterscotch candy for which he'd traded in cigarettes, bit the butterscotch to smithereens. Gus was as stable as the Rock of Ages. He bit the butterscotch to dust. If so stable, then how come she was dying? But the doctor had walked to the end of the hall.

Following, Andreas told himself that Derby was manly in the old style of smoking cigarettes and being evasive and aloof, whereas he himself was manly in the new style of not smoking and being direct and warm. But his arms hung like braids as he stared through the picture window of the nurses' station and watched the doctor disappear into the windowless little staff smoking room.

"Do you wish something, Mr. Kaligas?" the floor nurse asked, bustling past him with the contents of some errand. Andreas shuffled back down the hall to where his family watched the news.

Election night coverage was just beginning, and even though it was an off year, it was all there was in the way of news. The network got going with bingo-like scoreboards and called out the numbers for winners and losers, predicting outcomes on the basis of 2 percent tallies and "filling in" with media drivel until Andreas pressed the button and shut it out by remote control. They might tune back in for California, he suggested, though California would only be reporting after visiting hours and so what was the point. He suggested instead that Daphni and Maya take off again for the solarium and leave it at that.

"Gussie, is that guy telling you anything?" said Andreas after the girls had left.

"Nothing. Neither is the radiotherapist. That's one reason, I must say, for doing the head. I mean why should I die of boredom with all this cancer around? Death from boredom is so nineteenth-century."

"Is it?"

"I've no idea." Gus laughed thinly. "God, I'm restless."

"Do you have Jackson's number?"

"Tattooed on my arm from Daphni's needling, 'Mummy! Now this is his home phone, he told me! Now Mummy, you call him!' He teaches only the afternoon."

"You could have an interview."

"I suppose. Would you want me in bronze to lug around the rest of your life?"

"Gussie."

"I want to pretend I'm not getting worse, and so why the need for me in bronze? But I am, even if nobody will say it, nobody but Daphni."

"She's not saying that. What she's saying is that she's madly in love with a guy who makes heads."

"I guess. I guess I'm going to call him." Gus reached for the phone and dialed an exchange on the lower east side. When a voice answered, "Yeah," after one half-ring, she said, "Hello, is Jackson there?"

"Yeah."

"Then may I please speak to him?"

"Yeah, you are."

So this was the hero? Gus introduced herself and said she'd like to meet him and talk about a head.

"What time is it?"

"Now?" Gus looked at Andreas's watch and said about a quarter-past seven.

"I fell asleep. You want to meet now?"

"Why not come in the morning." Gus wondered at a hero who didn't know there were hours for visitors and hours not for them, and at a hero who slept through the evening news. "Come at ten."

"At ten in the morning?" He hardly ever woke before noon.

"That's right, and get off at Broadway and 168th, then cut through to the Fort Washington side. My room's the last on the right before the solarium, the seventh floor of Harkness Pavilion."

"This is tomorrow?"

"If you like, or Thursday."

"I'll try and swing it tomorrow."

"I wish I hadn't," Gus told Andreas once she'd hung up.

"How thrilling, Mummy!" said Daphni, predictably, when she was told. "I'm smothered with pride, and so will Nicky be. Let me show you his drawing so you can ask Jackson to comment. Don't say I helped him with the walrus part, promise, okay? Or with the signature of NIC." She rummaged. "I'll find it, but aren't we going to have so much fun?"

Gus marveled that Daphni was "womanly" beyond genetic feasibility, a queen from one of those claret-colored Romantic Periods, queen of hearts and a queen of passions and utterly audience oriented. A perfect first child, if Gus had read the psychologists right. But her child? It seemed that Daphni's personality was made of recessive genes, which meant that neither Gus nor Andreas had much to pass on of genes that carried hysteria. How then had Daphni made them dominant, not to mention domineering? Right there was a reason to study genetics if only Gus had all the time in the world. What was Daphni's question?

"I said aren't we going to have so much fun?"

"I hope so," said Gus.

"Well, here's that thing! You see the walrus? It's blue on account of the freezing water; clever, I think, but don't tell Jackson I thought of that. I've got to rush and tell Mr. Baum."

"And get to your homework."

"Right after, Mum."

Gus lowered the bed and released a cry that caught on a sob. Poor Mrs. Pargiter, dead in *The Years*. That poor frail woman dying from what was never named but what was probably. She was sure she smelled in Mrs. Pargiter's room the smell of. Gus remembered the words: "There she was—soft, decayed but everlasting, lying in the cleft of the pillows, an obstacle, a prevention, an impediment to all life." Then the woman was dead.

"Andreas, will you read to me please?" Gus was up to *The Years* from having begun with *The Voyage Out,* reading all of Virginia Woolf in order, with three to go before Woolf's own death. She was up to *The Years* but not up to it.

Andreas would read "1891," eleven years after the death of Mrs. Pargiter in "1880." As if Woolf had written on cellophane pages, the past seemed to be completely visible in the present. The characters grew old and remained the children they were.

" 'The autumn wind blew over England,' " Andreas read. " 'It twitched the leaves off the trees,' " and all over England, he read, the leaves blew, were burned so that the smoke blew. " 'The wind blew the smoke—for in every back garden in the angle of the ivy-grown wall that still sheltered a few last geraniums, leaves were heaped up; keen-fanged flames were eating them—out into the street, into windows that stood open in the drawing-room in the morning. For it was October, the birth of the year.' "

But Andreas read with an American accent. And Gus could well have read this part herself, since it was only Eleanor Pargiter sitting at her writing table working out sums. Andreas pronounced her "Allener" and not "Elinoor," which made listening to it difficult, no matter that if Andreas had gone to study in England, she'd never have met him, he'd never have been reading to her at all.

" 'Three times eight is twenty-four,' " Eleanor multiplied at her writing table. Her father was asking her to buy a little present for him for the birthday of her little cousin, his preferred niece. First an invalid's ceiling wanted mending, then Eleanor was coming back with the little necklace she'd selected. After a few more things, Gus could see, Eleanor and her father, the Colonel, would be presenting the little gift. Yes, there they were in the drawing room, the smoke from leaves burning in the garden blown in on the wind.

Andreas finished the section and Gus traced interlocking rings along her leg. Without taking her finger off the sheet, she retraced each ring to make the next, forming a spiral chain as organic as *The Years*. Gus was thinking of sad Eleanor.

"Darling, feel like talking?" Andreas asked.

"Maybe you could say something."

Andreas watched her retracing rings and tried to think of something cheering. "Christopher called last night and said that he and Susanna are getting a prize and coming east. Next week, he said. They're giving a paper and showing off some new operation right here in this hospital."

"But next week! I'll never be out of here by then."

"You don't have to be."

"But I *do*, Andreas. I told them last summer that we'd all go to that restaurant."

"Gussie, I'm sure they won't mind not going."

"But *I* mind; can't you understand that?" And then all the long day came trembling out, first her fear then her anger and then her pain. She was not getting better, but no one would say it. Again and again, fear and anger and pain. And, oh God, she was so tired. She loved Andreas. But getting lost on the way to treatment, and Daphni's insisting, and Derby's evasiveness, even the well-intentioned nurse, and then Jackson asleep. She was so tired. And she would have cried anyway, even without her brother coming next week and her not out, she was so tired. She loved Andreas.

Once he had seen his father weep, and for the same reason. His father the giant had wept himself to sleep like a child, complaining first of his fatigue (fear and anger and pain), and then shivering from being alone. The room had been white and he'd had to watch his father shiver in his sleep, the sobbing hanging like tapestries from the high white ceiling. He wished he might but hadn't dared do what he wished. Now Gus was shivering. Her sobs hung like banners while she slept beneath them and shook uncontrollably. Finally he dared do what he hadn't for his father: he climbed onto the hospital bed, under the sheet, and gave her his heat.

Chapter Two

A ndreas had just stopped playing and sat on the piano bench wondering what else to do with his restlessness until it was time to leave to pick up Gus when Nicky came out from his pillow nest underneath the baby grand. His face was crusty with dried lime-colored slime, and he was huffing breath in and out with cheeks that were two raspberry-colored hearts. His usually bright brown eyes were instead flat black, and he whined, "Paa, love and kiss," in a way that made Andreas ashamed once again that, once again, little Nicky had slipped his mind for a time, at least the part of Nicky that had the terrible cold had slipped it.

"Love and kiss, want you to."

"Poor Nic." Andreas opened his arms to the somnolent body, foul with diarrhea in the seat of the miniature Levi's, and crooned, "Poor Nic, I'm going to change you." He carried the damp limp child across the living room and down the hall to the changing table in Nicky's room. There were days when Nicky appeared to be toilet trained, days when he didn't. Whoever had first dressed him that morning had put him in double diapers for good measure. Still, the stuff was all over the place.

Andreas gagged. "Poor Nic," he said again, and turned away in order not to vomit on his own little boy. There was no point in making pee-yew jokes because those depended on Nicky himself holding his nose and laughing, shrieking "Fee-you Nic Da-ria," and Nicky was instead lying there as if anesthetized, with his tiny slippersocks in the air and his hands folded politely on his belly in an attitude of resignation. "Poor Nic," Andreas said yet again. He felt so guilty that his own child made him gag, as if Nicky were only equal to a family cat or dog; he felt so guilty that Nicky had slipped his mind the way a pet does when it curls up out of the way to sleep.

Andreas brought to the table a warm soapy washcloth and cleaned first the little sweating face, and then the bottom, which he creamed and powdered and wrapped again in doubled white cloth. "Ma's coming to love and kiss you too, Nic," he said, only Nicky was asleep.

After putting Nicky's rubber pants on him, Andreas carried the boy to his crib and put him down among the bears. Was there anything more moving than a child asleep? He would never again forget about Nicky, he promised he wouldn't. The palms of the little hands were upturned, the fingers curling over them like willows along the sides of ponds, and the love massed deep within his chest. He would always love their final child. The love rose and spilled from his eyes in tears.

Was there anything wrong? Her voice was so— "Naturally I'm upset, Andreas," Gus interrupted. "Of course I'm disappointed, Andreas." She doubted he could even find the damn thing. "Darling, I'll find something," Andreas assured her, "don't worry, Gussie." He hung up the phone and went to locate the long gray wool maternity jumper and the knee socks. He must tell the others not to be overwhelming about Gus's arrival, that she was upset, and he must find a sympathetic taxi whose driver would make an easy return. The jumper was likely to be around somewhere; she'd last worn it only three years before.

Gus disintegrated. She'd counted on the reassurance of wearing home what she'd worn to sign in, but tights were out of the question and the skirt didn't fit. In three weeks she'd become even more distended than she'd known, and she felt betrayed again by that body she grew to despise more each time it failed her. The whiteness of the flesh enraged her because it sheltered what she wished to strangle, smother, cut up, flush away. The flesh around her middle was *accommodating* the vilest life: make yourself at home. Not just sheltering, but receiving a stranger as if it were family: my home is yours. And she couldn't wear the skirt, and so she couldn't be wheeled to meet Andreas at the entrance. It was no use. Going home for a Sunday wasn't going to be exciting or even fun. She wouldn't be up to the celebration that had begun the previous evening with the resident's announcement that the doctor had said yes, when the girls had jumped all over the room with why didn't she *say* be*fore* that *may*be, when Daphni had begged, "Papa, let's *go get ready* and let Mummy *rest!*" Gus was exhausted.

"You kept a taxi waiting here while I got dressed! Then why didn't you say so? God, I can't stand it." She struggled from the wheelchair into the Checker cab. And all the way down and across New York, Gus went on complaining: New York was disgusting, New York was repulsive, she hated its guts.

"Gussie, what's the trouble?"

"It's not just a trouble," Gus accused. "It's not just troubling, Andreas, or too bad or unfortunate."

"What is it, Gussie?"

She held her breath to cut off the oxygen needed for sobbing, but the tears came pumping up anyway. "What *is* it, Gussie?" she heard him repeat. "You wouldn't know," Gus said bitterly, "how much this drive is killing me, or how I sit around that place and nobody tells me anything, or how I have to eat their disgusting repulsive food."

"What didn't they say, Gussie?" God, the pressure in his chest was awful, and he wanted only to watch the Central Park horses going clippety-clop.

"That there's more than before, don't you understand? That I'm puffing up like a—don't you *understand?*—like a—"

"Bullfrog?" And Andreas laughed, of all things.

"God damn you." But he couldn't stop laughing, and anyway, Gus realized, Andreas was right. It was like a bullfrog. She joined him, laughing, and said, "Like a bullfrog of all things. I'm sorry, Andreas. I love you."

"Here we are, sir," the taxi driver announced. "Need some help with the lady?"

Inside, no one spoke. They stood in a row and stared as if Gus were a ghost they shouldn't ask in. The girls wore dresses, matching ones that Andreas's mother had sent to them from Athens, on which Greek key embroidery ran from shoulder to modest knee hem and in which they looked awkward and unfamiliar. Nicky stared at the floor but gripped Frieda's hand. Frieda's eyes were on Gus and filled with pity for her dear old friend. Still nobody spoke. "Hello, everyone," Gus finally said, "remember me?"

Nicky flung himself against her shins and hugged her knees and cried, "Maa! Maa!" and wouldn't let go, so the others greeted Gus above him, Frieda last and longest. Then Gus put her hands on Nicky's head and shoulders and arms and rubbed the little frightened body until he let go and freed her legs. She sat down on the hall bench, wishing that she could kneel or take Nicky up in her arms, and Nicky stood between her legs and kissed her face as she kissed his three weeks' worth. Gus wept.

The trouble with Nicky was that during the pregnancy Gus hadn't known the discomfort was cancer. She'd thought it was only that she was pregnant at thirty-six and not twenty-three or twenty-five, as for Daphni and Maya. She'd thought it was tension, she'd thought her body was maybe too old, she'd thought it was because Nicky wasn't planned and she had thought of aborting him and thus felt guilty and thus, then, tension. She'd taken it easy on her digestive tract because the gas was uncommonly bad, but she'd thought she'd heard that tension settles in the colon sometimes or often. She hadn't known. And then the bleeding. Within a month after Nicky's birth, she'd begun to have rectal bleeding and much more pain, so she saw a proctologist who was dismayed at not having seen her much sooner. He was also dismayed to advise her that he'd recommend a colostomy, it was that bad. The trouble with Nicky was that he was both guilty and innocent.

"Come and play, Maa," Nicky coaxed, convinced that Gus would be home forever. "I miss you, look!" he said, showing her that on his elbow was a Band-Aid. "Kiss!" he insisted. She did. He shrieked, "Play!"

"In the living room, Nic." But it was no use. She could no more play with trucks on the floor than make love to Andreas with anything of the energy there had once been. It was all such a waste.

But their building was one that still allowed working fireplaces, and since the hospital signs warning DANGER: OXYGEN IN USE had made Gus yearn for conflagration, Andreas had built a fire for her. There were mums on the mantel and sun, though a thin November morning sun, coming in the big windows. Gus sat on the couch and asked Nicky to join her, suggesting that they might color together while she, on Daphni's instructions, would sink in and feel at home, drink espresso, and eat real toast made from Frieda's wheat-germ recipe. Pleasing everyone at once was what Gus had been so good at, and there was pleasure, a little at least, in that she still could.

But wasn't it funny, Gus said to herself, that Nicky and Daphni both looked like Andreas. And wasn't it funny that Maya was her, even to hair and nose and fingers, even to teeth. Do firstborn always rubber-stamp their fathers? Is it always only for the second that the female genes are organized and lobbying, petitioning for power? And the rhythm: does it always go male first, female second, male first, female second? Would she have had to have had a fourth to get another child like herself? Do male genes *rape* until the female genes have a chance to learn a martial art? How come she had two Byzantine children and one New England one? Was it perhaps that Maya was the one of the three who hadn't come by surprise attack?

"Mom's thinking, Daphni," she heard Maya say, and so Gus struggled back into presence and complimented Daphni on her fine espresso. "No she wasn't," Daphni told Maya, "she heard me ask."

"Darling, would you play something?" Gus asked Andreas, who'd never played more than in these last years, when he'd taken up, the way Gus had Virginia Woolf, playing Domenico Scarlatti, for time. He was playing for time the way Gus was reading, by having always unfinished business and thus a reason for Gus not to die. He was learning Scarlatti's 555 sonatas for harpsichord one by one and would be finished in six years.

Andreas sat at the piano and played Scarlatti, for which one always had to be agile though not necessarily gay, as he put it. Gus knew Nicky would dance if Andreas played, and she needed to get his weight off her legs as much as she needed to get him to stop bearing down so hard on his crayons, stop

tearing his papers and crying and making Gus want to scream
out loud. She wanted Nicky to dance and then collapse into
his morning nap. There had to be peace.

But Andreas finished and Nicky still seemed to be a con-
testant, so how about, Gus suggested to Maya, some *Mikro-
kosomos?* Maya loved Bartók and would have been willing to
play for a long time, except that her freshly washed hair kept
slipping out from under her purple felt hat and getting in the
way of her hands. "Dammit," said Maya when it happened the
fourth time. "Dammit, I knew I shouldn't have washed my
hair." But Nicky had rolled to a halt, on the floor, and after
covering him with her sweater, Maya announced, "That's that,
and now we can relax."

Frieda had been sitting on the floor knitting a sweater for
Nicky in stripes colored blood and grape and mud. She'd also
been studying Gus's face and felt sorrow and anger watching
Gus doze off and come back to a panic flutter while she tried
to get her bearings again. In her own practice, for Frieda had
been a dentist in Amsterdam until this past month, she'd say
right out that the teeth were rotten and had to go, and that
there would be pain. But Gus, Frieda knew, had too many
doctors, and since each wasn't sure what the other was saying,
nobody said much. The insecurity this created was terrible and
typical, and Frieda objected. Her doctors had made Gus an
adolescent approaching puberty, but with parents who had
never explained the facts of life. And why, Frieda sorrowed,
why don't those in a position to assure the normality of something, why don't they do it? Why don't parents demystify
puberty? Why don't doctors demystify death for their patients?
If doctors would only say, "X will happen because of Y, and
you will feel Z," Gus wouldn't have to be distracted by her
fears that it was not comprehensible, this thing happening to
her. She would be able to try and understand it as a *fact,* which
is indeed enough of a task. Frieda knew she wasn't the one to

say, "You're dying, Gussie," because Gus wouldn't feel she
was in a position to know. Perhaps Christopher and Susanna
would, perhaps Gus's brother and sister-in-law would finally
tell her. They'd certainly know, being doctors.

Gus started to laugh. She said to Frieda, "The girls didn't
share your opinion of that movie."

"We certainly didn't," Daphni asserted, "and we sure said
so. But we've got a little work to do beating egg whites and
so on, so you have your laughs and we'll be in the kitchen."

"Not yet," Maya said.

"Maya, we *agreed* that the three of them could be alone."

"I know."

"Well come *on*."

"For God's sake," Maya muttered, "that girl just can't relax
for a minute."

"I heard that," Daphni called over her shoulder. "I can *too*
relax, Maya."

Maya confided to the adults that Daphni was nothing but
a boss. "So I have to go now," she explained, got up, and left.

"It was so funny," Gus continued, "their telling us about the
movie. I'd said to Andreas that if you liked a cartoon about
marriage, it must be dreadfully pessimistic."

"It was." Frieda laughed. "I suggested they go see something
else, but they wanted to see what I'd found funny."

Andreas said he'd have sent them to a savage version of anything in order to buy time alone with Gus. "I amused myself
in the taxi by thinking I'd sent my kids to the movies as if Gus
and I were courting, but it was so nice to be alone, wasn't it?"

"We flirted. Frieda, you can't imagine; they're always there,
Daphni bearing down in that beige jacket and talking about
the hospital drama, and poor Maya sighing. It seems they
can't stand to miss a day, and I love their love, but I do
wish—"

"They didn't love you so much?" Frieda leaned on one

elbow and laughed, caw-caw. "One sure thing is they'll not go
again to one of my movies. They raged at me for having
missed an afternoon. It's the first time I ever saw Maya furious.
'Frieda,' she said, 'that ending was sick! That couple still
dressed up after the wedding playing slot machines at Las
Vegas, that's sick! That's *dreary*, Frieda!' "

" 'That's life,' did you say?"

"That's what I said. Maya said marriage wasn't dreary like
that and shut herself up in the bathroom to print that dreary
picture of you two, that stark one that seems to feature the
wrist I.D. and the I.V. pole."

"She brought it to show me last night. I didn't know what
to say." Gus finally felt she'd begun to relax for the first time
that day. "I've missed you, Frieda, missed all of your wonderful
negativism. They keep me so cheery up there, or try to. I
miss—"

"My bleakness?"

"That's what I miss."

Gus and Frieda had been friends for twenty-two years, since
the year Frieda came as an American Field Service student
from Holland to live during the school year with Gus and her
parents. Gus's older brother, Christopher, had spent that year
in the Korean War, putting all his medical training to no use
putting Band-Aids on the knees and elbows of servicemen's
children, and her older sister, Mimi, had gone off to try her
luck at college again. Frieda had become the sibling then, and
had been ever since, no matter that Frieda had suffered the war
in which all the rest of her family had been sent to the ovens,
while Gus had been a lucky seven whose father had sat at a
desk and decoded.

Since 1952, they'd had but twenty-one visits, the month of
August every year, when Frieda would join Gus at the Cape in
the house her parents had bought in the fall of the year Frieda

stayed. They should have had again that many months together.

Frieda sighed and picked up her knitting to knot on a
switch from grape to blood. Then her fingers flew into knit
and purl, and she looked up at Gus. She'd known in August
the odds were shifting. Gus had sat and read in the garden,
next to the dogwood they'd planted three years earlier to ac-
knowledge that the Wests were dead. And Frieda had seen a
second dogwood in Gus's place. She'd known in August that
she'd be coming back and had made arrangements for a sub-
stitute at the clinic long before Gus wrote that she was going
to be re-admitted. Of course Frieda would be the one to stay
and care for Nicky until the time.

"They tell me you're going to do the head."

"Let me tell you how the meeting went." Gus looked over
her shoulder to check that Daphni didn't hover. "Jackson's a
caricature just like Daphni's tennis player last summer, the one
with the vase-shaped forearms, or like the hockey player who'd
lost his front teeth and had his nose bashed. He's got a black
beard and wears wrinkled shirts, has sleep crust in his eyes and
teeth that haven't been brushed. An artist." Gus smiled.

"At first he sat there and wrapped his arms around his chest
as if he were in a china shop. You Break It, You Buy It. Terrified of ruining something or, rather, everything. I asked if
hospitals made him uncomfortable. 'Freak me out, I was in one
once.' So I asked what for, and you know what he said? For
the birth of his son."

Caw-caw, laughed Frieda, rolling back again onto her elbows and pushing the knitting away with her foot.

"Well he'd brought these snapshots, apologizing that they
weren't good before he'd show them, and what a relief. I was
thinking his heads could only be monuments: Madame Curie,
the Virgin Mary, Martha Graham. But they're not, they're not

melodramatic at all; they're not even idealized. While I looked
at them he looked at me, then he said he liked that I wore a
scarf, the way the life in my face was forced to break from
under bald stretched fabric. I took it off and explained that I
only wore it to treatment to bring some color to radiotherapy,
and to cover the fact that I'd not lost my hair as so many of the
others have. He said he'd always loved red and yellow, or something inane, and then we were restless again for a while until
the phone rang."

"Me?" asked Andreas.

"You." Gus explained to Frieda, "Andreas called and Jackson took it because I was in the chair, not in bed. At the end,
Jackson said, 'Nice meeting you,' and turned puce, I think the
color is, then apologized for what we must think of his being a
teacher for our girls. Then he dropped the phone and said,
'You see?' And I was sold." Gus reached for her braid and
retied its ribbon. "I think he will make my mornings nice, as
long as things have to be this way."

The November noon light was trying to cover them all
with some faint proof that they existed in nature and might
have some protection finally, even if it might only be the
thinnest light from a near-winter sun, and even if it brought
no heat. There were only two noises: the fire behind Frieda
and Nicky's breathing, though they were not so much noises
as sounds.

Into their near silence Daphni boomed that she was furious
with them all for not being merry. She was on the run from
the kitchen to say that her soufflé was perfection and they'd eat
in ten minutes. "But pep up," she instructed, running out
again, "and, Papa, you know you're in charge of entertainment
whenever Maya's got to be in the kitchen. I can't do everything, you know!"

Frieda crowed until she fell off her elbows and lay spread-
eagle. "That's better!" Daphni yelled from the kitchen, which

made Frieda laugh all the more, joined by Gus and Andreas and even by Nicky, who staggered to his feet from underneath Maya's sweater and fell again on top of Frieda to laugh at the way her convulsing body bounced him around. "Pee!" he cried, however, and did.

"Oh well, let's change for lunch, Nicky," Frieda said, picking him up and taking him off as if he were a basketball.

Andreas admitted to not having remembered that Nicky was there all that time, or to remembering and then forgetting again. "I must think Nicky's a dog or cat," he apologized to Gus, who replied that she did too, sometimes.

"Sometimes," he continued, "unless Nicky imposes himself, I not only don't know if he's in the room, I don't remember that he was born. Do you think I want to forget he was?"

"Perhaps at times."

"Do you ever?"

"Only at the hospital sometimes, and only if I need to forget the past few years and pretend."

"I know. Skiing, for instance, and canoeing."

"Body surfing at the Cape, tennis. And most of all—" Gus stopped. "Andreas, afterwards will you promise to lie on top of me full weight?"

"After lunch?"

"After the end. Will you?"

"Yes, and how about after lunch?"

"I'm serious."

"And you know I would have anyway."

"I want to know for sure that you will."

"I promise I will, Gus. Darling, I promise."

"I'm sorry, I could have asked you later."

"May I ask you later about after lunch?"

"Do." But she knew it would be impossible. "I'm going to cry."

"To Cry, New York? Where Playland is?"

"I keep trying to be serious."

"I know, Gussie, but it's the day of rest."

"For God's sake, you two!" Daphni blasted. "And where're the other two? It's time to *get going! * Maya's camera's *ready!*"

"We'll go to Cry later," Andreas whispered to Gus, helping her to get up.

"The traffic might be bad." She kissed him.

"Then we'll stay home." And he kissed her.

"That's nice, and I hate to interrupt, but the soufflé, for God's sake! Can't you get a move on?"

"It's her Byzantine blood," Andreas joked. "Too many Turks hung around in Greece for much too long. I'm afraid the blood spoiled."

Gus wanted to say that made two of them, then. But she left their exit on his half joke. For once they hadn't taken her blood first thing that morning; maybe it was improved.

The seating had been carefully planned to put Maya the farthest away from Nicky. Maya sat, therefore, on Gus's right, Daphni on her left, and Nicky between Andreas and Daphni. Frieda took the leftover seat to the left of Andreas on Maya's right. The table was round.

There was talk about school and talk about work, and finally there was the toast to the Goose, which began with Andreas saying, always, "The first time I met the Goose was"—pausing and continuing—"at the Vatican." Frieda laughed; it was always some ridiculous place.

"The Pope"—and Andreas rose to go on—"the Pope had proclaimed that he'd heard of this modern thing called dance, to which his cultural attaché said then how about being an audience for once in your life. Okay, the Pope proclaimed in reply.

"So there I was lighting the spectacle candles when in ran this American wearing navy blue sneakers and little sweatbands on her wrists. '*Rosa, rosae, rosa, rosarum,*' she was saying, *'tubam, tubas, tubat.'* I muttered so she could hear, 'Excusing me, *signorina,* but you're new in town?'

"She wiped her brow with one of the terry-cloth wristbands and said, 'How the hell does the neuter go, *sonor?'*

"I told her I was taking offense at her language and *sonor* wasn't how it went either. If she needed a guide she should apply at the Vatourismo desk under the holy-water font.

" 'I hate this place,' she screamed, 'just look at these Kleenexes!' It was true that she hadn't known to cover her arms in the old days when you had to to go to Rome, not to mention the Pope, and she had Kleenexes paperclipped on to make sleeves of her funny little American sleeveless shirt with blue poodles printed there. 'What's your name?' I asked. She said she was embarrassed to admit that she was the famous Goose of world renown, since nobody'd told her about the sleeves and she didn't know neuter.

"But if you're working among holy presences, even if you don't know one when you see one, you at least know one when they say they are. So I got down on my knees and touched my forehead to her sneaker. She hissed, 'Get up, you fool, I'm an American! Just clue me in about the neuter.'

"A farmboy from Bologna who had something to offer the famous Goose of world renown? I said, *'Signorina,* it would be my very esteemed pleasure if only there were time. But these are the very spectacle candles I am alighting. The Pope in all his glory will arrive in a moment. *Signorina,* you are but a moment too late.'

"The Goose wept bitterly. 'Here I came all this way to dance for an elected official. I like saying things to elected officials, as it is our American way, and yet you're denying me the words, o young farmboy from Bologna, of which you are full.'

"So that made me mad, and I told her it was her own damn fault that she didn't know the Pope was neuter beforehand, since she had a whole ocean crossing to figure it out, while I myself had only been on the goat path between Bologna and Rome, Rome and Bologna until it was coming out of my ears, and *I* knew it, I knew the damn Pope was neuter for God's sake, I told her.

" 'Very funny, *sonor*,' the Goose said, and threw up all her tranquilizers right there in St. Peter's. 'But the hell with neuter! His Latin can't be so rusty that he's forgotten how to talk masculine and feminine in a pinch to foreigners. And hey *sonor*, do I have to leave my sneakers on?'

"The dancing was swell, and the Pope banged his rings together in clapping. After that, it goes without saying, we all lived happily ever after."

"Hold it!" Andreas was obliged to hold it every time so Maya could get a shot of that last line. Her feel for the decisive moment was poor because she, like the others, including Andreas, never knew ahead of time to expect the end.

"Papa," Daphni confided, "your stories are never realistic! And what's so happy about that ending? Honestly, Papa." And then she cooked up a toast of her own in order to detail what she'd have made for lunch if she'd had more time to plan. Sugared grapes and quail. Which reminded her to remind the others what she wanted for Christmas was a subscription to *Gourmet* and the ten-session course in haute French cooking for which she'd seen a magazine ad. And so it was a toast en gelée full of floating which and wherefore clauses.

But so what, thought Gus, so what if Daphni is a fool from time to time. In time perhaps that nerve of hers would knock them dead in the world out there, unless, that is, she took too much more after her aunt Mimi and ended up scattered as the hundred colored pieces of the plastic "village" Nicky played with in his room.

Nicky gave them a song, and Maya, who since his birth had avoided Nicky at all cost, even took his picture and gave him a smile. Beside the point to worry whether Daphni'd be able to hold herself together or end up like Mimi and worship only the great Californian here-and-now. Gus relaxed again—the day a series of drawings-up and lettings-go—and was thankful for the jungle of the sixties and the jangle of the seventies that had made of her grandmother's dining-room table a round space in which kidding was permissible. There had been some awfully quiet meals when Gus was a grandchild.

"To Nicky," Gus heard, and joined the others in a drink. But it wasn't so simple, it wasn't simply that Gus had been softened by Andreas and what he brought from the Mediterranean. True, her blood was Puritan shirt starch, but his was the still stiffer stuff of noblesse without the oblige.

He'd been raised in a damask-and-brocade town house, a crypt in which he was to read Corneille's *Le Cid* to learn of honor, to eat foie gras and nothing from an Athens street stall, to play Debussy or else be whipped in French by parents whose blood was Greek. "What's more Greek than ships?" he'd protested to his father, a radically successful builder of them. "And why then this ugly French furniture?" he'd challenged his mother as she sat and snacked on petits-fours in Coco Chanel's latest afternoon suit. He'd been lonely and chilled to the bone by their silence and by the emptiness echoing in the subculture grotto where all the money was Greek but all the manners French. They both had had to learn how to thin out their blood.

"To Gussie," she heard. How much she loved Andreas's stories of meeting her on the Amazon, at the Pyramids, in the sewers of Paris. How much she wanted only to lie down with him. She acknowledged the cheers, manufactured a yawn, and pushed herself back from the table. "Dessert!" gasped Daphni, rushing for the caramel custard and spun-lace cookies. Dessert was a blur, except that Frieda said when asked that the reason she was so quiet was that she was having a fine time.

In the large creamy room, Gus and Andreas were finally alone. There was a fireplace, and Andreas lit the fruitwood they had brought down from the Cape after the summer while Gus took off the knee socks she might have bought during college and the maternity jumper she had gotten to accommodate Daphni. Andreas undid the buttons he had done up that morning, covered buttons of pearly silk, and the blouse fell forward and inside out because Gus hadn't remembered to undo the cuffs. The greasy black lines on her back and front were nothing new and by then one of the details one takes for granted when one knows the behind-the-scenes, adhesive tape on a stage floor put there to get the actors into the light. The bag was no longer a shock; the belly had been swelled before. Gus stretched herself out on her side, blond limbs predominating, and watched Andreas undress.

It was as so many Sunday afternoons had been, when they'd build a fire in their dreamy room and lie down together. Andreas undressed as precisely as he always dressed, putting his things one by one on a polished mahogany rack day in and day out. He was unchanged after sixteen years and played squash to ensure it, registering only in his face that the years had been sieved through him. It showed in his face that he had three live children and a dead father, a wife for whom he suffered, along with whom he suffered and was made exceeding glad as according to Scripture, a mother he hardly knew to that day, work that irritated and enriched him, bored and absorbed him, an energy for living and a terror of death coming before he was finished (and even then, still), a faith, but this of such an ambidextrous nature that he could believe the Messiah had and hadn't come and would and never would again, a pride that willed him to mock himself occasionally to keep all this in balance (he was Greek and knew the hubris folklore), a superstitious inclination but a trust, a tone for melancholy and a flair for flourish, most of all for flourishing. His hair was long as vanity made men's hair long, and lustrous and luxuriant in ripples that were curly waves in undertow back from the wide stretch of his forehead. He was graying, as was Gus.

Amazing that she had been a dancer, Gus thought as she looked down her own body, amazing that once she had taken both such good and such bad care of herself. Dancers are hypocrites who will not move an inch until they are warmed up, but who then will perform on a torn tendon nonetheless if need be, dancing on tour on auditorium floors that are concrete under a splintery veneer of some impossible wood that tears up the feet like acid and makes leaps' landings fearful. Amazing that once her body had been everything, as during the summer of company apprenticeship when news of the inside world was all that mattered because newspaper headlines about Adlai Stevenson running against the General never reached her there at the barre where turnout was not voter but first position, second position, third, fourth, fifth; amazing that she had paid such extravagant attention to that body that lay distended on her bed. How mortifying that she had so lost touch that she hadn't felt those cells piling up, moving around and massing, and that—it seemed at least—she had been a dancer for nothing.

At the time Gus had felt that quitting would be all that would be painful about having danced, and it was plenty painful having her muscles contract back into themselves— aluminium drinking cups shrinking down to flat disks for the pocket—and cramping as they did in those searing cramps that would wake her out of sleep and send her cursing around the room like a lunatic, calling out to Martha Graham to re- move the curse which drove her even crazier than she'd been in coming to the conclusion that she lacked commitment to the nearly wholly difficult life. At the time Gus felt that once the cramping was over and she was stiff again like the rest of the world, no more pain would come from having danced, nothing at least like the pain there was in seeing that she hadn't been alert enough to know what was what and what wasn't when, fifteen years later, she'd thought that all she was was pregnant.

Andreas spooned her, kissing her shoulders and speaking love. It was magazine-muted in their own warm room with the fire flickering into romantic ceiling shadows, and what (one might be inclined to suggest) a centerfold. Conjugal Romance in such centerfold perfection as there might be, given editorial discretion and a photo finisher to airbrush out the evidence that she was a colostomee, and pastel in an erection for him. Andreas kissed her shoulders, nudged his knees against the backs of hers, and slid his hand down the length of her arm to stick his fingers between hers for—hold that pose—the presto look of a figure-skating couple matching up line for line after hairpin turns over barrels or some such thing. Andreas nuzzled, settling in against an equally dopy Gus: her bottom arm was angled like a queen's caught in mindless midwave to whatever was on the other side of her Rolls window; Andreas's bottom arm looped over her head like the lip of a Venetian blown-glass pitcher; and together they lay there still-life—no action photo this one—and spoke no more words, neither moving at all until Andreas unlatched his fingers and pulled the sheet and the electric blanket over them to cover what one otherwise might have gone on studying and shooting there in the magazine light of fruitwood logs burning in the creamy dreamy master bedroom.

As they began to waken and heard Nicky on his plastic E-Z Rider tricycle revving himself around the living room, Andreas thought it was morning. Gus said, "Morning," and they waked wondering if it was or wasn't, looking at each other, Gus having turned onto her other side to face him. "Morning," he said. But it wasn't, they both knew by then; it wasn't morning that had the digital clock reading 3:49 and Nicky cruising on his tricycle, humming to get them up to play. Gus touched the smooth stretched skin Andreas had awakened with—the centerfold coordinator's pastel labwork —and enveloped him with one hand and a part of the other like a mourning veil. Her sadness filled him with pity and desire, and he kissed her cave deep, which made Gus cry and take her hands from him to her own face. Nicky would give them maybe ten minutes more.

And Gus felt the worst inadequacy in not knowing what to do with the fact that Andreas had wakened erect, and that was then why she kept her hands on her face and tried to keep them there forever while Andreas pushed them off to hold her face in his hands to kiss her again. She felt him pressing into her thigh as if with a small-child's fist, insisting, and wept to catch her breath in her mouth between his kisses. Andreas said, "Gussie, I love you, Gussie, I love you," with his hands over her ears so that, even with his face inches from hers, he seemed to be calling down a long padded hallway. And what should she do?

He smudged her face with his thumbs as if she were a drawing, pushing the tears on an upward diagonal from the corners of her mouth along her cheekbones and off into her ears. Gus had tears in her ears and laughed a little in spite of herself.

"You put tears in my ears," she told him.

"You put sunshine in my eyes," he sang, "and azure in my skies, so touch me, touch me, ba-bee!" Andreas was singing awfully loud and kept on singing, so she touched him, and he pumped his small-child's fist into her hands and kept on singing. Gus felt perfectly adequate to having her hands loved.

"Play!" Nicky crashed his tricycle into their door. "Jammed!" He had got his leg jammed or the front wheel jammed and began to scream, calling for "*Maa!*" and pleading, "Come! Maa, come, please!"

"Never mind," Andreas suggested to Gus, and finally Nicky was attended to by Maya of all people, who said, "Leave them alone, Nic. Can't you hear them singing?"

Chapter
Three

Gus sat in the padded chair and wished her room were on the east side of the building, so that a strip of morning sun might just then fall over her shoulder and into her lap. It was nine in the morning, with an hour to exterminate before Jackson would arrive to begin the head, and Gus had a chill in her that was realized at skin level by a damp sweat she had known only once before.

She picked up *The Years* and read over the part Andreas had read aloud, about the leaves and the smoke and the wind, about giving the birthday necklace to little Maggie, the Colonel's preferred niece, on the day Parnell died. But no, Gus thought, little Maggie was getting too much affection. One should rather love the littler one, Sara, who was deformed from having been dropped as a baby.

In the next section, called "1907," which was sixteen years later, Gus read: "It was midsummer; and the nights were hot. The moon, falling on water, made it white, inscrutable, whether deep or shallow." And Sara was lying on her bed listening to someone else's dance music, trying to amuse herself in the sleepless hot past-midnight by rummaging through "the Antigone of Sophocles, done into English verse by Edward Pargiter," who was her cousin. The doctor had told Sara she must lie straight, lie still.

But then Maggie comes in from the party she attended with their parents and unpins the blackened live flower she has worn, and then their mother comes along to scold and exhilarate. " 'I am lying straight and still,' said Sara. 'Now'— she looked up at her—'tell me about the party.' "

Gus found this scene so to her liking that she read it twice, and then again just those three pages. Gus and Mimi too had found ways to press their mother into telling of the party, just as Daphni and Maya had, with Gus herself the mother in the dress that rustled as, pressed to tell, she sat on the edge of a bed. It was perhaps too symmetrical to have Daphni and Maya, Mimi and Gus, Maggie and Sara; it was perhaps too even and predictably paired to have three sets of sisters; was that so? To have three different mothers sitting on the edges of beds after a party?

There is still music coming in through Sara's open window —it is from another party down the street—and the girls are able to urge their mother to dance to it as if she were a girl. But Gus and Mimi were never that good at urging, or there was never music being volunteered, or dancing had not been special to their own mother. And she hadn't danced for Daphni and Maya but once or twice; lately, the parties they went to were rarely dances because of there being so much in the world to discuss with a friend. What symmetry there was, then, was what Gus was drawn by. There wasn't too much, not for her at least.

But too bad, thought Gus, how the fathers in Woolf's world are always the cranks and spoilers, calling out that it's late and so come along, spoiling Maggie's and Sara's fun in being girlish with their mother, who is girlish still for having been spoiled by her domineering crank of a husband. Gus knew Woolf's own was this crank and spoiler and felt it was small wonder that her fiction fathers have no family friends, only subjects. Still it was too bad, she felt, since fathers like her own and then Andreas let happen those groggy, romantic, important last-minute-of-the-day talks that the daughters would be waiting up for, especially in the summer when it was too hot to sleep. And Woolf's were always interrupted.

When the children are afraid of their father, how unlucky it is to have the mother die as Woolf's did. It was lucky for her own children that they adored Andreas, it was a lucky situation altogether excepting, needless to say, her own luck. "Thank fortune" was what her mother had said whenever someone else might have said, "Thank God," and Gus's mother had meant it as a literal thank *fortune,* because she believed that God was not responsible for who was sick and who wasn't, not even for who dies and who doesn't. Heaven was maybe the great card factory in the sky, but God never cut the deck or shuffled. Her mother's sense of things straddled the fence between God Is All and God Is Dead and seemed to Gus the most realistic. For certainly if God were shuffling, everything would appear less random and chaotic, and certainly if people had the shuffle—it is after all a skill one can work at—lives would be more orderly as well. Why not, then, an interstellar gypsy lady who shuffles nameless decks of cards for everyone, one each at birth? How else could there be such a thing as luck, or unluck?

"1907" finishes with Maggie listening on the stairs to her mother apologizing for having forgotten to have a new lock put on the kitchen door. " 'I'm so sorry, Digby,' Eugénie said as they came into the hall. 'I will tie a knot in my handkerchief; I will go directly after breakfast tomorrow morning. . . . Yes,' she said," and "Then there was a pause. Maggie could hear soda-water squirted into a tumbler; the chink of a glass; and then the lights went out."

The chill that had been relieved returned, and there was still more time to extinguish somehow. Might not the mail come any minute? And just then it did. A note from Mimi:

Dear Gussie, who must think I am an absolute hedgehog!

I never even thought about your being sick when I asked you here for Thanksgiving. My analyst says aren't I forgetting something? and maybe—he suggests—I asked you here as a way of avoiding the fact that you may be very seriously ill indeed.

Honestly I have just been from the phone to the doctor's and back to write this, stopping only to send you flowers, hoping you are feeling better. I myself feel awful about this and hope you are not out of sorts with me. It's true that last time Andreas called, he said things weren't exactly looking up.

Best love, xxxooo, Mi.

Gus didn't know if Mimi had ever been dropped as a baby. She certainly didn't have, like Sara, one shoulder higher than the other, but Gus thought it was entirely possible that something had jarred her lobes, something like a harsh fall onto linoleum or rocks. Because for someone who had done every self-help program ever marketed—mind and body benders one on top of the other like filo pastry for baklava—Mimi was a wreck of a specimen, a heck of a success. For a moment Gus felt sorry for Mimi, that something had maybe happened to her that left a great chink in her brain which sent her careening around to fill it up with the here-and-now, all those facile philosophies about being your own best friend and knowing what doesn't amount to much about sex. It seemed Mimi's here-and-now chink would do her in whether or not it came to be called by its real name, hydrocephaly.

Then the sympathy vanished, and Gus put the letter back into its heavy bond envelope and with her big desk scissors from home cut it, even including thirteen cents in uncanceled stamps, into airy slivers that fell like cut hair into the lap of nightgown stretched between her knees. Then Gus tipped the slivers onto the floor to be swept up.

The rest of the hour, Gus reasoned, could be spent getting ready, beginning with undoing her braid and trying to kindle a spark in her long lank hair by overbrushing it. Sweating dampness was very unpleasant, as if her body were a basement, as if she were already in clay. She would have to change her nightgown just then in order to get away from the cold, and she would have to fill the bathroom with steam to compensate. Was she being vain? The chilly fear she felt was the same as when she'd stood before a box camera for the formal wedding portrait she knew her parents would mount in silver and keep forever on their piano. It was the fear that she wasn't really pretty enough to keep around forever and ever in silver or bronze, the way Mimi was.

Gus lay in bed in state and waited. Jackson was late by one minute, two, and part of a third, and Gus felt she must tell him how important it was that he be on time, though not just then. He was having a hard enough time getting into the room with all his things, which included a knapsack of tools, clay and wire, and a pedestal with a plywood deck. The coffee equipment he had brought was in the bulging pockets of his balding, middle-aged corduroy coat. He was camping in for the winter, it seemed. "Hiya," he said, breathing noisily through his nose as if making wind through bushes. His shirt was the same one as days earlier, faceless plaid in faded browns, but he'd pruned his beard. "How you doing? You ready?"

"Not bad, and I guess I am. If you want to rearrange things, go ahead."

"I'll have to. Just move this bureau thing out of the way. Okay if I collapse the cards?"

Gus smiled. "There's a nurse who apparently needs to set up my cards that way. She says it looks cheerful. She'll set them right up again since, according to her, I have the floor's best."

"I'm going to move the bureau over behind the door. Okay for the plants?"

"What little sun there is makes it all the way to the door," Gus said. "Do you have enough room?"

"Makes it like a submarine in here. Ever been in one?"

"No, I haven't."

"Ever been on a pedestal? This is for you."

"Haven't been there either."

"Let's see. Think I'll start by making myself some coffee while you put on your scarf."

Gus said she thought the scarf was corny, and must she? Jackson answered with, "The reason you wear it's not the point. It does good things for your face, I think. And I did like your braid."

He went to the bathroom for coffee water while Gus began to rebraid her hair and complain in silence that she had brushed it out for a reason. "Why didn't you tell me not to change?" she complained to Jackson when he reappeared. She'd deliberately chosen a nightgown to go with her brushed-out hair, to go with an invention of herself as a romantic on a velvet divan.

"Why should you have?" he replied with a shrug. "Now where's that scarf?" Gus directed him to her bathrobe pocket.

"We ready to roll? The way it goes is first I build the armature that I can stick the clay onto in wads, any questions?

Here goes." What Jackson made looked like a world, a group of spheres he knotted together clumsily with the same heavy wire, except that he made it concave in places and pushed the whole shape into an egg without even looking. "Don't worry, we'll give you a hairline so you won't look bald or anything. See how I stick the clay onto the skull? See, the whole idea's to put a lot on and take half of it back, and I know you might be embarrassed at first, but don't sweat it, it's normal."

"It is? Good. I'm cold all over and feeling nauseous."

"I think it's the fear of what we each look like. Only small children don't have it, I think. You feel dizzy?"

"Yes."

"Then I'd say you're normal."

"I wish you'd tell my doctors to say that."

"They don't say you're normal? It's always important to tell somebody they're normal when they feel lousy sometimes. I mean, under certain conditions like you've got I'd think feeling lousy is very normal. Like, sitting for a head a cold sweat's very normal. I'm almost done putting on the clay, and you won't be nervous once we get going."

"I'll look forward to that." Gus closed her eyes and willed the heat to come back on inside her. She told herself that it was okay, that she could relax, that Jackson was fine, and she rubbed her knuckles together like twigs, trying for a spark in spite of the fact that they were damp. "Shall I tell you something about myself?"

Jackson dropped a large dose of powdered coffee into his mug. "You can talk however much you like and it'll be fine. But what you say doesn't tell me what to do with the clay, understand what I mean?"

Gus nodded.

"I mean, there's stuff I wouldn't know about you without your telling me, like for sure where you went to college or for sure what your major was. But the rest you don't have to.

The rest I get from opening my eyes and paying attention to what I see, if you get what I mean." He gulped the hot coffee. "And now I'm ready to open my eyes. You ready to go?"

Gus guessed she was. "Well, I went to Wellesley and majored in sociology."

Jackson grunted agreement. "I would have said Bennington and dance. The hair and all."

"And once I danced, but there was no dance major at Wellesley."

"Once, huh? And now?"

"I've been a foreign student adviser."

"What for?" The shape was starting to come up out of the clay, starting with the brow. The shape was crude.

"When I realized," but she stopped. Who had ever before asked her for what had she been a foreign student adviser? Did she know what for? "When I realized," she began again, "that being a dancer meant having that be everything, I realized I couldn't be a dancer. Getting a master's in advising at Columbia seemed a good transition back into the world of speech."

"Is that sociology, the world of speech?" The excess clay was coming off nicely.

"But it's much less important than sociology pretends to be. It's talking to strangers about how are they liking New York."

"And how are they liking it?"

"It depends. The women are liking it better than the men are. The men are upset, especially for instance the Indians, who can't understand what the sexual revolution bothered to free people up for if not for sex. They might as well be home, they say."

"What, you don't allow sex?"

"The American women who come to International House come to be with the foreign women now. Or they come in order to practice a language. The attitude has changed from seeking the approval of foreign men to not seeking it, even to refusing it unless suitably expressed. It's no longer Open House, and that upsets a lot of the men."

"You got some way to fix that?"

"We're running a seminar: American Women."

Jackson stopped and thought. "And that's fixing it?"

"I've been in here for all of it so I don't know. And there are problems. The Arab students boycotted the keynote, for example. They said the West will never impose slavery on their men as it has on its own, the same thing Islam said downtown at the U.N. in response to the International Women's Year proposal. God, that was probably the worst funded, most ignored imaginable project the U.N. has ever committed itself to. Anyway, the seminar is set up to have speakers from diplomacy, that was the first, then finance, law, medicine, physics, engineering, education, city planning, government, and the arts, in something like that order. I'll let you know as we go along, if you're interested."

"Who's talked so far?" asked Jackson.

"The keynote was Assistant Secretary-General Helvi Sipila, the woman of highest rank in the U.N. Then the president of a large savings-and-loan association who also talked about money, power, and money power. I'm told Islam showed up for that one. I wanted to hear her; she came into money and power herself by that dumbwaiter route of shuttling dutifully between president father and vice-president husband, then chairman father and president husband, until both were dead from premature heart failure and she was left there hanging like a hammock stretched between dead trees."

"That's nice." Jackson had found the rough shape of Gus's nose. "I missed that last sentence," he admitted.

"This bank president who picked up the business by its top."

"Then I missed the last two. Can't concentrate sometimes, only on the clay. Just want to more or less get you, roughly, in one shot. Christ, is it hot in here! But less resistance from the clay, that's one thing. Let me just get you to the chin if you wouldn't mind keeping still that part of your face."

Had she talked on and on, and whatever for? Gus felt foolish and boring; she felt the series was foolish and boring; she felt being a foreign student adviser was, when you came down to it, foolish and boring. She hoped she wouldn't open her mouth for the rest of the morning. Maybe she was better off in the nonverbal world of dance after all. How pretentious to define American Women with speakers from each of the male professions! What for was right; Jackson was right to ask that question. What *was* it for?

Jackson worked the clay to achieve the chin's approximate shape, humming to himself an Asian-sounding tuneless tune. "Okay, foreign student advising, so. Then what's your husband?"

"A lawyer," Gus said.

"I mean what's the accent? Remember I answered the phone when he called?"

"Andreas is Greek. Daphni didn't tell you?"

"Daphni never says a word, just flirts with her eyes. Guess I should have known from the last name, huh?"

"Or the first," Gus explained, saying Daphni was that monastery he surely knew, the one near Athens with the Byzantine mosaics, the one that was in ancient times a temple to Apollo on the sacred road to Eleusis.

He knew it. "No, she never did say," he said earnestly. "It's a real nice name. Do you have another named Empire State? I mean, most people don't name their children after buildings, or civilizations either, like Maya."

"You were named for the President?"

"Jackson's my last name."

"Your first was after?"

"Nothing. I was named for nothing."

"Our third is named Nicolas."

"After Santa?"

"No, only after Andreas's father. I shouldn't say only."

But Jackson answered, "Well nobody's father's as good as the spirit of Christmas, right? Most don't even come close. Most are, I don't know, pretty spiritless."

"Andreas isn't."

"Mine is. Is yours?"

"Mine wasn't, no."

"You're lucky."

"Yes." Yes, she was, or had been, extremely fortunate. Gus heard her mother's voice say thank fortune, thank fortune for that. Her mother had said thank fortune for everything that was good and had probably said it, Gus thought to herself, right up to an hour before their deaths, right up to the moment before perhaps. The energy drained from Gus's face and pulled shut her eyes.

Jackson whispered that he was being too tiring and that he was sorry.

"No," Gus assured. After a moment she opened her eyes and smiled apologetically. "Let's go on. I'm okay."

"Let me rest for a minute, then. Brought you something anyway, looking at that walrus picture your kid did, you showed me, remember? Well this is my kid's. It's supposed to be of my parents' great dane. They live in Greenwich."

"Did I know you have a child?" Of course she did. He'd told her that first day. "But what a nice drawing. Is Max the dog's name?"

"Max is my son."

"Max Jackson?" Her laughter was an explosion. "I'm sorry, but. I'm sorry, it's that Max Jackson sounds like somebody's snapping chewing gum."

"And that's not the funny part. Want to know why Max in the first place?" Hi, hi, hi, went Jackson's laughter. "It's Maxwell after Maxwell Arnold."

Gus didn't quite get it, and then she did. "You meant *Matthew* Arnold?"

"He was only my favorite poet in college: Maxwell Arnold, 1822–1888." Jackson put down his knife and leaned his weight on the plywood deck of the pedestal. Hi, hi, hi, went his laughter, hi, hi, and he just about knuckled under and went down. "My wife, Marty, one day asked me why Maxwell, how come did I want to call him Maxwell if it was a boy? So I told her." Hi, hi. "You see, Marty was an English major." Hi, hi, hi. He supported himself with his right arm on the metal footboard. "So anyway, when it was a boy we decided we liked Maxwell better than Matthew anyway, and that's how come we've now got Max Jackson like chewing gum. His name is Maxwell Arnold Jackson. A girl we would've called simply Eva after nobody in particular. Eva was the name Marty picked."

"Your next child can be Eva then, can't she?"

Jackson stopped laughing. He turned the talk back and around to Matthew Arnold's poems and boasted that he knew "Dover Beach" if she wanted to hear it. Gus said she did.

"Dover Beach: '. . . Begin, and cease, and then again begin/ With tremulous cadence slow, and bring/ The eternal note of sadness in.' " It was Jackson's most loved poem, he explained, and the reason he stayed out of head shops where they sell those posters with some wrongly taken lines from the poems one has always loved, put on a sunrise or a sunset or a rainbow or a field of daisies to groove on, stoned. He literally feared seeing "Ah, love, let us be true/ To one another!" with no mention of the "darkling plain/ Swept with confused alarms of struggle and flight,/ Where ignorant armies clash by night." Jackson told Gus that if he ever saw "Ah, love, let us be true/ To one another!" put on a field of daisies, he'd puke.

Gus asked if he would hand her the Bartlett's *Quotations* from over on the table. She thought she'd read Bartlett's quotes for Arnold. She'd never read Arnold, believe it or not.

"I've looked him up in Bartlett's," said Jackson, "since Marty took all the literature. We're divorced, maybe I didn't say."

"You didn't say."

"Eighteen months ago, but let's get going."

Gus opened *Quotations* to Arnold. "What? It goes Dostoyevsky, Baudelaire, Matthew Arnold, and then Ulysses S. Grant!"

"Yeah, I noticed that. One night when I was stoned I tried to figure out why, and you know what it is? This took me an hour to figure out: Charles Baudelaire and Fyodor Dostoyevsky both have seventeen letters, and Ulysses S. Grant and Matthew Arnold both have thirteen. Check it out."

"Letters?"

"C-h-a-r-l-e-s-B-a-u and so on. Seventeen, seventeen, thirteen, thirteen. Brilliant, huh?"

"F-y-o-d-o." Gus would count more quickly were she sure of the spelling, but she had to limp through Dostoyevsky finger by finger. Not so Baudelaire: *"Ecrivez mille fois BAUdelaire!"* a college teacher had once scrawled on the title page of a sophomore paper, called *"Le Cadavre dans l'oeuvre de Charles Beaudelaire,"* in which she'd misspelled the man's name thirty times.

"Isn't that swell?"

And Gus said it was, rather. Did he mind if she didn't talk but read instead? Bartlett's patches of poems and essay bits would read, she knew, like poster slogans, but it would give her some idea of Jackson's favorite man in college. Bartlett's too, perhaps, since he'd given Arnold nine columns and Baudelaire only one.

> Fate gave, what Chance shall not control.
> His sad lucidity of soul
> Yet they, believe me, who await
> No gifts from Chance, have conquered Fate.

Four lines from "Resignation," and maybe she'd read the whole poem. But not much that she noticed until "Dover Beach," and then a stanza from "A Wish":

> Spare me the whispering, crowded room,
> The friends who come and gape and go,
> The ceremonious air of gloom—
> All, which makes death a hideous show.

And then the final bit on Shelley:

A beautiful and ineffectual angel, beating in the void his luminous wings in vain.

But Jackson had used her reading to advantage. With her head tipped down and her eyes seeming shut, he could see nicely how her bones were set down and what her face consisted of. Her skin fit those bones like a leotard and made of her face a dancer's body, a streamlined torso with flat cheekbone breasts and the mound of chin. It came in at the waist where her nose and mouth made a navel of the space between, but she wanted legs, and so he imagined sinewy legs coming down from the chin and fell in love with what he'd made, wanting to enter her there and fill her with love and pain.

"It seems to me," he heard her say, "that there are better ways of reading Arnold."

Articulating the eyes, spoiling the dancer's body, Jackson

saw that he'd floated off but didn't see that where he'd arrived was not at Gus. "There!" he announced, believing that he'd just had sex.

"How did you do?"

"This clay goes like frosting. It's like I'm Betty Crocker and Duncan Hines in person."

"I'm glad there's one advantage to this hothouse heat. Do you want to show me?"

"Sure, if you want to. Or you could wait for Daphni and Maya if you prefer. I'll tell them in class they can have a look."

"Then I'll wait," said Gus. "They'll be very pleased."

Jackson took up the plastic and wrapped the head. Then he shook Gus's hand and said she was the nicest person he'd ever met in every way. He just wanted to say that, he told her, and left. On the other side of the door, he stopped to rest for a moment. The tears skipped down his beard like stones being skipped on water.

The subway stop was an indoor block from the elevators that went to the private patient wing, and Daphni had run like a taxi in traffic to get from the subway to her mother's room before Maya did. It was no contest. Daphni arrived three minutes sooner but sat and heaved to get her breath back. "Hi, Mum," she gasped finally as Maya strolled in and cooed, "Hi, Mom," and kissed Gus sweetly. And there they were, Gus thought to herself, there were Daphni and Maya in one of those see-through gelatin capsules.

"He said we could look! Jackson said it, honest!" Her side ached, but Daphni shouted, "No! Me!" when Maya matter-of-factly began to remove the plastic. "Me, Maya!"

"Do it then," Maya said, "and can't you try to keep your voice down?" She helped Gus up and slid the sheepskin slippers on her mother's feet. Gus picked up a shawl and headed for the bathroom with a tottery shuffle.

So Daphni got to her feet and approached the pedestal as if it were a communion altar with the body and blood of Christ underneath the drape. With the care of a priest she lifted the plastic; she was prepared to find under it the makings of a miracle. What she found was the back side.

"It looks like Mom has her hair in rollers," Maya said.

"It's the wedges of clay, you dope!"

"Daffy, I know that. I said it looks like her hair's in curlers."

"Well it isn't. You better help me turn this thing; the face part's on the other side. And don't call me Daffy, my name doesn't happen to be that, you know."

"And don't you be so bossy!"

"You shut up, Maya! It was my idea, and I can do whatever I like!"

"Then you turn it around yourself, you big shot!"

"I will, and if it falls it's *your* fault!"

"It's *not!*"

"Well I'm sorry, it is. Don't try to get out of it."

"You're such a liar: it's *not* my fault, Daphni!"

"Yes it is."

"What is?" Gus asked as she came from the bathroom.

"Nothing," said Daphni. "Maya's just being uncooperative once again."

"You liar, Daphni!"

"You see, Mum?"

"I'm *not!*"

Gus asked, "Are you going to turn the head around or aren't you, Daphni? Or are we supposed to admire the back that looks as if my hair is in curlers?"

"You see!" Maya yelped. "That's what *I* said, Mom, and Daphni said I was a liar."

"You called *me* the liar, Maya," Daphni said indignantly.

"Wait," said Gus. "Why not just turn the head?"

"Because I need *help!*"

"Then why didn't you say so?"

"I *did*, for God's sake! No one would help!"

"That's not true, Mom," said Maya.

"You just check the record, Maya Kaligas!"

"Wait," Gus repeated. "Can't I help turn it?"

"Yes, anyone can who wants to at this point." Daphni's voice was spun sugar. "I'd really appreciate your help, Mummy, thanks, and we'll just ignore Maya."

"We won't ignore anyone."

"You hold it steady and I'll turn the base, Mum."

The turning was over in eight or nine seconds.

And Maya spoke first. "But I thought you'd be smiling! That's not your face, Mommy!"

Gus said, "It is quite austere, rather grave in fact."

Daphni was speechless. Her hero had betrayed her with a head that wasn't the least bit peppy. Her personal hero had broken her heart.

"This is only the first draft," Gus said to Maya, "and Jackson did say that I wouldn't be smiling." To herself she looked the way Virginia Woolf did toward the end: she looked frighteningly thin and unspeakably sad. The resemblance chilled her, she looked so frail and extinguishable. "It's a working draft," she said to try and be comforting, "so it's only approximate."

Maya said it was not even close, it was not even more or less like Gus, it was somebody else.

"He must have to start somewhere," Gus reassured her.

"Well he ought to have started somewhere else, and I'm going to wrap it up again. Jackson's nuts if he doesn't think you're pretty." Maya turned the face away from them by twisting the plywood deck and shoving the pedestal with her foot, which took four seconds. The plastic was back on in three seconds more. "And you're not depressed, and you're not sunken in, and you're not a bald man."

"That's supposed to be my scarf."

"Well it's wrong," Maya argued.

Daphni had gone to sit on the edge of a dinette chair as far from the head as she could get. She was bent in half and hugged her knees to keep from shaking herself apart. Her heart seemed to palpitate with hatred. She vowed never again would she trust Jackson: how could he have been so inconsiderate of her feelings, how could he have broken a sacred trust, how could he have treated her like that? He had broken her heart as if she didn't matter at all, and she would not in a million years forgive him, not ever.

Because they would all blame her, she thought, for Jackson's insensitivity. She'd been used by Jackson, tricked into convincing the others that what they all needed was Gus in bronze. She vowed never to love another man. She'd become a nun in a convent in France in the Middle Ages, and Jackson, in disgrace and to atone, would have to become a monk. They would correspond because talking would be prohibited, and in those letters he'd say how he'd die without her forgiveness. Wasn't there a way, he'd write, to soften her heart? She'd write back that her heart had been broken in two, and she thought that his death was the only answer. Only God could heal her heart, she'd write to Jackson, and if God did she'd let him know. But maybe it would be by then already too late.

"Mum," Daphni whimpered, "am I a fool?"

"You sure are!"

"No, she's not, Maya. Daphni, you're not."

"Well she is because this was a lousy idea!"

"This was just the first day. Daphni, please stop crying."

"Oh what a fool I was!" Daphni moaned and rocked.

"It serves you right!"

"Maya, stop that! Daphni, please, can't you stop?"

"Oh God, I'm doomed!"

"And you deserve it!"

"Please," Gus pleaded, "just get out of my room! I want

both of you out of here right this minute!" Her eyes were wild with the pain in her side, and her voice had taken off from within her. "Go!" she screamed.

Could they not see the tornado of pain advancing, whirling, ripping into her? Could they not hear it roaring through her? She bit the flesh of her right hand between the thumb and the index finger and left a violet ring of pain. Even this was no use, she told herself, even the process of getting to bronze was utterly futile. Why had she bothered if Jackson wanted only to sculpt her as a cadaver? She pressed her fists against her face. Because if she was already dead, why did she bother? She tugged on her braid to transfer the pain to the base of her skull, then tore at it to rip it in half. Didn't anyone *know?* The scissors with which she had cut Mimi's note caught her eye, and she picked them up and cut.

It was time for bed, Andreas suggested to Daphni and Maya, who, to his surprise, rose obediently and left the room saying he was right. He moved to the couch and, glad for the warmth they had left in the cushions, stretched out to absorb it all. The routine was maybe fatiguing him; it was maybe too wearying having to go from the office to the hospital. If only the woman sitting in the wing chair were Gus. Perhaps he'd better eat something.

He asked Frieda if she'd eaten yet, and Frieda mercifully said she hadn't but was thinking of grating some cheese for a fondue loaded with kirschwasser. She'd already cut the bread, she said.

He knocked on Maya's door and entered her black and white room with the deep purple rug. "Will you sit?" Maya asked. She was deep under the covers and lay on her side with both arms around her pillow in the embrace that let her get to sleep. "It makes me so sad to see Mom get angry and cry like that, it makes me so lonely. I wish I were older so I could help."

"But she needs to get angry."

"I don't like it if she's angry at you."

"She wasn't, Maya, she just needed someone."

"And was that why she was angry with me? You know I didn't mean to spill my ginger ale."

"I know."

"And Daphni didn't mean, you know, to scream so loud."

"I know, Maya. It's so very hard to be alone and then have all of us in that little room."

"Does she hate us to visit?"

"She loves us to visit."

"Are you sure, Daddy?"

"Yes."

"It just makes me so sad to see her cry. Does she want to come home still?"

"Very much."

"Are you sure? I'm afraid she doesn't now."

"She does."

"But then why did she do it?"

"I don't know, Maya."

"I wonder. Are you sure she loves me?"

"Yes, I am. Can you get to sleep now?"

"I think so, Daddy."

Andreas switched off the little chrome lamp just above Maya's head and noticed the eerie glossy surfaces of the photographs and book jackets that covered the white of Maya's walls. He wondered, as every night, how she could sleep in such a room that glinted all night from the publicity for her favorite films and books. It was as if her walls were mirrored in glossies but as if, behind the hard bright surfaces, whatever action there was might go on: the sea go on rolling, the dogs go on barking, the Hollywood lovers go on loving, the shoot-out go on being shot out. How Maya found that restful, if she did, was beyond him. He bent to kiss her and sat until her breathing seemed to have gone to sleep.

In Daphni's room the walls were rose colored. She sat on the edge of the little maple canopy bed that had been her mother's and brushed her hair. Beside her was the journal she wrote in every night with colored felt tips.

"Have you finished your writing?"

"Not yet. I had to wash my face." Daphni's skin was clear, but she believed in friction and faithfully scoured her face with the same type of wiry plastic cloth that she used on the copper-bottomed pans.

"Can you write tomorrow?"

"I have things on my mind, Papa."

"Shall I come back?"

"If you wouldn't mind. I do have to get my thoughts for today down. My hair's done at least." She put the brush on her bedside table. "Is Mummy worse?"

"A little bit worse."

"I know," she said. "She seems very worse."

"She's tired of being there."

"That's not it. Why on earth did she cut it? I hope it's not because she hates Jackson. I couldn't stand it if she did."

"I doubt it has to do with Jackson."

"I wish it all went faster. I wish I could figure out why she did it."

"I'm going to check back in exactly ten minutes."

"I'll try to be finished."

"Light out in ten minutes."

"You don't have to be condescending, Papa. God, you're all so *touchy!*" Daphni unlocked her journal and began to write. "Would you mind?" she said. "It's private, you know."

Andreas left the room trying to remember if he had gone through that phase of making other people want to kill him. But he thought not, since he thought he wouldn't be alive now if he had. His own father had despised phases of any sort, having had time only for finished products and people who had likewise arrived at the top of the line. Which was why, and of course Andreas knew it, Daphni had always been indulged, no matter that he personally wished vengeance on the one who'd invented the adolescent. He wished for that person a bullet each to the brain and the heart. There was no worse invention than adolescence, except perhaps fascism.

Frieda sat and studied the flame from the sterno can. Its violet-blueness reminded her of the skies at the Cape at the end of the school year she'd spent in the States before returning to her Dutch foster family in Amsterdam. She'd not wanted to leave, just as she'd been afraid to leave Holland, and just as she'd been terrified on the train that had brought the children from Germany the night it was still possible to get children out. The violet-blueness of the skies was what leaving meant; it was what it meant to be adopted and then have to leave and be readopted somewhere else. There was no more lonesome a color than the violet blue she stared into.

Andreas returned in ten minutes, closed the felt-tip pen, and locked the diary. Daphni's face in repose was much more lovely than ever it was in action: her full mouth slack, the pink lips parted but no voice behind them. She looked, asleep, the way Greek village brides have always looked: skin young and fatty, face passive and vulnerable, hair black and thick and womanly.

He wondered how to be a father, especially alone, and a dumb panic filled him with apprehension and dulled momentarily the growl in his empty stomach. And not only Daphni; all three of them, especially alone. It *was* too wearying having to go from the office to the hospital. He could no longer fully concentrate, working, but then was still more helpless once outside the office. How was he to answer them? Switching off Daphni's bedside light, Andreas admitted that Gus was beyond him.

Chapter
Four

Jackson got a seat on the subway after the stop at
Columbus Circle. He had planned to look over the
Poetical Works of Matthew Arnold, a Yale-blue
leather-spined 1895 edition that came from the
blue-leather Great Works bookcase in his parents'
library, but there was a man across the aisle stroking himself.
About Great Works Jackson knew his parents didn't know
their ass from their elbow, but their library was blue, and
who was he to criticize anyway? He freely admitted that he
liked Arnold because of all the water poems.

He propped up the book and peeped over it to watch the
man who chewed gum and stroked with the same slow
circular motion. He had put socks in his jock, maybe, or else
was a triple-X film star with a firehose phallus. Jackson didn't
dare look above the slowly circling jaw to see where the eyes
stared, if anywhere. Would he stroke all the way to 168th;

could he keep it up for a hundred blocks? Jackson liked the idea of a triple-X film star riding the subway, stroking and chewing, to Riverdale and back one day, the next perhaps to Flushing and back. He liked the idea that film stars did that between films.

At 168th Jackson closed the Arnold and hopped out the door. From the platform he watched the man keep up his stroking and chewing; his eyes were closed as if he didn't give a damn that Jackson had grown up in Fairfield County in a big Greenwich house and been prepped and educated at great expense in order to run for President somewhere. The stroking man seemed not to give a damn, as if he were the star and Jackson just another nobody riding the subway. Jackson could hardly wait to tell Gus.

And when the elevator opened, there she was. He joked, "You the new security guard?" She didn't smile. "And what's with the chair?" She didn't answer. "I brought Maxwell Arnold. I just saw this guy who"—he looked around and nodded to the waiting attendant—"what's going on? Where're they wheeling you to?"

Gus said with disgust that the doctor had first canceled and then reordered treatment, delaying the decision until there was no longer time to call him.

"No problem, you want me to come along?"

"You won't like it."

"Better than waiting here. I can stay all morning, so we'll do the head after the treatment, no problem, okay?"

The attendant slid up and said, "Hittin' the road?" He pressed the elevator button and grinned when the doors instantly hissed open. "You wanna hold that, please," he asked the person inside. "We gonna wheel in."

The commute was a long one from high on the Fort Washington side to underground on the Broadway side, but the orderly made the trip spectacular, singing and skidding Gus along to "Be-Bop-A-Lula" and "Yakety Yak," Jackson trailing after with admiration. His second exhibitionist of the morning, he marveled.

"Thanks very much," Gus said, and stuck out her hand to shake the attendant's in what turned into a black power shake. "We still got the return," the man answered her happily.

Jackson's knees buckled, looking around at what he saw as cadavers. He told himself he never ever should have come along. Gus said he should wait in that windowless room where the outpatients sat, and that she would read the Arnold if he didn't mind. It mightn't take long.

He sat on a frame chair and listened to the newer patients compliment each other on their neckties and knitting, waiting to be called for what they couldn't speak of. Jackson had thought the stroker the day's item, then he'd thought the showman was it; but the day's item was his own exhibition. He crossed his legs and tucked his fingers in to hold them still; then he kneaded a knot in his neck and another in his forehead and stripped his fingers of cuticle; then he re-crossed his legs and stuffed his fingers in, this time to hold the legs still. There was no hope, Jackson told himself, there was no hope.

The skulls of the inpatients, those who'd progressed, were identical, the men's and the women's, and he, who thought he knew anatomy, felt ill. Without hair, without flesh, they were identical, ancient-looking, tragedies. And the isolation! All of them having to do it alone when they're not even themselves anymore! The rage and the panic vibrated through him. There was no hope. "Hey man, le's go," the showman called, and Jackson could see a blurry colored scarf behind him that would be Gus. He didn't know if he could stand, but the patients gave him encouraging smiles and said good luck.

In the hall, Jackson vomited the chili beef soup he'd had for breakfast.

"How old are you?" he asked Gus when they were back in her room and he'd finished explaining that it must have been a minor bug that made him throw up in the hall like that.

"Don't worry, I vomited my first time too, and I still feel like it every time. Thirty-nine."

"You are? You're only nine years older than me, you're not even forty! I thought you were older on account of your control. Is it a phase to not be angry, if you don't mind my asking you?"

"It's a phase to be angry, they say, and they're right. I've been angry, but I'm much less so now. I'm waiting to have confirmed what I know." Gus stood on the footstool and backed into bed, contracting to pull her legs around, gripping the sheet and then letting go when there was no pain, only discomfort.

"How do you know you know?"

"I had this dream six months ago: I was watching a monkey giving birth, a lab monkey they brought from her cage fairly late in labor. Everything was going fine, the baby's heartbeat and everything, but when the baby was delivered it was dead. And instead of being bloody, it had this white stuff all over it, white sparkles like the shiny specks in talcum powder. The vet stuck his hand in and brought it out white. He pressed on the stomach and all this white sparkling powder came out. There was no placenta."

The stinging acid juices gathered in his mouth, and Jackson flew to the toilet to unload the misery. Reappearing, he said he was sorry and slumped into the easy chair.

"My brother is coming, and he will confirm it," Gus said softly, and took off her scarf. "My brother's a doctor. Now tell me: how do you like my hair?"

"I noticed." He smiled lopsidedly. "I mean it's terrific but why didn't you get a nose job or a chin job? I mean: nothing

like your model getting plastic surgery right in the middle!"
He pushed himself from the chair and lifted the plastic wrapping from the head. "We got work, you and me," he said to the head. "Hell, where's that tool? Jesus, Gus, you really weren't thinking at all." He found the tool.

"Yes, I was thinking, Jackson. How could I have cut two feet off my braid if I hadn't been thinking?"

"Hell, how would I know? But this doesn't even look like you now!"

Gus paused. "Nor did it yesterday."

"Well Jesus Christ. And now what the hell should I do?" She was correct, he had to admit. The face he'd made had come from his imagination. Melodrama. "So why'd you cut it?"

"Lying on a braid's like lying on a staircase. Or having an industrial zipper glued to your spine. That's what I told Andreas, and he protested but I looked him in the eye and said *it is*. It hurt, that's why."

Jackson made a few passes with the tool. "How long did you have it?"

"Thirty years."

"No wonder he protested." The scarf had been wrong anyway, too severe, and her brow was not that bony.

"I wish I'd cut it earlier, instead of figuring I'd get better."

"Ever think of a bun on top?" He was completely reworking the eye sockets.

"It was arrogant. I was lucky I wasn't bald."

"Yes, so you said."

"It was arrogant of Maya and Daphni to scream and say I didn't have the right to cut it, and I said so."

"Arrogant how?" The mouth was wrong too, he saw.

"They aren't my doctors. That braid was only there by the grace of something or other. You saw what it's like; imagine taking a thirty-inch braid to that waiting room."

"Aren't you almost done there?"

"I finish this week."

"So why'd you cut it?" The nose was okay, it seemed.

"I told you: it hurt."

"Right, you said that."

"Also, I said this too: a thirty-inch braid in the therapy area has the same effect as a Cadillac in the narrow lanes of a mud village. You saw it."

"I still don't get your point."

"Out of place; get out of here."

"And what?" he asked. "You want to belong?"

"I *do* belong!"

"You just said you were about to be done."

"Yes, with treatment."

The nose wasn't right after all. What the hell was she saying? "I still don't get it. You want to belong but you're nearly through with treatment and won't ever see those people again, so you cut your hair and belong. And you screw up my head, and you frighten your family. And then you explain it with rehearsed lines like the narrow lanes of a mud village."

"That wasn't rehearsed."

"And it's not your speech, Gus." The mouth wasn't right yet. He thought the upper lip was too flat. "Which is okay with me, but I still don't get it."

"Too bad, because Dr. Harding gets it."

"Is he your family? Is he in the middle of doing your head?"

"She's the radiotherapist."

"So she saw me throw up; big deal." But those new eyes were perfect! Full of energy, partly furious.

"Jackson!"

"Yeah?"

"I want you to understand why I did it."

"Then say it again."

"You just want to believe like the others that I'm killing myself."

"No, I don't think I do."

"But you do. My brother's coming Friday, and he'll think it's fine."

"So the doctors all like it fine, is that it?" He'd needed to agitate her to get what was missing the first time, that edge on the placidity, that energy.

"That's *garbage,* Jackson!"

"How about garbage in the narrow lanes of a mud village? You know, thrown out windows by the peasants who don't mind the smell?"

"I'm not pleasing doctors! I don't care what they think about me!"

"But if you belong, then it seems to me—"

"I don't *belong!*"

"Then I misunderstood you?"

"I said it, but I *don't* belong."

The new mouth forced him to change the cheekbones, but now he could see how they should have been. He'd seen it all wrong the first time out, when he had seen her as a torso and not as a face. Perhaps he'd needed that falling in love with her briefly and hard. Perhaps the head had needed it in order to be brought to life. The only problem was keeping track of what she was saying in order that it not collapse. It had to do with belonging, he thought.

"So now you belong with the doctors, right?" Could he get by with that?

"You've confused every point I've been trying to make! I agree I didn't cut my hair to be accepted by the patients, but I didn't do it for the doctors. It wasn't trying to hurt myself but to make myself feel better, and now I can't even think what I meant. I hated the ugly face you made." Then Gus waited for him to say something.

"I didn't catch it."

"I said I hated the face you made."

"Ah."

"Well?"

"And so you cut your braid?"

"No."

"Meaning?"

"I didn't cut it just to get back at you."

"Glad to hear it." He made her a truer chin and softened the jaw line to make it firm without being rigid.

"Forget it, you've confused it all. I don't care if you understand or not, I'm just sorry you feel that I didn't think, because I did. In the meantime you've wrecked my reasoning." She pressed the button to lower the bed.

"I didn't wreck it, look." Jackson turned the pedestal. "Isn't that right?" Did he need to ask? There was nothing wrong with it.

"How did you do that?"

"Just paying attention." He grinned.

"It's fine." Gus raised herself. "It's me."

"Yup." He stuck the point of the tool where her ear would go. "I meant to do this the first time around. Guess the drama distracted me. Anyway, now we've got it begun. Do you like it?"

"I do. It's—"

"Lively?"

"Yes. And thanks."

"Do you mind if I still keep the braid?"

"I promised Daphni and Maya you would. I had to."

"Good." Jackson lunged for the reclining chair. "I'm exhausted. Let them have a look again if they want. I don't have either one in class today."

"I'll tell them."

"I'm relieved and exhausted. We did good work. You mind if I rest?" Jackson closed his eyes and fell into sleep.

Gus stared at the head for another moment. He'd made her

on the edge both of laughter and of rage, and she was lovely. She lowered the bed and followed Jackson, on her sleeping face as on his a shallow smile of deep satisfaction.

After school the girls took the bus to the hospital because Daphni insisted they needed to talk and needed lots of time for it. She was bringing meringues and had suggested that Maya bring contact sheets so that Gus would know how much they loved her. The bus took forever.

"We've got to find out what happened, Maya."

Maya nodded. The mold for the seat was too big for her. She grabbed the metal upright and wished Daphni would shut up for once. There were no good-looking ads to read and no interesting people except for one old goat chewing cud. Maya wanted to scream.

"I bet Frieda knows what happened; I bet she just isn't telling us. Papa knows too, I bet, I bet even Nicky knows. I bet they're just not telling us."

"I'm trying to concentrate, so will you shut up? I've got some dates to memorize."

"How *can* you! We've got to *talk this over!*" Daphni glared at Maya's profile. "*Maya!*"

"Will you shut up? Everybody's looking, Daphni."

"So what? *Something terrible* happened, and we've got to talk!" Daphni had no idea of how many people were watching her because she hadn't counted as Maya had when she looked around for something to fix on. Twenty-nine people were watching her. "*Maya!*"

"Will you cut it out! Stop calling me Maya."

"Your *name* happens to be *Maya,* and *I* happen to have something to discuss with you! I'm *worried,* Maya, that Jackson is responsible, don't you understand? What if he *drove her!*"

Maya leaned forward over the bookbag in her lap and, fastening it there with her elbows, covered her ears with her hands. She couldn't stand *scenes,* especially Daphni's. T-o-e-s, g-u-m w-r-a-p-p-e-r, l-e-a-t-h-e-r b-o-o-t-s, m-o-r-e l-i-t-t-e-r, she hummed and spelled as if she were fixed on a life-saving mantra, meditating.

Daphni saw Maya's curved back as the thing she'd like to stomp on until Maya repented and was bloody. She'd like to thwack Maya between the wings karate-style until she was bloody and repented. She'd like to take Maya's own braid and cut it off so she'd know it was *important* what their mother had done. Daphni gave Maya's braid a yank. H-u-r-t-s, Maya hummed and spelled, and reached for it, pulling it into the safety of the trenches under her nose. "*Maya!*"

It would have been so easy to tip Maya onto her head, dumping her ass over chin like junk tipped from a dump truck, but she didn't dare. The problem for Daphni was that Maya never got back. She didn't know but thought that if she over-did it either on purpose or by mistake, Maya just might get back once and for all, by tying Daphni in the bathroom, gagging her, sticking a funnel in her nose, and pouring in lethal amounts of developer, stop bath, and fixer.

Dr. Harding knocked, smiled, opened the door, and, still smiling cheerily, said, "Hello, Gus, mind if I sit for a minute?"

"Lovely, but what are you doing up here when you ought to be downstairs broiling people until they burst? Like hot grapes. Have a seat." Gus closed *The Years.*

The therapist sat on the edge of the bed. "I feel badly about this morning. Has Dr. Derby been in?"

Gus nodded. "And now you've changed your minds again?"

"No. He said he was going to tell you we're not going to finish the treatments, and that's where we're staying." The smile wavered and she took off the glasses that pressed foot-prints into the bridge of her nose.

"My blood?"

"Yes, we miscalculated."

"That's what he said, that it was my blood. And so you're retiring me."

"Yes." She was accustomed to saying "Cheer up" at that moment, but instead did an odd thing. She kissed Gus's face twice.

"So this is early retirement, is it? No gold or silver watch, nothing. Only that after all these years I didn't turn out to be management material after all. Not even a tin watch. You folks aren't easy on loyal employees, are you?" Gus smiled weakly.

"No, not easy." She paused. "But you've pulled more than a few surprises on us, Gus."

"Yes. I'll go home now."

"Are you asking me?"

"Yes."

"I thought so. I know we want to look at your blood for a while, if that helps, but otherwise."

"I know." Gus gave a wan good-sport smile. "Do you like my hair?"

"Yes, I do. I'll be sorry to lose you."

"I'll be back," said Gus before considering which way the radiologist might have meant *lose you.*

"And so will I. You'll be here a while."

"Did you say a week?"

"You know I'm never specific."

"That's the trouble with you: all those years of training gone to waste. Aren't you ashamed, Dr. Harding, to be so vague with all that training to be specific? I've never understood that in doctors. Baby-talk to the patient, talk to each other in code. God, and not even a retirement watch."

"First thing in the morning."

Gus grinned. "That's better. Now are you sure you didn't say a week instead of a while?"

"I think I said something in between."

"Thanksgiving's in nine days, you know."

"We know about Thanksgiving."

"Can you keep it in mind? My husband's turkey is better than the hospital's, but don't let me rush you. First the watch, and then we'll see if you didn't mean a week after all. What's the matter with my blood?"

"Low on everything."

"My brother and his wife are coming."

"I know," said the therapist. "We have a meeting set up with your brother."

"Good. I hope you'll talk code with him; you can, he's a doctor."

"I know. His wife and I were in medical school together."

"And Susanna and I were college roommates."

"Please give her my best."

Gus gave a sly look. "Your second best. I'm keeping your best." She pressed the button to bring herself up. "Want to help me? Because even though you think you're retiring me, really I'm just getting out of bed. The girls will be here soon, and I've got to brush my hair. Are you sure you like it? I have to defend it. They hate it, for instance. I'm ready to go home, you know. Can you hand me that shawl? I was hoping it would work the way it did the last time. It didn't, did it? Still, I figured I'd get through it and get to take the chance it offered. I hate not finishing. Fluid." She put her hands across her stomach. "Isn't it?"

"It's the masses. We wanted to shrink them again."

"Can't you boost my blood?"

"Not enough."

"Besides, it isn't worth it? Diminishing returns and all? I never know what to do with myself once I'm out of bed. I guess I'm just showing off for you. Shall I say something in algebra?"

"I'm sorry for what we've put you through."

"I know. Derby meant to say the same thing, though it didn't come out right. I'm sorry too. What time is it? Where are Daphni and Maya? Unless they took the bus today. The man who threw up corrected my head, if you'd like to see it. Perhaps you can help me with the plastic. I know why I'm up: it's so they'll see the head unwrapped before they get going on my hair. God." Gus held the metal footboard as if it were the handle for a waterski tow, letting it pull her weight to it. Then she put her forehead on the row of eight knuckles. "I've had a miserable afternoon, since Derby. But I'll be glad to be home. Do you like it? Lively, isn't it?"

Dr. Harding stroked the spine that invited a touch of some kind. "How like you it is," she said, massaging her own eyes with her other hand. "I'm sorry it didn't work this time, Gus."

"I didn't expect it. Imagine being that good with clay! But we'll see." She wished the tears would come. "My husband's in Boston today at a federal court case. The only time in weeks I haven't been able to call him, wouldn't you know? Please keep doing that."

The radiotherapist used both hands to bring warmth into the bony back that had her own black lines disfiguring it beneath the crumpled cotton nightgown. "And if I can't find a tin watch, will plastic be okay?"

"It will be fine. I wish I could cry, there's this awful pressure. I guess I figured I wouldn't get rejected at least. My body doesn't like surprises."

"We're not rejecting you."

"Kicking me out, aren't you?"

"Losses outweighing the gains, that's all, Gus. There's no magic number to these treatments."

"Twenty-one, it was, last time. And twenty-one this."

"But it's not like Berlitz. We have to measure the effect, not just fire away." She massaged down the arms and unclenched the fingers.

"I hope he doesn't have to stay in Boston; I hope he's not late. And I need to see Christopher. Why aren't the girls here?" She lifted her head. "I'm not able to cry. My body's not letting me even do that."

The doctor watched Gus maneuver herself into position and took a step forward but was waved away as Gus backed into bed and lowered herself onto the pillows. "I'll see you first thing in the morning then," Dr. Harding said, touched the footboard, and left. There was nothing more painful than sending a favorite patient home to get on with dying. She reached into the pocket of her starchy white coat to find a Kleenex.

At six, Andreas bounced into the room. "And we didn't even do as badly as I feared. And it's not going to drag on until tomorrow." He dropped his overcoat onto the chair and kissed his wife. "And I even said a thing or two in my native Greek."

"And how is your native Greek these days?"

"Very fast and rushing to catch the shuttle."

"You chatted with the crew and told them, but confidentially of course, that your father built their ship?"

"The crew was there on paper only. Their lawyer was Greek, and we talked about the election and Caramanlis."

"And Mercouri?"

"Well no, but I was rushing. We got off for sixty-forty, and I'd figured seventy-thirty would be the best we could get. Their lawyer wasn't too hot, perhaps he's been here too long or not long enough. But sixty percent at fault is a bargain! He could have proved seventy easily. Then Senator Kennedy was on the shuttle."

"Was he? Did you tell him we're neighbors at the Cape?"

"We weren't introduced." Andreas smiled his own politician's smile. "How was your day?"

"I'll tell you later. I want to hear in the finest detail what went on in Boston and everywhere else." She was badly in need

of information of any sort, she explained to Andreas, just anything that seemed to him at all distracting or educational, any
sort of fact or figure, any data there were on any subject at all.

"What subject?" he asked.

"Any subject," she said.

He loosened his tie, filled two glasses with ice and poured.
In fact he did feel a bit like fooling around. "Well now," he
began, "Boston's quite a nice town but it isn't the capital.
Washington is, but D.C. for District of Columbia. The Columbia River is in Washington but not in D.C., and that's because
of there being two Washingtons, not counting the President.
I'm just a naturalized citizen and have never seen the Columbia River, only the Potomac that Washington crossed in a
famous painting. Shall I go on?" He gave her the glass and
performed a small bow.

"Yes, please. Cheers."

"Cheers. Charleston is the capital of West Virginia, and
the capital of Idaho is Boise. There are more state capitals that
begin with C than B."

"Is that true?"

"I have no idea."

"Do a lot begin with F?"

"None, because certain letters of the alphabet were only
annexed later on after all the capitals had been named. F was
annexed very late due to an oversight, and it only exists today
because of the Louisiana Purchase. F was thrown in along with
a lot of other stuff, which means that since 1803, the country
we call France has all along been, technically that is, Rance.
No legal document exists that says we loaned them our F. In
fact, you might say that since 1803, Rance has been going
around illegally as France. Or, perhaps more accurately, Rance
is still pretending it owns F, when in fact it should be paying
us a little something in rent. The problem is that Rance is too

proud to admit that they were so poor they had to sell their F, and especially now that F has turned out to be an extremely popular letter."

Gus said, "I guess they're embarrassed."

"History is one embarrassment after another, isn't it?"

"I love you, Andreas. I've loved our life."

"So have I. I still do."

"So do I."

Andreas sat on the bed and bent to kiss her, all the features one by one, beginning and ending with the mouth. "I love you," he said a half-dozen times. "Are you okay?"

"Almost."

The doctor hadn't knocked—he never did—and so they didn't know he was there until he spoke. "Good evening" was what he always said no matter what, and he said it then but added an apology. He looked miserable, and Andreas offered him a drink and said there was no need to be embarrassed.

In that case he would gladly accept a glass of something, whatever there was, scotch, neat, if possible. It had been a monstrous day and he was on his way home anyway. He hadn't brought his clipboard and made no gesture to dismiss Andreas. Instead he sat on one of the frame chairs and held the glass on the kneecap of the one leg he had crossed over the other. His face was broken in with exhaustion.

"How are the girls?" His smile was pitiful. It was as if he wanted to express to Gus, "I care about you, Augusta, please won't you understand?"

"The girls are just fine, thank you," Gus replied.

"They're lovely children," Derby said, "and you both must be proud of them."

"Yes," said Andreas.

"I have two lovely grandchildren." He made another attempt to smile, but it was floppy. "I'm sorry I missed my own two growing up. I didn't know them. I haven't been this tired in years, and I don't know why I'm telling you this: I just lost a boy who'd been badly burned."

Gus had thought he looked to have lost a patient but hadn't dared ask. Andreas, who hardly knew the man, hadn't known what to think.

"We're supposed to say it was a mercy. His father's a doctor here, and he just told me he'd never made time, or been given it, to know his son. His ten-year-old boy played with matches last Saturday. He'd told the boy they'd go to a soccer game, then couldn't make it. The boy just died. The only time they spent together was in this place, and the boy was unconscious most of the time. His name was Teddy. I didn't know what to say to my colleague." He took a long sip. "I never had time for my children either, but at least they lived. At least we know each other now to some extent, though it's not the same, I don't think it could be. If you had seen Teddy. I think I had better be going now."

Dr. Derby handed his glass to Andreas and thanked him for having offered it. "What I wanted to say," he added then, "is that we won't keep you any longer than we have to, Augusta. We don't have enough time to spend at home, and that goes for everyone."

Chapter
Five

Gus woke at five but didn't know the time because she was wearing the tot-size plastic Cinderella watch whose movable hands she'd spun for two days, contentedly unmindful of the actual hour. But it was Friday morning, she knew, and even if it was dark in the room that didn't face east, at least it was Friday. If Dr. Derby kept his promise, as had Dr. Harding with the watch, she'd be home in two days. Meanwhile, Friday meant Christopher and Susanna and blood, healthy blood coming up to boost her along.

But she'd sweated awfully during the night and had to ring for the nurse on duty to give her a bath. She wanted to be clean for the blood; it was the nicest of changes to be receiving rather than giving out the blood that was daily run through machines to see how many more were missing of those disk-shaped platelets (plate-shaped disklets and then chicklets, Gus called them) vital for coagulation. At last count she'd had one-tenth the normal amount of chicklets, which meant presumably that her blood could race from her wrists thinner than exhaust, quicker than she could say "emergency," and that wasn't all.

Because if her megakaryocytes, the platelet makers, were off the assembly line striking for better working conditions, equally uncooperative were her granulocytes, the white blood corpuscles, and the fanciest arbitrators in the business had been unsuccessful at getting them back on the job. Gus called the granulocytes coyotes, little wolves on prairies, which had nothing at all to do with strikers but which went to show how easy it is to mix metaphors when you're trying to cope with things that 1) you've never heard of and 2) are fundamental to life.

Was it a problem that she called her blood things chicklets and coyotes? Gus asked the nurse who was finishing with her bed. "No, dear," the nurse said, "whatever you like. There you are, dear," she went on with the next breath, "how would you like to slip back in?"

Gus would like to. There was almost no better feeling than being slipped into all that white, even the hidden layers white, even the pillows and the mattress, the sheepskin pad white as a lamb and springy as a permanent wave. Her sister, Mimi, had suggested that Gus use her own sheets so she could have color, flowers, stripes, and dots. But Mimi didn't understand that the point isn't to make the hospital seem like home, but to make being sick seem like being a child, which had to do with white sheets because the coloreds hadn't been invented when Gus was six and sick in her tonsils, from which she got better.

Gus saw that the nurse's watch said five-thirty and gasped at having rung for a bath in the middle of the night, as well as at having four hours to get rid of before Christopher's visit. Wrapped in the shawl crocheted by Mimi of Popsicle-colored yarns, she would wait. She would read *The Years*.

"1917," and Eleanor goes to Maggie's for dinner. Sara no longer lives with her sister, who married Renny the Frenchman, but she's there for dinner along with a homosexual Pole called Nicholas.

An air raid: they huddle in the coal cellar wrapped in quilts and dressing gowns. "To the New World!" they toast with Renny's wine merchant father's French wine. And then:

"They listened. The guns were still firing, but far away in the distance. There was a sound like the breaking of waves on a shore far away.

" 'They're only killing other people,' said Renny savagely. He kicked the wooden box."

And then the bugles sound and they go back upstairs, Eleanor and Nicholas to talk about this New World they drink to.

"It is only a question," he said—he stopped. He drew himself close to her—"of learning. The soul . . ." Again he stopped.

"Yes—the soul?" she prompted him.

"The soul—the whole being," he explained. He hollowed his hands as if to enclose a circle. "It wishes to expand; to adventure; to form—new combinations?"

"Yes, yes," she said, as if to assure him that his words were right.

"Whereas now,"—he drew himself together; put his feet together; he looked like an old lady who is afraid of mice—"this is how we live, screwed up into one hard little, tight little—knot?"

"Knot, knot—yes, that's right," she nodded.

"Each is his own little cubicle; each with his own cross or holy books; each with his fire, his wife . . ."

"Darning socks," Maggie interrupted.

Gus would agree with Eleanor that she wished Nicholas to go on talking. When, Gus wanted to know, when?

When, she wanted to ask him, when will this New World come? When shall we be free? When shall we live adventurously, wholly, not like cripples in a cave? He seemed to have released something in her; she felt not only a new space of time, but new powers, something unknown within her. She watched his cigarette moving up and down. Then Maggie took the poker and struck the wood and again a shower of red-eyed sparks went volleying up the chimney. We shall be free, we shall be free, Eleanor thought.

Was Nicholas talking perhaps of death? The soul expanding, adventuring, forming new combinations, free. She would see. She would first see Eleanor home on the omnibus.

It was a shallow dream Gus had, and the colors were watery thin ones. The ocean was the color of the Atlantic, even though she held a fat Caribbean child on either hip. They were wading —the children, twins, were only two or so—or rather she was wading while they sat on her hips. A wave knocked her over, and then something—it was very hard to see because the colors were so pale, as if it were a pitiably thin negative, too thin to print—something happened, which was one of two things. Either she lost the twins—or—they lost her.

Gus sucked her breath in. She wasn't supposed to dream anymore; the medication—especially the newest, stronger—was supposed to sterilize her dreamlife. She wasn't meant any longer to see the wave knock her down as she was wading.

"They listened. The guns were still firing, but far away in the distance. There was a sound like the breaking of waves on a shore far away."

Gus let the breath out and was dizzy with having held on too long. Its being shallow made the dream eerier, ghostlier, too far away in the distance, too much like the breaking of waves on a shore far away.

" 'They're only killing other people,' said Renny savagely. He kicked the wooden box."

Hours, still. She would ring to ask when the blood would get there, regretting having opened *The Years*. It was possible that Christopher was meeting just then with her healing team, and was on his way to confirm what she knew.

The blood arrived.

And eventually so did Christopher.

He entered his sister's room looking boyish as a breeze and smiling his half-moon smile, as if he hadn't just come from the meeting with her doctors. He always did. He had the looks of a movie doctor—the Tab Hunter of Open Heart, Gus had called him for years—and had felt it to be to his disadvantage to look so boyish and movie cute. Haw, haw, you don't mean to say you're the *doctor!* But what should he do? Paint on crow's feet, graft himself a paunch? Yellow his teeth and wear Ping-Pong balls along his jawbone? Make his *hands shake?* Was what they wanted the Sloppy Joe of Open Heart?

Boyish as a breeze, he kissed and hugged her, and Gus began to tremble from the inside out. She couldn't let go of him but didn't have to. It seemed that Christopher was prepared to hold on to her for the rest of her life.

And what a relief. Gus sobbed until it hurt too much to stay sitting up with her arms around him. What a relief it was to know that he'd come to help her understand whatever it was, her charts for instance, and tell her something definite for once and for all. She had needed to have confirmed the thing that nobody would, and Christopher confirmed it in the way he held her against his own certain loss.

She lowered herself onto the pillows and closed her eyes but couldn't think. Finally she asked, "Did you get the prize?"

"Last night." With his sleeve he wiped his eyes.

"And the operation?"

"Later this morning. It's only slides we're going to show."

"Susanna and you from the elbows down?"

"The wrists down. The star of the show is the heart."

"I'm proud of you both. A prize from the biggest hearts in America."

"Yes, it was extremely heartfelt and rather strange."

"Now let's talk about me." Her smile was weak.

He took a breath. "You're in trouble, miss. I see you flunked radiotherapy, and that your megakaryocytes are truant. You've got an incomplete in chemotherapy, I see, and a white blood count that tells us, frankly, that you're what we call an under-achiever." Out of breath.

"How about 'Gets Along Well with Others,' sir?"

"You got an E for Excellent."

"I get your message. You're sending me to the principal."

"I wish our tutors could help you."

"They're not all that bright anyway." Gus took air in, but it caught on something that made her give a little cry that sounded animal. "They're really not all that bright anyway," she said, and closed her eyes to try and think.

When she woke up again, her brother was in the easy chair. "I fall asleep so much," she complained.

"Your medication is getting stronger." He looked at her chart and was reminded he ought to return it to the desk. Christ, she could take a lot of pain, he said to himself. Her medication was nothing, so far. But how naive he was for never having been sick a day in his life. "I'll just return this and be right back."

Gus realized that his being straight with her was brotherly-sisterly, which instinct had somehow asserted itself over his very training as a doctor: namely, to avoid being the bearer of bad tidings, at all cost. Gus wondered if this avoidance weren't less in order to save themselves personal suffering, and more because they truly believed themselves omnipotent, with such a slim margin for failure that it was hardly worth facing up to.

Christopher excepted, and Dr. Harding, Gus found doctors were disgusting fakers and lame-excusers all. And Susanna excepted.

"*I detest doctors!*" Gus said as Christopher walked back into the room. "I'm *sick* of their shuffling around like Japanese maidservants, lying through their teeth Good Morning Augusta, Good Afternoon Augusta, Good Evening Augusta. I'm sick of their vacant diplomat's language which says nothing in case it might disagree with what another might have hinted at. Does a patient have to come right out and ask, 'Hey doc, what time's my ship sailing?' in order to find out what the manifest says? I'm sick of them all! They make me *sick*, just sick to God damn death."

Christopher sat down again. "Gussie, didn't I ever tell you what utter babies we are? Spoiled brats who can't stand not to win? Look at us: the most pampered profession in the country, the most difficult to join, the most looked up to, the richest. What do you expect of spoiled kids who are the elite and know it? Do you expect them to admit how little there is to learn? Or that medical school is mostly running around on no sleep in order to feel desperately busy, and so nobody will complain when you soak them for their savings a year or two later?"

"Yes, I do. It's sickening."

"I don't disagree."

"They couldn't even tell me in plain English they were letting me go, writing me off. And then they couldn't tell me when."

"They told me Sunday."

"Yes, I know now. Dr. Derby told me. But all they do is make excuses and avoid me, and then be so busy they just have to run, so sorry and all. That's not how it should be!"

"No, it isn't."

"Do you talk to your patients, Christo?"

"All there is to say, which is something like 'This operation isn't off the drawing boards yet, but it's your only bet in spite of the fact that the odds are not calculable.' That's all there is."

"Well just imagine being a patient!"

"I do, I try to."

"You're a depressing conversationalist."

"You're not all that cheerful yourself. Spirited as always, but." He stopped, and tears came into his eyes. "I love you, Gussie."

Gus took a breath and called, "Look out, Hollywood, here we come! A romantic brother-sister act: Antigone and the dead brave Polyneices in reverse!"

They had once put on *Antigone* as a puppet show, reinventing the dialogue to suit their being ten and fifteen. She had played all the women and he all the men for an audience that consisted of Mimi, their parents, and an English family named the Whomevers, who were invisible but who came anyway every time there was a performance of one of the classics.

"We've already done Antigone and Polyneices, remember?"

"I said in reverse. Now you bury me, Christo. I hope it's easier than the time Antigone had."

"It will be harder."

"That's melodramatic."

"Yes, it is. Are we invited for Thanksgiving?"

"Would you come? I'd so love to have you and Susanna there. Mère is coming; I'd like to ask Mimi too. Will this be my last holiday?"

"I don't think so, I hope not."

"My last Thanksgiving in any case."

"Now you're the one being melodramatic."

"Yes, I am." Gus smiled a new moon, a thin white curve, a beautiful line. "But I feel calm for the first time since I've been here. I was so afraid they'd keep me here until I was dead. Once I'm home I won't leave."

"I think they know that."

"But Dr. Derby doesn't approve, does he? I don't care." Gus listened to *care* and rhymed it. "But Christopher, you haven't commented on my hair. Do you like it?"

"Not much. Did you cut it for any particular reason?"

"Not that I know of. I'm falling asleep again. Wouldn't you like to see the head? I'm so glad you're going to come for Thanksgiving."

He took off the plastic, not wanting to see how some clown had fouled up, and carefully folded it before looking. "But it's good!" Christopher exclaimed. "It's you, your eyes, pleased with yourself. Your mouth as if you're saying something. I'm amazed, Gus. Who is this guy?"

Gus lowered her bed and closed her eyes. It was good he was pleased. "Ask Daphni and she'll tell you Michelangelo."

Again he sat, again he watched her. The cut hair wasn't Gus, it was somebody else. He closed his eyes and remembered the day their parents were killed. He had been in Boston for a conference and had telephoned in the evening, and Gus had asked if he'd seen the news. She had said that Mimi was on the news and would probably be back on at eleven to say "All things must pass" into the microphone. Mimi had been at the Beirut airport and had seen everything but, along with the others, understood nothing until the moment the plane exploded. "I have been to see the Cedars," Mimi had explained to the newsman in such a way that for all he knew, she might have been talking about the terrorists who had caused the plane to be blown up, "and all things must pass."

Mimi would fly into Boston, Gus had told Christopher, and they would meet at their parents' house on the Cape to decide what to do. She and Andreas and the girls—Nicky was only a pregnancy then—would leave to drive up just after the news. Andreas and the girls had seen it, but Gus had been late getting back from a conference on the Mideast. She had said to Christopher that Andreas thought it a good thing to watch (how else was what had happened imaginable?) and so she would. Would he meet Mimi?

The next morning they had stood in the side yard around the hole Andreas had dug. Mimi was complaining that she should have told the newsman to go blow, and that she was sure he had made a fool of her. But "All things must pass," she intoned again, placing their mother's and their father's reading glasses, extras for each and kept in the desk inside, at the bottom of the hole. "There's nothing else to bury," she said quite accurately, helping Gus and Christopher set the dogwood's roots into the ground that would be watered until nightfall.

Gus and Christopher walked then for hours while Mimi slept. The house was on a mile-long beach, and they walked out and back to one side and then to the other, the early November cold having emptied the beach of strangers.

"This ought to have been Thanksgiving," Gus told Christopher, "and we ought to have finished a big dinner during which the three of them told us about their trip to Lebanon. We aren't supposed to be here now. What happened, Christo?" Christopher said he didn't know either. "And I was at a conference on the Mideast," she went on, "but I didn't know it was their plane. We talked about terrorism. Christo? I want to pretend we are having our walk after Thanksgiving dinner. I want to imagine Mother and Father playing Scrabble right now with Daphni and Maya, and Susanna and Andreas talking, and Mimi somewhere but not in shock, don't you?" And Christopher agreed. Gus continued, "I can't imagine them in that plane waiting for someone to agree to something and wondering which side and what. And the heat, and then the shots, and then the fuel tank exploding. Did they hold hands and thank each other for their marriage?" Again he said he didn't know either.

They moved the fingers in leather gloves they held as hands and continued walking. " 'I am the resurrection and the life, saith the Lord; the God of the spirits of all flesh.' You know, Christo? It was the chance they always took." And Christopher nodded. "Did you smile at the part I did? 'I heard a voice from heaven, saying unto me, Write . . .' But that was the last thing I said to them, 'Write!' And they did, too, and I want to write back. They'll want to know who their grandchild would have been."

"Should."

"Should have been, yes." Gus walked to her brother's other side to change the hands held for those from their pockets. Her hands had cramped around the earth she had put on top of the dogwood roots, the earth was so cold.

"There's a fishing boat," said Christopher, "but it should be too late in the day for that."

"It's almost dark enough to see the light. I knew that one day we'd be burying them and walking and looking at the lighthouse."

"We didn't bury them," Christopher said.

They turned at the point to walk the last stretch back to the house. The wind had come up suddenly to water their eyes and dry their mouths, and as they walked into it their foul-weather gear was pressed flat against them. The yellow waxy jacket Gus wore made another shell for the egg-shaped child who wouldn't be born for nearly a month.

When Jackson arrived he found the head unwrapped, as Christopher had left it when he'd gone to show slides to cardiology. There was the back of the head to do, the braid, and the neck needed to be leaner. Jackson worked for a long while in silence.

"Hi."

"How you doing? That new medication must be a trip."

"A knockout, Daphni says I mutter."

"Some. You know what she said to me yesterday after class? That first came her father and then came me. Then she got all fouled up and said she meant only as an Artist, that she deeply admired My Work and didn't mean Personally or anything. Daphni's a hoot."

"Hoot?"

"I'm real nuts about melodrama. Where's she get it from? From her father?"

"We think she tends to take after Andreas's father and mother."

"Both?" He couldn't remember whether the braid had been fatter. "That's what I call a heritage! My genes are all stamped Submissive, and so when I get worked up I feel I'm a failure. My parents also tell me that to make sure I know it. Are your parents difficult?"

"Mine are dead."

Jackson dropped his tool and bent to retrieve it and to hide. He had thought he'd continue with melodrama, and why he loved it and why they didn't and thus were difficult. Dead? Now what could he ever say? Had he ever met anyone under forty whose parents were dead? "How so?" he said inappropriately, and rose to hide behind the head.

"Blown up. Are you hiding?"

"I'm hiding. I'm nervous. Blown up in a car?"

"A plane. A terrorist tactic backfired. The terrorists wanted to make a speech and then let the passengers go free. It was a planeload of university professors, American. But the terrorists wanted safe conduct and haggled with the Lebanese until threats were made and then a shot fired, then back and forth and the fuel tank exploded and everyone died."

Jackson stepped to one side. "I read about that. It was famous." He thought that his own life had never seemed so pathetic, conventional, boring, simple. That was his first thought. Next he thought, "Christ, how awful!" and said so.

Gus smiled. "Was your first thought how come nothing interesting happens to you? I think I saw that in your face."

"If you really must know, it was a little, only a little. You should have said something."

"Such as?"

"Who knows? My parents were torched on the Beirut runway! Don't spring it on somebody after a week, Gus."

"I thought you liked drama."

"I said *melo*drama; I hate surprises! Jesus Christ." Jackson wiped his forehead. "You got me sweating. You certainly know how to keep the advantage!"

"I wouldn't call it an advantage," Gus said calmly, "to have them dead."

"I didn't mean that. I'm sorry, but it's shocking, Gus."

"I know."

"Well, then don't get angry at me, Jesus Christ! I just want to know how you can stand working with Arab students after that."

Gus lowered her bed and put her fingers over her eyes. "It has nothing to do with the Arab students. My parents were in their seventies and had loved their retirement as much as their teaching. They'd had happy and very fortunate lives and always said a blast into death was better than a painful leaching out of existence. I'd like to rest now and be alone."

Jackson turned off the spots that illuminated the head. "Yes," he said, and had to say it again, "Yes," because his voice had disappeared.

He left the head unwrapped and went to the solarium to study the George Washington Bridge. The big window looked right out onto the bridge, and Jackson pretended himself into a glass-bottomed boat, from which he was examining a bridge-size wrecked liner that had sunk in barely enough water to cover. It was interesting to be so close to a wreck, except that it was such a monster in relation to the cute little trucks and buses that swam like fishes across its crisscrossed lower deck. Jackson didn't want it to end because—he wondered this with a fearing sort of seriousness—what would he do in the mornings without Gus? How would he ever spend the morning time he had learned to put to use again after years of sleeping it away? And with winter coming.

He turned his back to the window through which the river and sky were gray as the bridge. No sol for the solarium that gray raining November Friday, and the room had a chilly look in spite of the fact that its air was warm enough for orchids. More crisscrosses, Jackson noticed, in the wallpaper with its trellis design colored lettuce green to appear younger than it was. And more crisscrosses in the lattice backs and sides of that indoor porch furniture made of aluminum bamboo cushioned in lettuce vinyl. Lettuce lattice trellis crisscross buses fishes glass. There was so much to think about.

Susanna was looking at the head when Jackson went back into Gus's room. "Hello"—she smiled—"I'm Susanna Frye, Gus's sister-in-law." She spoke very quietly.

Jackson said, "Nice to meet you."

"And who are you?" Susanna asked, to his surprise.

"Oh, sorry, name's Jackson, thought you'd been told or something, it's me who did the head." He looked over to Gus, who was asleep. "How embarrassing," he said out loud, not meaning to, and with that they stopped shaking hands.

"The head is very fine, such a good likeness."

"Thanks, but I was about to leave so I'll cover it up if that's okay."

"It's fine; shall I help?"

"It's okay." The plastic rattled enough to wake Gus, which was the thing, Jackson realized, Susanna wished to avoid with her offer of help. "I'm sorry," he told her. He'd handled the plastic like a cape, to show off, and he'd blown it.

"Ahoy," Gus called, "are we in a storm?" She whirred the top third of her bed back into sitting position.

Hi, hi, hi, Jackson laughed, thankful for the relief. "Look," he said, pointing, "land."

"Susanna! I'm so glad!" They kissed. "Then you've met. Susanna and my brother are the prizewinners I told you about."

"Yes, congratulations," Jackson said. Susanna nodded.

"Tell us," Gus urged, "how was it?"

Susanna sat on the arm of the easy chair. "Well, the talk went on forever about how hardworking the two of us were, though never without a ready smile. College yearbook stuff to prove how perfectly suited we were for each other, even with Christopher's lost years in the army. So romantic, when as you know we couldn't stand each other at first."

"Why," Jackson interrupted, "or rather, how so?"

"He was coming back from the army and was at a terrible disadvantage anyhow, but I was determined not to let him sweep right over me and take all the interesting work I'd been promised. Women doctors have had to possess very long hours and very short tempers, and I always have. Anyway, last night: this wonderful old surrogate-father under whom we did our residencies went on as if he'd been God himself and we his little creations learning cardiology in the Garden. And then he went into the Frye/West jokes."

"What's that?" Jackson said, again meaning not to speak.

"It's that West is Christopher's name and Frye is mine and, so goes the joke, that after finishing our residencies here at Presbyterian, we got all these offers to Frye West. California, Texas, Illinois: Frye West, Young Man, and all that."

"And did you?" Couldn't he keep himself silent?

"Not at first."

"Is that the joke?"

"I don't know what the joke is. It's just always referred to as a joke, and it always goes Frye West."

"Did you get married then?" Maybe they didn't mind that he had to interrupt?

"Yes, only the jokes always refer to it as incorporating or consolidating. Anyway, it went on and on, and finally the man admitted that he'd lost the plaque." Susanna shrugged.

"He'd lost the *prize?*"

"He'd lost one of the two plaques, which was why all the delaying. *Which of us should accept it?* The poor guy was lost."

Jackson thought it was interesting that when he and Marty left the Ugandan school they'd taught at during their Peace Corps years, nobody worried about who would get the one plaque. He wondered if Gus and Susanna would be interested in hearing about that. Not especially, he decided. Anyway Gus was talking.

"—hope you told him to toss it onto the floor and you'd both dive for it on a count of three."

"And fight to the end!" Susanna's laugh had a crinkly sound something like aluminum foil being balled. "Finally he made us each put a hand on it while he put an arm around each of us, and that was the presentation. And you know? There was hardly any mention of the operation for which we were getting the prize."

Gus thought to herself that it must be quite a dreary profession that honors its successful members with such bad jokes. How dreary, then, to be a famous woman doctor, which thought then reminded Gus that the night before had been medicine night in her series at International House—American Women in Medicine—and she must remember to call Ellen, her assistant and replacement, to find out if it had gone well.

"Enjoyed meeting you," Jackson was saying. "I'm late for school, Gus, *hasta mañana.*" Out he ran.

"What a nice young man," Susanna said.

"He's saved my life," Gus answered, wincing, "so to speak. Christo told me. Have you seen my charts?"

"I haven't, but he told me too."

"I guess the tumors are after my kidneys, my liver, and my duodenum." Gus shivered.

"Yes."

"Not good odds."

"No."

"I would fill up with poison. I wouldn't be able to digest anything. And my blood's lousy too. Why haven't they told me?"

"I don't know, Gussie." Susanna rubbed her hands together.

"I'd like to see the first of the year. Is that more than I'll get?"

"I wish someone knew."

"But if there's a possibility no, there's a possibility yes as well."

"Yes, there's hope."

"Worth betting on?"

"Yes." Misery.

"Is that what you tell all your patients?"

"Yes." Susanna risked a grin, and Gus responded.

"Then I'm going to change the subject. How's your cat?"

Susanna relaxed. "Spot has some kind of neurasthenia."

"Which is?"

"Unspecified complaints, exhaustion." Susanna left such an ambiguous silence that Gus felt she ought to backtrack. "Your cat?" she asked. There was that crinkled foil sound again. "Isn't it nuts?" Susanna laughed.

When Gus said that she would take Spot's neurasthenia to sleep for a little while, Susanna said she would go and look up some of her old friends and then come back for the afternoon. Fine, Gus agreed. From time to time there was nothing better than time alone.

Which in itself was interesting. Gus would not have guessed from looking at her life, which had open doors everywhere and was peopled nearly every minute of the day, that she could have grown to love her own company. Dropping to sleep, she wondered how she could have found it boring being out of the mainstream, how she'd been bored with having to fill her time while everyone else was doing something and she was doing nothing. Was one theory that her insecurity had been with wondering whether she was in bad shape or not—and thus her fretting and thus her boredom—but that there was security in knowing she was done for? Maybe it was that as she got sicker, it was what others did that seemed trivial and boring in contrast to her own matter of life and death. Or maybe it came down to chemicals, that her cancerous body manufactured new chemicals to compensate, so that there was a certain chemical adjustment, a gyrostabilizer built into cancer patients to keep them steady in stormy seasons. Perhaps what seemed to be conscious and unconscious resignation was only a chemical balancing act, a trade-off. It was true that she and all the other cancer patients she had known had learned serenity.

She'd been asleep for two hours when Andreas arrived from his lunch with Christopher, during which her brother the doctor had admitted that the only thing Gus had going for her was that she could still eat and pee.

The omelets had come and gone untouched, but Andreas had two scotches and half of the wine to Christopher's martinis and the other half. And they'd wept over coffee.

Andreas took advantage of Gus's sleep to stare at her face and weep some more. He hadn't come to terms with her dying, not really, not for years and years, no matter, even, that they'd talked about it in the form of Jackson's head for Nicky, and in the form of paperwork that had to be attended to. Weren't those just in case? "Just in case" something goes wrong; just in case "something goes wrong."

"Hi, darling."

"Gussie." He kissed her with more than his usual tenderness.

She raised the bed. "Your eyes are red; is the air worse than usual?"

"Yes." Andreas added, "And Christopher and I had a lot to drink, and we talked about you, which is mostly why."

"Why you had a lot to drink or why your eyes are red?"

"Both. Did you and Susanna have a nice time?"

"We talked about how little time. She went to find friends, and when she came back we talked about whether I'd have known early enough if I hadn't been pregnant. That's what I asked her, but of course she said there's no way of knowing that. Then she went off to find friends again. They're going to come to New York for Thanksgiving."

"Yes, that's good."

"And I'm going to call Mimi."

"Okay." His stomach roared with hunger.

"Didn't you eat?"

"Our lunch was liquid. I should have put a roll in my pocket." Again his stomach protested with a whining buzz.

"You should get something."

"I guess." He sat. It was such a long way to the cafeteria.

"I could call Mimi."

"Okay." He stood. The protest was a rat-tat-tat. "Do you want something, Gussie?"

"Not me, I've had three bags of blood."

Chapter Six

Maya took many pictures of the taxis arriving, of the drivers handing things to the doorman, of Jackson emerging with his plywood platter and the plastic-wrapped head, of Mimi's gardenia bush descending the step to the street like an overweight goddess needing hoisting up again onto the sidewalk, of the basket filled with get-well wishes in letters and cards, of Andreas handing the pedestal to Daphni, who passed it on to one of the lesser personages, some spearcarrier or other who lived in the building, and finally of Gus, who stepped into the limelight in the daze of one who's been marooned, or trapped alone somewhere near death, and rescued.

Gus peered and then smiled into the camera, squinting against the sun that slanted over the awning and into her eyes. Who had come to watch her totter, she wondered. "Look, Maa!" Nicky sang, and made a spiral with his tricycle, bearing

down around and around. "Great, Nic," she said with slight
enthusiasm, sure he would topple onto his head by way of
stopping. "Hi, Daphni. Hi, Frieda," Gus said, stepping into
the shade to look into their faces. How come nobody jostled
her, or hustled or greeted her? It was as if she were royalty
in person come to midmorning tea, as if everybody knew that
it is illegal to touch royal persons and so hung back waiting
just to catch a wave, a smile, a wink. Do royals wink? Gus
doubted it.

Someone sounded pitch. So that's why they stayed grouped
together, hands behind their backs like that! Out came re-
corders, tambourines, and triangles, an instant upper east side
Hare Krishna outfit. Tink-tink and rattle-rattle, the orchestra
played a little salute. Rattle-rattle, tink-tink, a second number
which Maya finished with a laughable vamp of a whine from
her kazoo; the end. Then they cheered and rushed her as if
she weren't the least bit royal.

Gus went up first, and she and Andreas both said yes to
the doorman's observation that it had been quite a home-
coming. And for once, he made a smooth landing at nine,
rising right up to the level instead of bouncing around six
inches above and the same below, playing the brass lever like
a one-arm bandit being pumped for everything it was worth.

"Smooth landing," Gus said encouragingly. She had become
used to them, of course, in the hospital glider types.

"Don't want to bounce you up too much, right, Mr. Kaligas?"

"Right, Joe."

"Thanks, Joe."

"You're welcome." Joe pulled the brass cage door open
and shut. "I'll bring the others right up," he said, and disappeared.

The first smell was the simmering hot chocolate, and that
was enough to make Gus weep. She stood and watched her-

self in the hall mirror. There it was again, the gray wool jumper that went from her shoulders to the floor, which had come from England for her first pregnancy. She answered Andreas that she'd like to sit on the couch and be wrapped in the cashmere blanket that had also come from England once, but she didn't say it out loud and so he called to her again, "Gussie, where would you like to sit?"

"I haven't moved," she said.

"Darling?"

"Look, Andreas, everything is me but the hair. I'd look just the same as always if I hadn't cut it. What on earth did I do that for?"

Andreas put his back to the mirror to block the image. He touched her face. "You look more like your mother now, that's all."

"I know, I look exactly like her."

"She was beautiful too." Andreas kissed her.

"She's gone, of course." The thought of the waste made Gus choke on her weeping, and that was not even to mention the loss. "And so am I going to be gone," she said.

"No, you're going to be here."

"I cut it before Christopher came, as if he had nothing to tell me I didn't already know. Now I know why I did it, but I didn't see back in the hospital, not until I looked now and mistook myself for her. I thought I was seeing her just now, she stood here so often, right here to take off and put on her coat. It had nothing to do with it hurting to lie on, or with the radiotherapy patients. Did you know that?"

"I wasn't sure." He wanted to squeeze her.

"I want to look."

Andreas moved to stand behind her, but Gus asked him to leave the mirror. She couldn't get over what she had done and needed to examine herself. She was the photograph of her mother her father had always kept on his dresser, the photograph which still stood on his dresser at the Cape, an 8-by-10 in a silver frame, taken when her mother was thirty-nine and just finishing her doctorate. Gus was then fifteen, she remembered, and had asked her mother for a copy to put in her scrapbook with the program from graduation. Christopher was getting his B.A., their mother her Ph.D., both from Harvard. Gus had put a picture of Christopher on the same page but couldn't remember which one it was. She'd written "Mom Commences" at the top of the page in fancy script.

"Mom Commences," Gus said to herself in the mirror. At thirty-nine, her mother's career was just beginning. "Andreas?" He was just two steps away. "Can you take my arm? Can we have a fire?"

She loved the living room with its baby grand in front of the tall south windows, the all-year indoor window boxes flowering up geraniums, parsley, dill, and impatiens, the wooden tooth molding across the corniced window tops, the cashmere up around her neck. The drug was making her thinking floaty—or—foamy, only not shaving-cream foamy but root-beer-float foamy—or—scummy, gassy and light and bubbly but scummy foam. And where should the head go?

Daphni carried the pedestal and Jackson the deck. Why not by the window, use the light? Fine, anywhere. Daphni rushed for the cocoa.

"Marty's spending Thanksgiving in the West Indies," said Jackson, "so I'll have Max from Tuesday afternoon on. I'm asking a friend, if I can get a hold of her, to drive us and the head to Greenwich on Wednesday. The foundry's nearby there."

"Our last day is Wednesday?" Gus wondered if Nicky had noticed Jackson or the head, so intent had he been on his tricycle. "I want Nicky to know that you're making this head. Will you let him watch when you come tomorrow?"

"Anything you like."

"Whipped cream and cinnamon!" Daphni gave the first cup to Jackson. "Frieda's coming, by the way. It's just: Nicky fell off and smashed something, his knee I think. We came on ahead. Don't you love your hot chocolate fixed like this, Jackson? Children tend to like marshmallows, but adults don't. Maya still uses marshmallows."

"So what!" said Maya.

"Nothing. Here's for you, Mummy; here, Papa. Here they come now, that's Nicky screaming. How do you like it?"

"Good," Jackson said, watching Andreas walk to the door, "but I wouldn't say smashed, I'd say Nicky nicked his knee not badly."

"That's fantastic!" Daphni cooed. "Nicky nicked his knee not—how about something like noticeably instead of badly? Nicky nicked his knee not noticeably!" And she beamed.

"Because he landed on his shoulder," Maya informed them, "and I was there but you were in the elevator."

"The door was open, Maya!"

"So what? Did you see him fall?"

"Did you?"

"As a matter of fact, I happen to have."

"So? Big deal!"

"Just stop showing off, Daphni."

"Then you fix your own cup of babyish cocoa! You're such a child, Maya!" Daphni sighed and turned back to Jackson. "Pardon us," she said apologetically. "Mum, want some more?"

"Your mother's asleep," whispered Jackson to Daphni.

Nicky ran in and woke Gus to kiss the wrist he'd landed on, and his screaming stopped immediately. The fall hadn't even broken the skin. "Better!" Nicky chirped. "Want drinking for Nic!"

Daphni poured cocoa into a plastic cup. "Nicky doesn't use marshmallows, only Maya," she said, spreading a quilt of whipped cream speckled with the spice. "It's wonderful to

have you here. Art is so important to have in the home, I always say. And it's wonderful to have the head where it be-
longs. Nic, where's Frieda? She's going to want some chocolate,
being Dutch."

Jackson rose to leave them with the apology that he had
to find Lib, his friend with the car and the—needless to say
he didn't say—wide-open thighs. He was sure they wanted to
be alone together, he said, and so he'd run along and set up
his—transportation. Could he use the phone? She was also
the one with the most unapologetic libido, nineteen, with
gourd breasts and all the rest, in her first year at Barnard. He'd
told her he loved her libido that first night, and she'd asked
what a libido was, was it Spanish or Italian. He'd guessed at
its being Latin and told her she ought to look it up since she
had the best. "You're right, it's Latin!" she'd written on an
outsize postcard she signed "Love, Lib." Her real name was
something like Dorothy. No answer; he'd call her again from
a bar, or go up there and hang around for her. If she wouldn't
drive him to Greenwich, who would? She wore crinkly shirts
from India that made her nipples stand up like flowers, and
her skin was so smooth. "You don't have pores," he'd told her,
"do your fingers have prints?" He dialed her again. Lib had
drug-lidded eyes and had been all over the world by nineteen,
including to death's, so to speak, door to check out where pain
was at. Everyplace but Uganda, as far as Jackson could tell.
Still no answer.

"We wish you'd stay but understand how important it is
that the clay get a safe ride to the foundry." Daphni lowered
her eyes so as not to hint that she'd hoped. "And it is your
day off from students and so on, isn't it?"

"It's that I better find Lib, her car, the ride for the head."
She would ride him like a trapeze in bed. "Well, I'm off." He
blushed and dashed for the door.

"Oh dammit," Daphni muttered, "what on earth's left but

homework?" She shuffled dejectedly to her room. "I couldn't care less about the *Times,*" she said to Frieda, who stood in the way still holding on to the Sunday paper she'd been handed from one of the taxis.

"I could," Frieda said. "Bloody Marys and the *Times* by the fire?" Gus nodded yes.

"I think I'll print," explained Maya, and Gus nodded yes again. Nicky'd nodded out and was drooling on the skirt of her jumper. "You want me to put him away for you, Mom?" Again she nodded.

In fact she hadn't decided what she'd like to have done, what she'd like to do. She didn't think it was the *Times* but took the first section anyway, since there were two, her hospital one and the one delivered to the apartment. She didn't think she wanted silence.

" 'First Greek Election of Decade,' " Gus announced to Frieda and Andreas, "and 'Cancer Linked to Societal Ills.' " She wanted to talk. "Of course it's linked to societal ills. Do you know how last century it was TB? And now it is cancer. Whom do you think will write *The Magic Mountain* for cancer?"

" 'A spokesman for the oil producing nations reported yesterday that that production will be cut over seventy-four percent over the coming months.' Is that true, Andreas?" Frieda asked.

"Here's Czech humor for you," Andreas reported back.

PRAGUE (AP)—An elderly man disregarded the red signal and refused across the street.

A car braked to avoid knocking him down, skidded, the back door opened and a shopping bag followed by a young girl spilled out.

A spectator cried out and rushed towards the car, which landed undamaged at the curb. An old woman was crying in the car.

The careless pedestrian turned out to be the father, the driver the son, the girl who fell out the daughter, the spectator another son and the lamenting woman inside mother of one and the same family.

All ended well. The car was unscathed, the girl got up on her own, the picked up the spilled purchases and piled into the car.

"It's called 'Family Is Involved in Involved Mishap,' " Andreas informed them. " 'An elderly man disregarded the red signal and refused across the street.' Have you ever heard anything more Czech?"

"Are typos Czech?" Gus closed the first section and picked up one more comfortable to hold, the Book Review. There might be another fine biography; it had been a good biography year. Who *would* be the Thomas Mann for cancer; not Solzhenitsyn. There wasn't a good biography that week; just as well. The Quentin Bell of Virginia Woolf had set her to reading everything Woolf ever wrote, and there wouldn't be time. When Europe did better with the damp there was no more TB, if that wasn't too gross an exaggeration. What would be the damp behind cancer, finally? And when would they know? And who would write *The Magic Mountain?* And would she read it?

"I love that mishap," Andreas repeated. "Czech mishaps are the best there are."

"Remember my mishap?" Gus took a piece of paper from Nicky's drawing pad and began to write. What she didn't like about Sundays was that nobody listened; everybody read out loud and nobody talked and nobody listened. Every scrap of news read out was an interruption. Her mishap was this:

ATHENS—A young American mother and her child were waiting for the light to change.

On the same corner, a crowd watched a vender demonstrate a plush dog that hopped, wagged, and barked.

Many in the crowd laughed. The child said, "Mama? Give!"
A man with gold teeth showed the mother how many coins
to give the vender for the demonstration dog.

In Constitution Square, she wound the dog and put it down.
It hopped and wagged. It opened its mouth also. It didn't bark.
The child cried, "Broke!"

All ended well. The mother barked the way the vender had
been barking, which was why everyone was laughing. And the
child was happy.

But it wasn't accurate: what about, Gus asked herself, the
shame at not knowing how to ask in Greek how much for the
dog, sir?; and what about the rage in discovering it didn't
work?; what about the relief to know that the people had
laughed at the vender and not at her?; what about the embarrassment of barking in Constitution Square to please her
child? Gus guessed it wasn't a newspaper mishap, balled the
paper, and tossed it past Frieda and into the fire. The news
was so isolating, no matter that it was designed to keep
people in touch.

Andreas took a sip of his Bloody Mary and said he had
another Czech mishap for them. He put the newspaper on the
floor and checked to make sure he had their attention. "It
was a normal day in Prague," Andreas began, "a very normal
gloomy day in Praha, the Golden City of Europe. I was
having a hard time selling postcards that day in Wenceslas
Square, where the trolleys have to loop around the immense
statue of what's-his-name on a horse, and I was wishing that I'd
stayed instead around the Castle where Kafka postcards sold
pretty well. Not many tourists came to Praha that first spring
after the sixty-eight, uh"—Andreas whispered it—"takeover.
'A nice place to live, but I wouldn't want to visit,' we used to
joke to each other, we humble postcard folk."

He took another sip and floated to his feet like a princess.
The movement touched Gus and transformed the isolation she

felt to the fun of a schoolroom show-and-tell. "The rain,"
Andreas moaned emphatically, "day after day this gloomy
spring rain made me keep my cards under cover and my head
in the armpits of huge sooty statues. I longed for the olden
days of"—he sneaked a look over his shoulder and whispered
—"D-u-b, if you know who I mean, God rest his soul. It never
rained in those days. My postcards were always out in the
open then. My whole career was Czechered because of that
gloomy rain.

" 'What gloomy rain,' the Goose said the first time I met
her, 'got any of those Kafka postcards?' She wore such an
odd hat I was bound to inquire, 'Eengleesh? Freench?' She
said, 'Hell no, Merikansky; gimme two of those cards with the
real sad eyes.'

"The Goose kept her change in an open-ended plastic
rectangle marked Courtesy of Lew's Realty, which I remarked
on. 'It's my hat case,' she said by way of noting my interest,
after which she did a terrible thing by taking off her plastic
hat and snapping it into one long band, which snapped rain
all over my postcards even though she didn't notice. 'Get it?'
She'd folded the band into a rectangle the size of the case
but then unfolded it and put it back on as a hat. 'Cute, huh?
I haven't taken it off since I got to Praha, what with the rain.'

" 'May I ask why you are here, madam?'

" 'I came to teach the big boys Czechers.'

" 'Czechers?'

" 'It's a board game between red and black pieces.'

" '*Le Rouge et le Noir?*' I mumbled in case there were
nearby police, in case it wasn't an approved book. I was
extremely literate and extremely nervous. The new approved
book list wasn't out yet.

" 'Come again?'

" 'Nothing, here's your change,' I said mournfully and
with much characteristic Czech melancholy, for I was a

gloomy Czech vender who used to be an intellectual before
it began to rain every day."

"Cheers," Frieda said, rolling onto her elbows to crow at
the cheerfulness, "you'll make me an optimist yet!" With
a push off the floor Frieda gathered the paper and made a
pile. "Are we done with this? I want to talk happy and no
more mishaps, and no more societal ills for the moment. It
used to be that I was the one with the gloomy news; it was
better that way. I think we should all have another drink."

"To my being home," Gus suggested.

"Yes exactly, to that."

Being home meant eventually being in her own bed at
last, the king-size Andreas had purchased so that when she
came home to die he wouldn't bother her. They had put a
sheepskin pad underneath the sheet, to imitate the hospital's
bedsore prevention notion, and even if there wasn't a motor
to raise and lower her, Gus was comfortable, at home, alone
for the time being but by choice and not by default. She had
asked to be alone in order to hear them going about their
business, for which she had longed in the hospital: the relief
of knowing her world was nearby without having to have it
on top of her. The relief made her breathing even, oxygen to
the brain and peace and knowing:

... That it had happened correctly, that she'd needed the
time. The word *leaching* had surprised her when she'd said
it to Jackson—her parents having blasted off instead of leaching—but leaching it was. The leach field gets water out of the
house, brings it into the soil: life leaching out as waste water,
leaching into the earth again. If she'd blasted off she'd never
have had the time she'd needed in order to see Nicky learn
her name.

... That it was right to have married Andreas, let Daphni
be born, and not attempt to go back to dancing except on
Saturdays. Wrong. She'd already made the choice about

dancing; it was only Daphni she'd had to choose, and only Andreas. They'd entered her life simultaneously, both strangers she met her first day on the job as an adviser. Correct. But she'd chosen, first one and then the other, and she'd been correct.

Relief. How even her breathing was, contentedly regular. Words she'd read in "1918": "A veil of mist covered the November sky; a many-folded veil, so fine meshed that it made one density." . . . "Now and then as if a door opened and shut, or the veil parted and closed, the roar boomed and faded." And if she'd blasted off she'd not have known *The Years,* or any of Virginia Woolf.

Gus picked up the book to read again about the mist and Crosby, the saddened old former maid to the Pargiters, hobbling on pained legs and talking aloud into the mist that made everything and everyone invisible.

> "Them guns again," Crosby muttered, looking up at the pale-grey sky with peevish irritation. The rooks, scared by the gun-fire, rose and wheeled round the tree-tops. Then there was another dull boom. . . . Crosby pulled herself together and tottered across the road into the High Street. The guns went on booming and the sirens wailed. The war was over—so somebody told her as she took her place at the counter of the grocer's shop. The guns went on booming and the sirens wailed.

She'd not had a live-in Crosby to raise her, the way Andreas had had a Sophia whose task it was to ruin her legs raising him up to adult from newborn, teaching him everything from alpha to omega. Sophia was dead now. Gus hadn't had, and neither had her children, a withering surrogate, thank fortune. Gus smiled at her mother's thank fortune and thanked that fortune for having had her mother raise her, love and cherish her, choose her. She didn't know the answer. The question was: who was going to raise Nicky?

Gus put her fingers over her eyes as compresses. She had a way to get away, a memory that always worked when a sadness took her by surprise and she didn't want to think of sadness. She pressed her temples with her thumbs and felt the fingers' weight on her lids. It always worked:

Waking up with the first, thin morning light, lying in the damp of the rock walls veneered in whitewashed plaster, listening to the roosters, waking not entirely from the dream in which she had been, as usual, coasting weightlessly twenty feet off the ground and the sea. It was Ios, the March of their first year of marriage, her first trip to Greece to meet for the first time the grandparents of the child she carried. Andreas was sleeping.

Dressing in shivering haste, tiptoeing on cramping cold feet on a floor that was chill as wet sand in the night, outside, where the whitewash was tinged pale chartreuse by that earliest light. Knowing she shouldn't remember the house by that color but by something that would last an hour, for instance the geraniums.

Running down the steps from the village to the bay—the steps each long enough for one donkey and wide enough for two—running onto the sand and running until her feet were warm and she was full of blood and muscle. Lying to rest, propped up and pivoting on an elbow to see what kinds of shells there were, or pebbles if pebbles. No shells or pebbles that she could see, only large and small gray rocks with perfectly drilled holes in them which made them—what? whaat? —light as air.

Coming off the elbow to measure with more accuracy the weightless stones she had landed near, but it was still true that the stones had no bulk. They weighed, even the largest, no more than a quarter of a bar of soap. Thinking: fake stones! fake Hollywood stones such as would be used in a movie called *Stone Age!*, such as would come out of a studio

volcano in *Lava!*, such as would go tumbling into a bathtub
Pacific in *Quake!*, fake, fake! Thinking she was dreaming.

Did they float? She threw them into the air like bubbles
but they came back down. She threw them onto the water's
surface but they sank. The perfect holes went through even
the flattest and most small—the size of her thumbnail—and
even the largest and most round—the size of her fist—and
there was no explaining. Alone on a foreign beach, the sun
an untrue yellow, the bay making its way toward her in near
silence and with minimal haste but surely, as if the bay were
in kimono, coming toward her little step by little pigeon-toed
step.

Rush rushing, standing still and filling up with a pleasure-
ful panicky thrill of simple dumb unknowing whether it was
the gods, or not, who'd made those magic stones. Zeus! Was
he going to come in person to take them back, as a swan, as a
bull, as the bay, as the sun, as that eerie odd untrue early
light? Was she going to have Zeus make love to her and
then lift off the stones she'd hidden in the hammock of her
maternity shirt? Closing her eyes and counting sixty, nothing
happening.

Running, running, beating it out of there feet on fire,
racing up the steps until she saw her first person, who was a
real Greek man leading a donkey down the steps. Good
morning—having no breath for speaking but gasping out
what little she knew how to say in Greek—good morning!
Watching him descend and ride his donkey across the beach
and back up onto the path over rocks on the other side; breath
caught, making her own way back to the place where she'd
left Andreas asleep.

It was pumice come from the island of Santorin, he explained, ruining nothing. Santorin with the famous cliff that
was in fact the crater wall of a volcano, said he, and they
were going there next. Pumice ruined nothing, nothing, said

she, about having been where the gods play games and tricks on people.

Feeling her face change under her fingers, her cheeks rising up to her eyes with a smile, with a laugh at having never had such a fearful and thrilling experience as she'd had that morning, even including the one a day or so later when she saw the Santorin cliff itself, six hundred feet of schist and scoria, marble, pumice, and cinders in green, black, red, and gray, when she learned that they in their little boat in twelve hundred feet of water were sailing right across the center of a live volcano.

Chapter
Seven

Mère's arrival at JFK was, of course, traumatic, and it was the last time she would fly Olympic if they were going to give her trouble the next time too, she told them all. She was totally inconsolable, she told them, for keeping waiting her son and grand-daughters just because Olympic couldn't get its baggage compartment open. And what was her dog supposed to do in the meantime? Wait? Wait one hour and a half?

It was the fourth version Gus had heard since seven-thirty that Wednesday morning, when Andreas, and then Maya and Daphni in turn, began telling the story Gus had missed hearing, because she was asleep, on their return from the airport the previous evening. The only relief was that when in New York Mère always stayed at the Pierre, and so at least Gus was listening to Mère's version of the story for the first time. But it was temporary relief.

"I told them to open that baggage door instamatically! Because my dog and I want our *valises! Impardonnable!* I said, *Vous êtes inepte, irresponsable, intolérable! Vous êtes irrespectueux, enfin! Vous ne me connaissez pas?*"

"Hold it." Jackson put down his coffee cup. "How come you speak French, I mean why speak French to Olympic Airways if I might ask?"

"No, darling, Greek," Mère answered. "It was *invraisemblable,* I tell you!"

Frieda spoke inaudibly, "And *imprévisible,* and *indigne.*"

"What, darling?"

"I said *indigne.*"

"*Exactement, chérie, quel traitement indigne!*"

That she meant Mère's behavior was *indigne* was the reason for her looking to Gus, who would know she'd meant it that way, but Gus was clearly paying no attention. Frieda looked then to Jackson, who looked at his boots. Had the impression been recorded that Frieda was sympathetic to Mère? Unfair! Gus finally looked up and gave Frieda a weary smile to thank her for seeming to keep things going.

"I've got to be going," Jackson said, "since my friend's waiting for me downstairs in her car."

"So quickly? I have not seen the bronze!"

"It's just clay, madame, but you're welcome to have a look if you like." Jackson popped the balled napkin into his cup and swung himself onto his feet. "Under here, madame," he said, folding back the plastic he was so tired of taking off and putting on.

Mère looked and didn't speak, and so Jackson concentrated on her scent, which was a rain-heavy cumulonimbus cloud that had saturated all Mère's belongings. Silent still, Jackson studied the pancake film that made Mère's skin almost creaseless and satiny, and the smoky eye shadow, and the tinted chestnut lashes. How horribly bland and unformed, Jackson told himself amazed that Mère had lived so little interest into her face. Lib had lived more by nineteen—and her face had not yet by any means taken shape—than Mère seemed to have lived in all of her seventy-odd. Had she kept her face as still as it was right then her whole life long, and whatever for? Why was no experience registered there?

When they fell they hardly marked the surface, but they fell resolutely from her lower lashes and off the jawbone cliff onto her Paris suit. Jackson counted ten of them before there was a discernible quiver in that chin to prove what he could hardly believe: that she had been moved to tears by the head. Her breath came out a long exhaust, and it was another few seconds before she had the new breath fully in enough to say, "It is perfect."

"Yeah? Thanks, madame."

Mère gave him a flat look and then turned to Gus. "*Dieu, c'est triste,*" she said in the way she had said it to Edith Piaf, that other sparrow she'd known in person. "*C'est triste et c'est trop.*" Mère sighed.

Jackson covered the head and realized that yes, he agreed, he was sad it was over. No other head had moved him as this had, and no other person as Gus had moved him. What Mère meant by *triste* was whatever she meant, but he was sad too. Only now what was Mère going on about? She was energetically searching for an answer to something, but what? The free world's economic crisis? What to do about monopolies, rape, or blackmail? How to keep the leaves on the trees in autumn? Or was it some weird kind of contest to see who could best imitate someone solving some real kind of problem or other? Or was it a joke?

"I will *accompagner,* I *insiste,*" Mère was saying. "I will have the *aide* of Joe, and we will locate the *voiture!*"

"I'm sure it's only by the curb"—Jackson caught up—"and I can swing it on my own, no sweat."

"*J'insiste!*" Mère was getting into her coat.

"Suit yourself. Okay, and so I'll see you two Monday."

"Good luck," Frieda said.

"Yes, good luck at the foundry. Happy Thanksgiving."

"Same to you, Gus. Take it easy." There was something else he wanted to say, which had something to do with the fact that he wouldn't be seeing Gus for five days. "Uh, take care," he left it.

"O-kay now," droned Joe. "O-kay a little t'yer left now, o-kay, t'yer right, good hold it 'ere." Were they joking? Hadn't it been Joe himself who had bounced hell out of Jackson and the head only three days earlier, the Sunday morning they'd taxied over from the hospital? Hadn't that same Joe, in fact, shut the brass elevator grate against Jackson's foot?

"Cool it," Jackson muttered. He'd been required to sit on the mahogany bench in case of an emergency, and Mère faced him ready on her feet. When she said whatever it was she said, Jackson noticed the fortune she had in gold crowns in uppers alone.

"Very good," Mère observed about the landing.

"Thanks, Mrs. Kaligas," said Joe. His tone was vilely obsequious, in Jackson's view.

"The car, is it red?"

Jackson said, "I can't see. It should be a Saab."

"That I wouldn't know," Mère said modestly.

Sure enough, it was still a Saab and still red, still sitting at the curb Lib and Max had dropped him at an hour, or so it seemed, ago. Jackson heard Mère say the obvious, that his friend seemed to have left the little one all alone.

"Jesus Christ, where's Lib?"

Max pointed east.

"She been gone long?"

Max nodded a diagonal nod; it wasn't clear to him yet which was which in the nod world.

Jackson put the plywood platter on the roof of the car. "Holy shit"—he whistled—"Jesus *shit,* man!" Long enough to have gotten a parking ticket, he noticed. "Shit," he repeated, and took in a breath, fixed a smile, and turned. "No sweat," he told Mère, "so thanks for your help and all."

She was giving Joe a tip that would almost have paid the parking ticket, and Jackson wanted to punch them both flat out and tell them to get and stay out of his life. That he didn't was partly a function of matter over mind—he hadn't been raised in Good Manners Greenwich for nothing, in other words—and partly of his relief at seeing Lib round the corner, a Bloomingdale's shopping bag jerking off the end of an arm.

"Made it," she gasped, having run the minimal distance from the corner.

"You went to fucking *Blooming*dale's?"

"Got us some lunch, some delicacies." Lib squinted over Jackson's shoulder. "Hi," she said.

"Oh Jesus," said Jackson, matter over mind again, "excuse me. Look, this is Lib, Mrs. Kaligas. I thought you took off."

Lib switched the bag and they shook hands. "Hi," she repeated, "I'm Dorothy Martin."

Mère gave an impression of not being confused, and after expressing her pleasure in meeting whoever the young lady might be, she said, "I would like you to make two." She tipped her head in ticktock fashion to Jackson and beyond him to the head.

Jackson checked beyond him. Did she have any idea how much that would run her? He asked.

The figure Mère answered him with was twice what he was charging Gus. It was probably also more than what Pericles gave Phidias for doing the Parthenon and all that other stuff combined. It would mean more than a thousand free dollars after casting fees, a lot more, more like two.

Mère asked, "Isn't that correct?"

Jackson ejaculated air with a "pah" sound, and he did it on purpose to keep his lips from breaking into a "shucks, ma'am" grin. Slowly, he cautioned himself, con-trol. So he waited for the answer to flash on the screen: first, she was no naive cookie, he reasoned, and second, she had the dough—maybe he had the order wrong—and third, she'd obviously, or should have, asked Gus what to offer. The answer flashed in: SAY YES, YOU ASS.

"Very acceptable," he said.

"Very well. *Au revoir.*" She offered her hand.

"*Au revoir,*" echoed Jackson, and likewise Lib.

"Oo voi mon'ti," Mère said to Max, who was nodding out on the stoop of the Saab.

"See ya later, that means," Jackson suggested, but Max didn't have a single bye-bye in him. He didn't even have a wave.

Another hour later, they were still nowhere near Greenwich for all the Merritt Parkway traffic leading from the city to the long Thanksgiving weekend. But Jackson was all content, and he said to Lib that were he ever to croak from an overdose of mainlined pleasure, it would be right there in her Saab, with Max sleeping in his lap, the head in the back, money pouring into his pockets (he would finally be a rich artist, he said, and soon), and the effects of hashish pouring into his brain. The picnic lunch from Bloomingdale's had been a smash hit too.

However: what an effort it was for Lib to work her car's clutch to keep from stalling while all the lanes of traffic were braiding together into one neat plait. "Wow," Lib observed, "there's so much to take into consideration! Is this the right parkway?"

"Sure." At least he thought it was.

"Wow, just look at that *shine!* You don't see black cars much anymore. And it looks like black ice!" Lib rolled down

her window and stuck her head out and as close to the
Continental polish as she could get. She gave her reflection
a glowy smile and involuntarily touched the black glass surface.

"Your prints on record?"

The voice so startled Lib that she laughed. "Sorry," she said,
looking up at the passenger. "Wow, what gorgeous *teeth* you
have!"

"Say what?"

Lib let out the clutch, and the Saab popped out like a light
bulb. The man in the Continental laughed. "Say what?" he
repeated.

"Nothing," Lib said, but in the direction of her windshield.
The car had been idling so long it wouldn't start up again.
"Jesus," she snarled, watching the man's electric window
seal him off. "Do you realize I told that dude he had nice
teeth? He could have killed me!"

"What dude?"

"That black car dude!"

"Does he?"

"What."

"Have nice teeth?"

"Well of course."

"Then what's the problem? I mean, if he had no teeth or
awful teeth maybe he'd've thought you were insulting him."

"That's not *it,* Jackson! The guy, for God's sake, could have
punched me!"

"What for?"

"Jackson, where've you *been?* I mean I might as well have
said you got good rhythm!"

"I don't agree at all. If he's got good teeth, he's got good
teeth. He smiled, didn't he? What do you expect?"

"Don't you under*stand?* The guy was *black!*"

"So?"

"Don't you *understand?*"

"*No!*" Max stirred. "No," Jackson whispered, "and keep your voice down."

"Oh fuck off. Jesus Christ, Jesus fucking Christ! There they are again." Lib watched the electric window disappear into the black glass door, and out of the same corner of the same eye, she saw the black arm stretching out to touch her face. The man was tapping politely on her window. "Here fucking goes," she said to Jackson, and rolled down her window.

"Say *what?*" The man exploded with laughter.

"I'm sorry, I only said you have nice teeth."

"Is that all? Is *that all?*"

"Yes."

"Then why you so scared, honey?"

"I'm really not."

"And that's okay, honey, cause anyway, you got nice tits." And there was that nice smile again.

"Okay, okay see you." She rolled up the window. "Oh brother, get me out of here! Won't this traffic *move?*"

"Well you're both right," observed Jackson, "because he has nice teeth and you have nice tits."

"Fuck off."

"It's true."

"Jackson, will you shut up? You're so fucking dumb!"

"Well at least I'm not dumb enough to leave a fucking two-year-old kid all by himself!"

"I did it so the car wouldn't be ticketed."

"And what do you call that thing?" Jackson jabbed at the windshield.

"That's an old ticket, and I meant to say towed, so it wouldn't be towed."

"That's ridiculous, Lib!"

"My name isn't Lib."

"Fucking Christ, what's the difference?"

Lib got the car to move forward a car length. "I'm sorry, I shouldn't have left him alone. And it's fine for you to call me Lib. I'm glad I have one."

"Libido? Me too."

"That hash."

"Me too, we both are." Jackson curled the fingers of his left hand inside and underneath her thigh. He closed his eyes. Wasn't it nice of Lib to drive him to Greenwich, and didn't she have the most beautiful thighs he'd ever touched. Never, never had he experienced such pleasure as there was in feeling Lib's leg flex under his palm as she pressed and released the accelerator.

The jumbo jet taxied to the head of the runway and took off for the nonstop to New York from Los Angeles. Mimi supposed that she should be thankful to have gotten a seat, but since it didn't make sense to be grateful for the discomforts of that horizontal skyscraper, she decided to concentrate instead on the horrors of flying jumbo style.

She imagined a crash into the desert and all those hundreds of passengers disappearing under those old familiar shifting sands.

She imagined a crash into water and all those hundreds of passengers bobbing in the sea until one by one they are jerked under by sharks or whatever.

She imagined a crash into mountains and all those hundreds of human ice sculptures sitting around being blue and dead.

What did she have in mind: Palm Springs? the Mississippi? the Poconos?

Yes, give her another Manhattan, she told the steward. The environment was getting on her nerves. Did she dare imagine a crash into Manhattan? No.

One of her therapies processed everything as if it were some Kraft product, some emotional Velveeta cheese, and she decided to take a look at what her fantasies possibly meant. She decided to process her crash fantasies and figured it didn't matter one way or the other that she was a little drunk and depressed. Who would know? She thanked her lucky stars that the people nearby her were asleep.

Her lucky stars. Mimi wondered if Gus had inherited their mother's superstition that Miss Fortune up in the sky there was responsible for what was in the cards. She doubted that Christopher had, on account of its being so wildly unscientific, though she did remember him once telling one of her kids about the Sandman. "Mister Sandman," she'd heard him singing, "send me a dream." But that was one thing. Whether or not he'd be capable of singing to a kid a song that went "Oh Miss Fortune, spare me an ace" was quite another.

"Mister Fortune" made better lyrics, and Mimi thought it was all rather Roman that fortune was female. Witlessness and caprice being why Rome fell, and Fortuna being the goddess of all that (or was she simply making this up?), she became annoyed at Rome, the Pope, and all of Italy. Whether or not she was making this up, it wasn't fair to blame women for the fall of Rome. No woman was in charge anywhere, that was for sure, and so it wasn't right to hang some imaginary woman over it all, call her Fortuna, and call Rome failed, blaming bad luck. Was this what her mother believed?

And what did she mean, unscientific, anyway? What's more scientific than the solar zodiac and the lunar zodiac and all those other stellar factors? Astromythology was a real science, at least it was in California, and if Christopher was too hardcore to appreciate it, that was his tough luck.

Where was she.

So she should thank her lucky stars that they'd made it past Palm Springs without crashing into the desert. And how about just a cool glass of water from the steward? How lousy it might have been to watch all those passengers get buried alive by tons of sand shifting over them.

Where was she.

Drowsy. And in spite of her important thoughts, it seemed more wise to doze off for the moment. Nothing was more authentic than sleep, and no human potential therapist had to go and teach her that one.

No dice. No matter how authentic sleep was, Mimi couldn't drop off. Besides, it might be time for the snack. She consulted her watch, the gift of her twenty-one-year-old daughter, and found it was only L.A.'s noon. The Cinderella was a serious watch, as opposed to the Nixon, the Agnew, the Ford, the Kissinger, the Goofy, and the Donald Duck watches; Cinderella was the only one with a human face, at least this was her daughter's thesis, the daughter who wore the Cinderella one herself to remind her of her origins, whatever that meant. That Mimi had this totally political daughter was—she even said so herself—one of those common anachronisms one came across a lot in L.A., where there was really no such thing as evolution.

Which was an odd coincidence. In preparation for seeing Andreas's mother again, Mimi had looked something up in the dictionary, though maybe it happened another way, which was that she was looking up a spelling and (*that* was it: she was looking up unfortunately—or it must have been fortunately—to see if there was that *e* in it or not). Her eye caught Fortuna, and she learned by accident that the Greeks called their lady luck Tyche, whom she had never heard of personally. So she thought she'd ask Andreas's mother about Tyche (that *was* it), and so she'd looked up Tyche to see if there was anything, which there wasn't, only something called *tychism,* which as any fool could read is a theory that says evolution is just a matter of luck. Now that could probably be a theory of evolution for L.A., was all.

Other than that, where was she.

The snack wasn't bad, a salami omelet she wouldn't have touched earlier in the year because of cholesterol and processing chemicals. There she was: processing. But what? Oh God, that was always happening to her. She was *always* finding her place again on the page, only to find the title page blank, as was one of her masters' way of putting it: Zen, if she remembered right. The hell with it.

The book she was reading was a smash success about adultery, a number-one for three months in ten major U.S. cities because it was a how-to that went simultaneously paper and cloth: *Adultery and You,* by Dr. Apple Amen, a spiritual guide to extramarital relations (went the blurb) and so forth. She'd bought it because—she knew it was true—who else bought that sort of book if not people like her? Who else, except people not like her, could walk by an airport display of a book like that, where she could choose it in any one of ten pastels and three primaries, and not get caught. One therapist had said she shouldn't try to fight that herd impulse to buy what was obviously supposed to appeal to so many people; another had said she should. Add plus and minus and you get zero, said her daughter, Cindy, by way of analysis. Follow yourself, Cindy said.

Big help. Mimi had bought the magenta version of *Adultery and You* and found by page three that she was not interested in going on. If there was anything she had tried ad nauseam it was adultery, and she had no need for some spiritual doctor telling her it was a bonus activity. She would tell the steward she'd found it on the floor when she could get his attention for another Manhattan; that was the ticket.

And she would have been perfectly happy to pay the difference and fly First, if there had been a seat available. From First, she felt she knew, it was far less easy to imagine hundreds of passengers dropping like leaflets from the belly of

the crashing plane, one of whom was sure to have a cut that
would attract a herd of bloodthirsty sharks. And all the Man-
hattans in the world were free in First.

Mimi stretched her long legs into the aisle. They were Gus's
legs too, and their mother's, and Maya's and Cindy's. She
didn't think they were Daphni's—she thought Daphni's were
less American, if she remembered right—and had no idea
about Christopher or her father or her son, Jojo. God she had
hated Christopher. Her first suicide attempt, in fact, was a
hunger strike at the age of two, to protest the birth of Gus because Christopher was in favor of it. Or maybe she'd made up
that part about the hunger strike, but it didn't matter because
it was at least subjectively believable. She did remember hating
Christopher enough to punish herself with hunger, in order
to make him feel guilty for not liking her. Mimi wondered
what her mother would say about all that, and suddenly she
was weeping.

What a liar. She had never in her life attempted suicide because, as everyone knew, she was in utter terror of death.

"It makes me apprehensive, Andreas, having Mimi in the
air. Mère's enough. What can I say to her? She'll tell us
Cindy's practically mayor of L.A., and that Jojo's become a fish
and lives on a commune where talking is forbidden. She'll
want to correct the drugs I'm on, she'll be back on pills now,
now since that health guru died on the talk show. I think it
might have been a mistake."

He was lying beside her. "Inviting them here?"

"Not Christopher and Susanna, the others, distractions. I'm
frightened of what I'll tell Mimi."

"You can tell her to go to hell."

"That's what I mean."

They were lying on their backs side by side as if in a
meadow watching clouds. The firelight put shadows on the
ceiling that late afternoon. He held her hand.

"I want to finish *The Years,* for instance, and once she gets here I think I won't be able to."

"Shall we finish it now? I can read to you or you to me."

"I would like that. It's long; it's the 'Present Day' chapter. They've all begun to get together."

"Good," said Andreas, "since so are we."

It is one of those sunset summer evenings in which everything is edged with light. And Eleanor's in her seventies, Gus explained to Andreas, her face brown and her hair white. She has been in India.

Ah, Nicholas Pomjalovsky is back, the Pole they call Brown for short, who talks about the soul and everything. He is at Eleanor's, and so is North, who is Eleanor's nephew. Eleanor is so beautiful, so deep brown and white! Gus decided to read aloud, in British, North's going to Sara's for something to eat:

> He glanced at the name of the street on the left. He was going to dine with Sara but he had not much notion how to get there. He had only heard her voice on the telephone saying, "Come and dine with me—Milton Street, fifty-two, my name's on the door." It was near the Prison Tower. But this man Brown—it was difficult to place him at once. He talked, spreading his fingers out with the volubility of a man who will in the end become a bore. And Eleanor wandered about, holding a cup, telling people about her shower-bath. He wished they would stick to the point. Talk interested him. Serious talk on abstract subjects. "Was solitude good; was society bad?" That was interesting; but they hopped from thing to thing. When the large man said, "Solitary confinement is the greatest torture we inflict," the meagre old woman with the wispy hair at once piped up, laying her hand on her heart, "It ought to be abolished!" She visited prisons, it seemed.
>
> "Where the dickens am I now?" he asked, peering at the name on the street corner.

But Gus couldn't keep up the British. It was harder in scene-setting sentences than in ones that said some queer old British

expression or other: "Dirty brute!", what Crosby muttered
about "the Belgian who called himself a Count" but left a
"blob of spittle...on the side of his bath." So Gus gave it up
and went on in American reading through the untasty dinner
shared by Sara and North, who was just back from Africa.
"Are you asleep?" she asked Andreas. He said he wasn't. On
back to Eleanor leaving for the gathering with North's sister,
Peggy, who is a doctor.

> "Oh, well—" Peggy laughed. She was about to say that aero-
> planes hadn't made all that difference, for it was her line to
> disabuse her elders of their belief in science, partly because their
> credulity amused her, partly because she was daily impressed by
> the ignorance of doctors—when Eleanor sighed.
> "Oh dear," she murmured.
> She turned away from the window.
> Old age again, Peggy thought. Some gust blew open a door;
> one of the many millions in Eleanor's seventy-odd years; out
> came a painful thought; which she at once concealed—she had
> gone to her writing-table and was fidgeting with papers—with
> the humble generosity, the painful humility of the old.
> "What, Nell—?" Peggy began.
> "Nothing, nothing," said Eleanor.

"Woolf's world is so touching," Gus stopped to pro-
nounce. How touching it was going on with Eleanor and
Peggy, and then back to Sara and North, and then on, and
back, and on and on until everyone is gathered for the party,
and there is page after page of British greetings and sayings
that go as conversation—snide, often—for Gus to read aloud,
amused by the utter forgivability of the snideness because of
how, in the end, touching the English are. "Isn't it, Andreas?"
The foreigner tries to make a speech, and again he tries
twice. They are all gathered around the table, but none wishes
an ending and none wishes, it seems, thanks. But Gus wanted

to know what Nicholas might have said in his speech! She hoped there might be someone else, someone at the party, who'd ask him what he would have said.

"What I was going to have said? I was going to have said —" He paused and stretched his hand out; he touched each finger separately.

"First I was going to have thanked our host and hostess. Then I was going to have thanked this house—" he waved his hand round the room hung with the placards of the house agent, "—which has sheltered the lovers, the creators, the men and women of goodwill. And finally—" he took his glass in his hand, "I was going to drink to the human race. The human race," he continued, raising his glass to his lips, "which is now in its infancy, may it grow to maturity! Ladies and gentlemen!" he exclaimed, half rising and expanding his waistcoat, "I drink to that!"

He brought his glass down with a thump on the table. It broke.

"Perhaps," Gus said to Andreas, "Nicholas has no business talking about the soul and the human race in its infancy. In that way he's altogether too foreign. But look how late it is!"

"The dawn!" said Nicholas, getting up and stretching himself. He too walked across to the window. Renny followed him.

"Now for the peroration," he said, standing with him in the window. "The dawn—the new day—"

He pointed at the trees, at the roofs, at the sky.

"No," said Nicholas, holding back the curtain. "There you are mistaken. There is going to be no peroration—no peroration!" he exclaimed, throwing his arm out, "because there was no speech."

Gus knew that was it, what she most loved about *The Years:* no peroration because there hadn't been a speech. She touched Andreas's hand and turned to watch him breathing his almost noiseless breath of sleep, his head tipped toward her, his mouth a silent suggestion of contentment. Yes, in all its dreamy driftiness about the soul and the human race, there was hardly a more exact book.

And to think that one Sunday she'd read about the biography and, Monday, picked it up and Wednesday finished it, and Thursday begun *The Voyage Out,* Virginia Woolf's first novel. Here she was at the end of *The Years* and straining against the end of her life, as had Woolf, as had Woolf in writing it. Virginia would be dead herself in four years' time and was straining right then against the end, but no peroration. There was no speech.

Chapter
Eight

For all the sixteen years of their marriage, the turkey had been Andreas's specialty. He had never seen one dead or alive until that first Thanksgiving in the States, when Gus had taught him how to cook it, but that she was two months pregnant with his child had its impact on his wanting to learn and her wanting to teach. They hadn't by then decided, but there was that chance that they had some sort of future together.

Gus lay in bed to think it over then and now. Then she had been concerned that it had happened too quickly, and now it seemed it hadn't happened at all soon enough. Then she had been afraid to take him to her parents' for Thanksgiving, but now she couldn't imagine why, even though she could remember exactly. She'd wanted to make the decision "alone" about whether it was possible to have loved Andreas from the first hour, about whether that was "reason" enough to love him in sickness and until death, about whether that child "deserved" to be born, about what she was "doing" anyway with that life of hers that had gone from ten years of studying dance to one week at International House and right into Andreas's lap in her own single bed. Unprotected, even.

Now Gus admitted that she had feared their disapproval. She was ashamed to be doing something Mimi would do, something consequently so unlike their own good Gussie. And Andreas represented the Mimi in her that had to be punished by skin-and-bone bird in her crummy apartment, and not a plump one at the Cape. How could they approve of her marrying some Greek stranger who had knocked her up? "Beware of Greeks bearing gifts," they could only have joked just as if she were Mimi, or so she believed.

Of course they hadn't joked at all and were pleased to be the witnesses for the living-room wedding on New Year's Day, and of course they thought her marrying him was the best decision she'd ever made, the part about Daphni notwithstanding or, rather, included. All four of them cried when the vows were said and, because none had ever cried at a wedding, then burst into laughter to solemnize the exchanging of rings. Afterward they ate lobster and toasted each other three bottles' worth. "The first time I met the Goose——" Andreas had said for the first time, telling her parents how it had happened.

Just as Gus was wishing someone would open the door, Andreas did and brought her a tiny pot of mint tea. "Good morning, can I help with your bath? The turkey's in." In that bathrobe he seemed to masquerade as his mother's son.

Gus decided to tease him. "Teachers are so perverse in how they say, '*Can* you go to the bathroom?' Well I *guess* you ought to be *able to*.' So you have to raise your hand again and ask, 'May I go to the bathroom, please?' so the teacher can smirk and answer, 'Yes, you may.'"

Andreas raised his hand and asked, "May I help with your bath?"

"Yes, you may. Was that a present from Mère?"

He undid the sash and shrugged the pale blue silk to the floor, then stepped out of it as out of a puddle. "Was what," he said. All he wore was his wedding ring. "Look." His penis rose like a cannon.

"Don't," she said in spite of herself.

"It's just a salute."

"Well it makes me sad."

"Me too, Gus, believe me." He sat on the bed.

"That's ridiculous: I was just afraid."

"Of me?"

"I'm afraid so. You wouldn't, would you?"

Andreas thought that she was kidding. "Become a rapist just to please you? Forget it, no way; there are limits, you know. I'd shoplift for you just possibly, but not rape. No capital crimes, and that's final. My reputation as a lawyer out the window on one crime of passion? I'd honestly like to please you, ma'am, but a felony's out. Can't you possibly think of a misdemeanor?"

"Bathing me?"

"Good idea. I'm quite sure that's a misdemeanor in Massachusetts." He helped her up and held her against him. "Please don't be afraid of me," he coaxed.

"It was just a passing fancy, or a passing alarm." Her mouth came to his collarbone, and she kissed the wing shapes and said she loved his every inch. Then she shivered.

In the bath, Andreas worked first on her back. It was barely fleshed out, and he stumbled over her vertebrae; she said she guessed the muscles had decayed to the point where she couldn't have lifted an angel if she'd tried. The turkey's back was better than hers, stronger and meatier. But the air was nice and warm, wasn't it?

"Shall we wash your hair?" It seemed a good thing after all that she had cut it because, were it still floor length or thereabout, he didn't think he could've managed.

"I wouldn't mind, nor to have it blown dry. It's handy it's short."

"Yes."

"You hate it, don't you?"

"Yes."

Gus laughed. "At least there's the head. Are you glad I did that?"

"I'm very glad, Gussie."

"Will it be consoling?"

He rinsed her left arm. "I hope it will, I hope something will." He poured a bowl of water over her head and shampooed it quickly.

When she raised her head, she was dizzy from having hung it and there was water in her ears. "The Augusta West Kaligas Consolation Prize is awarded to her be-lov-ed husband," she said, although she wouldn't have if she'd first looked at Andreas, who, she saw then, wept.

"I'm sorry," he ventured, "I know it's upsetting enough, but I don't want you to die." He had never spoken the word to Gus. "And I don't want a consolation prize."

Her wet hair rained onto her shoulders and down all her swollen and sunken planes. And she shivered in the warm air. There was the longest silence, in which Gus realized how much she would lose but how much she had won. She'd been had and held in sickness and in health, and loved and cherished until death. It was more than most could even dream: that promise kept. And she loved Andreas more than life, she knew for certain: the value wasn't the value of life but the value of him. She stared at him, shivered, and was speechless. He wouldn't understand if she said she'd just realized she could give up her life.

There was a knock. "May I come in?"

"Yes, Maya," Gus answered too quietly and, louder, "yes."

"I thought I might help," Maya explained needlessly. The tears were evident on her face too. "I just wanted to see you," she confessed, also needlessly.

"Sweetie, come in," Andreas invited, "and help us finish before we catch your mother a cold."

Maya took off her slippers, rolled up her pants and stepped into the shallow bath to prop Gus up, standing, while he washed her legs. He used the bowl to rinse her and helped Maya get her out and wrapped in terry cloth. Gus shivered like a refugee. Maya worked on her hair with a brush and a drier and didn't want to stop until every surface of every hair was drier than the driest wood, until flames nearly flashed out from it. She didn't want to share her mother with any of the others coming.

Finally, when the thin hairs were flying like spider's webs in the wind, and were irritating, Gus asked her to stop. "Why not help me get dressed?"

"Well Daphni is, but maybe she would let me help too, though I doubt it since she didn't get to do your hair even to watch." Maya wrapped the cord around the drier too slowly, to prolong, and Gus realized that essential to accepting dying was being let go of.

"How do you like it?" Daphni had arranged the new jumper on the bed in such a way that it looked to Gus like a very flat person lying in state.

"Can you hold it up?"

"There, don't you just love it?" A cashmere plaid in red and yellow. "And here's the blouse, see?" Yellow.

Gus would never have chosen anything so bright, nor anything so obviously expensive. But for such softness she would have spent her last dime and settled for any color at all. She stroked the cashmere and said, "Yes, it's wonderful."

"We got it in the maternity part."

"Yes, thank you."

"Nicky loved it the most."

Just then Gus wished a nurse would come in and rub a cream into her all over, to make her feel less dry and stiff, and to help get her blood going. Maybe it was that she had cancer of the heart now or tumors on all the major vessels, but something didn't circulate right. Her limbs were asleep and itched and hurt. Gus hesitated to ask them to help her relax but, after hesitating, asked them. If Daphni and Maya wanted to help, they'd have to rub.

"Are you kidding? We'd *love to*," Daphni boomed. "You just lie right down, isn't that right, Maya?"

They were apprehensive the way a mother is over a new-born child, and the touching was overly gentle by consequence. Yet it was for Gus a wholly sensuous, excellently sensual experience and, perhaps, exactly as it had once been the other way around, when she lay them, as infants, on her big bed and patted and stroked them with tenderness creams.

"Are you having cramps, Mum, in your calfs?" Daphni kneaded, in case, the leg she'd put herself in charge of.

"Do you like me squeezing your arm like that?"

"Should I do your feet?"

Gus guessed it only natural that they avoided her torso, for fear of hurting and for other fears too. She then turned obligingly onto her side to let them get at her backside.

"Your fanny is gone, Mummy! She's a straight line, Maya!"

"Doesn't take long if it's not being used; the muscle disintegrates."

"Maybe you should jog with Frieda." Maya smiled shyly.

"Well, we'd have to ask Christo and Susanna!"

"I was only kidding."

"Oh. Well."

"How about my left arm here? Then we're done."

"I'll do it," they both said, and did.

Andreas emerged from the bathroom just as Frieda, though she had knocked, ran in. To cover her embarrassment, Frieda covered her eyes and asked if this was one of those illegal massage parlors. Then she looked at the floor and said that Mimi had called from her hotel and was on her way over, and Mère had arrived. Andreas walked past Frieda to the bureau, and she could hear him putting on his underwear. She turned her back to him and asked how Gus had liked the red and yellow. And the slippers.

"These, she means." Maya opened the box to reveal what was vinyl but looked like glass. "They're Mère's idea."

While Gus dressed herself the other three tried the slippers on and sighed at how none of them was the princess. "I must be it," Gus said confidently, "but where are my sheep? Just imagine wearing an open-toed glass platform slipper instead of an old sheepskin scuff! She's never, obviously, been sick. Will someone return them?"

"I'd wear them if they were in my size."

"You would," Maya said.

"What's wrong with that? I happen to find them quite hilarious and immodestly stylish, if you know what I mean. As opposed to your boots, Maya."

Gus suggested, "Then you return them, exchange them to fit." Again she brushed her shoulder-length hair and wondered where the rest of it was.

Frieda stayed to zip up the cashmere jumper and wished she hadn't been embarrassed by seeing them naked in front of their children, if that was why.

Mère said, "Perfect, *n'est-ce pas?*" and examined the fit.

"Except for the slippers," Gus said, returning Mère's greeting kisses and explaining how her feet had shrunk.

"*Tant pis,* they were only silly fun things." She ignored the part about the feet, which was just as well, since Gus had decided that her feet had swelled. She didn't know which it was, to be honest: shrunk or swelled or both or neither. And there was the buzzer.

Mimi had fumbled the lobby meeting because of the pies she was sure she would drop. And wasn't it typical to have run into Susanna and Christopher in that way? And she hadn't had a thing to say in the elevator, wasn't that typical? Christopher was bringing the wine but hadn't come close to dropping that, nor Susanna the mints. She was sick of being the family fool.

They all blared their greetings to each other and kept the volume up until they were seated by the fire in a ragged horseshoe. The moment of silence was a reminder that they'd spent little and very ancient time together, and whereas what they had in common was Gus, what they really had in common—rather, what they had that they could talk about—were the parents who'd managed to keep up with everyone equally. If only the older Wests could have been there, everyone noted privately, they wouldn't be sitting around the fire complimenting each other on dresses and neckties, like cancer patients restless for treatment. They wouldn't be talking about the dead.

"I remember on their last visit, before Egypt, how they went to Daphni all of us together, which is so close to me. It was the first time for us, though I had been to Delphi of course on their prior visit." Mère was stranded: she was twenty-five years older than Christopher, the next oldest, and so how could any of them understand her grief? Did they even understand her English?

"I was there too," Mimi said, "remember? We met in Greece and all went to Daphni, and then I went to Turkey and Afghanistan looking for Jojo before Beirut and the"— she hoped she'd choose the right word but she didn't know— "incident."

Gus shivered. *Incident,* was it? And when she was dead would they all sit around remembering just who was where? The Augusta Incident. Once more she shivered.

"And they were in Holland too that trip," Frieda put in.

"That was the longest day of my life," Mimi informed them.

But what could one say? "How so?" "Do tell?" Did she want to describe the day right there, describe it *again?*

Apparently so. "I'll just never forget it, the terrible heat, the sickening black smoke, the boom, that roar, and that awful reporter and all the microphones. What did they *expect* me to say?" Mimi left the room.

"If you're ready for another drink just tell Papa, because I'll be in the kitchen." Daphni gave Maya a jab and a nod and Maya joined her.

"Anyone?" But the glasses were full.

Susanna moved to Mimi's seat next to Gus and asked her how she felt. "Okay," Gus replied, "but I'd like to ask you a question later."

"May I ask you a question now? Have you a fever?"

"Mine was what should I do if I do. It's just above normal, but I feel funny. My hands are so cold."

"Let's go into your room." Susanna went to get the tool kit she traveled with, which naturally caught Christopher's eye as he listened to Andreas playing Scarlatti and tried to think of what he would say to Mimi, who had returned and taken the seat next to him. "Excuse me," he chose to say, getting up to follow the other two.

They listened to Gus's breathing while she watched them in the full-length mirror behind their backs. They bent their heads, she folded her hands. "You have a cold," Suzanna said.

Gus watched herself laugh, throw back her head on a diagonal, her jaw jutting up like the Washington Monument with its hard edges and too-slender shape. "You're joking!"

"No, it's a cold," said her brother.

Gus went on laughing but ceased to watch herself. "Oh Lord, I thought it was something circulatory! I couldn't believe a cancer patient could have a cold! Can a paraplegic stub a toe, and isn't it crazy? Oh God, I didn't know what to think! Can a paraplegic?"

"Of course," said Susanna.

"I thought my blood was running in place! I thought my heart was about to go! But do I have to stay in bed?" It was odd, she thought, that she treated her dear old loves as doctors.

"Not unless you want to," replied Christopher, taking the arms she extended to him and lifting her. She was frail as a very aged lady, someone's ancient great-great-grandmother, yet her eyes were the twinkliest in the room.

"Thank fortune," Gus said to make them both smile. "Now I'm ready for the turkey. A cold! Imagine that." She couldn't wait to tell Andreas they'd found her guilty of a misdemeanor rather than a felony.

They helped her into the seat next to Mimi, whose hand Gus took and held while the others talked about Scarlatti. Mimi said, "You know, I hardly knew them. Greece was our first time, and Beirut would have been our second. In forty years nearly. And Mère didn't even remember I was there!"

Gus checked and saw Mère was out of the room. "But don't let Mère bother you; even Andreas doesn't."

Mimi barely caught it because of her thoughts heading into self-pity at losing her family, all but Christopher, who might possibly take a day off if she died like the others. It caught by a thread, and Mimi postponed her bitterness. "What a really good guy Andreas is," she said simply.

Susanna and Christopher conferred in the hall. He'd call Derby, they were suggesting, to ask that he stop by after he'd finished feasting. It was a pneumonia possibly, most likely, and pain from the coughing would drive her wild. Derby lived

—they'd looked him up to find out—in the neighborhood. He should call in to order an I.V., in case he wanted their opinion, though not so much to arrest the pneumonia as to spare Gus discomfort. In their opinion, Derby was too conserving with his pain relief. Was he waiting for her to beg? Some did.

Daphni rang a bell, and Mère called, *"A table, tout le monde!"* in her falsetto. With artichokes the size of softballs, with almonds whose shells were honey colored, and with persimmons that gave the appearance of being lacquered, Mimi had sculpted a centerpiece the previous evening, her fruit flown jumbo from California. Andreas's turkey was plumper than ever, its skin a native American color, and Daphni's trimmings were chestnutty, oysterly fragrances. Mère had written menu cards in her gala European script, and Maya was taking it all down in still-life frames rich as the Dutch masters' with their delftware and their vegetables. Nicky sang an improvised song and pretended he was a baby by making elaborate infant droolings, like nonretractable yo-yos gone dead on the ends of their strings. Finally, all ten plates were served and all held hands around the table's circumference for a silent grace that brought tears to the eyes of all but Nicky. On the one and the other hand, how could they give thanks and how could they not?

"A jumbo, full!" exclaimed Mimi.

"The luggage compartment locked!" Mère emphasized.

"Our flight? They gave us a turkey omelet." Susanna laughed.

"Disgusting," Daphni assured them all, "in theory and in practice."

"How was it?" Gus couldn't help asking.

"Disgusting."

"How about playing squash tomorrow?" suggested Christopher.

"On!" Andreas winked; the glee of a truant.

"I'm going to the dentist tomorrow."

"*You* are?" Gus laughed at Frieda's irony.

"More of everything for me!" Daphni helped herself. "Mimi, have you been to the artichoke capital of the world? And tell us generally what's California like. Naturally, I'm hoping to live there."

"You sound like me," Mimi volunteered before someone else did, "and California is scatterbrained or evil, depending."

"On what?"

"On who's scattering the brains."

"How fascinating! Papa, did you know that was true?"

Andreas was thinking of Robert Kennedy.

"Frieda, are you here for long?" Mimi asked.

Frieda gasped and pretended her mashed potatoes were still hot. "As long as I can be." She hoped Gus hadn't heard the question.

"My plans are vague too. Another relationship down the drain, another alcoholic shadow the California sun made from nothing, down the drain. Come and go, they do." But she sighed delightfully and revealed the perfect set of caps installed by the L.A. dentist who did all the stars.

"Well, who wants more, or is it whom? Mum, which is it?"

"Who."

"Do you?"

"No thank you, Daphni."

"But you loved it, didn't you?"

Gus raised her water glass. "Yes. And if you don't mind being drunk to with city water, I want to, that is I need to tell you all that I, two things, that I, three things: I thank you for being here, one, and I love you and." She lowered the glass, holding its stem to the table with both hands, wishing it weren't true that she could no longer hold a piece of crystal in the air as long as a minute. "And I will miss you."

In the silence Andreas filled the glasses, but the silence

endured, no eye daring to make contact with another, no voice risking understatement, each aware of the deep unspeakable importance of Gus and yet each feeling, in the presence of strangers, uncomfortable. As if indeed there were strangers there.

Gus continued to stare at her hands, enduring the silence until, "And I know I am loved and will be missed," she broke it. "It's time to hear how Andreas met the Goose, or something." She shrugged. "Or anything."

In a wax museum, Andreas thought, at a taxidermist's, a statuette factory, a rock garden, if he were to get inspiration from them. Gus still stared at her water glass, then looked at him to ask if she had said something wrong. He stood in his place next to her, then bent to whisper something which nearly made her smile.

"The first time I met the Goose," he began, "she was just off the boat, and I, as a lover of the sea, was there by the dock.

" '*Ohayo gozaimasu,*' said I.

" 'Nope, New York City. Never been to Ohio in my life. Hey, you know where the king lives?'

" '*Watakushi wa Sony desu,*' I said to introduce myself.

" 'Again, only this time Wichita, huh? Can't you cool it with the geography? New York City,' she hollered.

" 'Tokyo,' I said, 'name Sony.'

" 'So, sonny, you know where the king lives? I missed my boat or else he'd be here.'

"Was she meaning Emperor or Prime Minister? And how was I to believe that someone so rude and crude wasn't an ill wind bringing no good, to refer to an English saying, or, to refer to one of our own from a little-known Haiku, 'I know not / Whether it will be astringent, / This first-plucked persimmon.'

" 'I happen to be the famous Goose of world renown! And a world-famous Moat Biologist!'

" 'Your business?'

" 'To consult with the king about the Imperial Moat.'

" 'Your business card?'

" 'Look, you jerk, I don't need to carry business cards!'

"As everyone knows, you simply don't go to Japan without your business cards, and I was suspicious. I happened to know the Imperial Moat and knew it was in terrible shape, but I didn't trust this astringent persimmon.

" 'Come on, sonny, look: I've come all the way from New York City because of a cable from the king. As we all know, the king is very good with salt water, you being an island and all, but as a marine biologist domestically he doesn't have it. In fact he knows not a thing about moats! Now be a good boy and take me there.'

"I told the Goose to follow me, I would drive her to the Palace.

" '*Arigato,*' she said unexpectedly, to which I of course said you're welcome, for our first exchange in my native tongue, consisting of *arigato* (thanks) and *do itashimashite* (don't mention it). A humble beginning it was, but not unlike that of my forefather Sony, who turned out to have good luck with transistors."

Andreas stopped talking and took down all the wine in his glass, only nobody followed him. Maya said, "Hold it!" and took a picture in case it turned out to be the end, but then Daphni came right out and said, "Then what?"

"Then what what?"

"Then what happened," she encouraged, "between you and the Goose."

"I'll need some more wine."

Daphni poured. "Okay then what?"

Andreas looked around the table, all eyes on him. He bent to kiss Gus. "All right," he said, "all right," to let some thoughts scramble together. He kissed her again. "All right, well: now Tokyo traffic's a glut on the market, and we were driving around for days before even getting near the Palace. Luckily the air is filtered in my car, so we didn't pass out from the monoxide, and there was plenty to eat by stopping every five hours for noodles and other snacks. Also, I taught her more Japanese than just thanks. All in all, we were well entertained, and after many days had passed, we reached the Imperial Palace wall and the moat.

"The Goose exclaimed, 'Ye gods, he sure wasn't kidding! I've never seen such a mess of a moat! Is that him up there?'

"It was. The Emperor paced the battlements right there in person. Imagine my shock when she rolled down her window and called up, 'Hi there!' She then said, 'Stay put, sonny, let me just tell the king that I'm here.'

"'Hi again,' the Goose called up to the battlements. 'It's me, I made it. No, down here, sir, I'm down on the ground. No, it's okay, don't bow or you're going to lose your balance, but come on down and let me in.'

"'That crazy guy,' she came back to the car to tell me, 'imagine bowing on the battlements! But he'll be right down. Come and say hello.'

"I got out of my car and prostrated myself on the wooden bridge over the moat. 'Hey whaddaya see?' she asked, and then lay down beside me. 'I lie for sun,' I answered to my best ability, which was definitely not good enough, since I knew that being American, she wouldn't know a thing about divine right and all that, and wouldn't know about him being the sun and all.

"'Ye gods, is this thing ever *filthy!* And just look at those carp on their very last legs!'

"Then the Emperor showed up and told us how embarrassing it was for him to be divine, and that he'd really prefer shaking hands so would we please get up from being prostrate? I translated by poking the Goose and pointing up. Inside

I was shaking like a rattle. '*There* you are,' she said. 'Gee, you look terrific!'

" '*So desuka?*'

" 'Yeah, really, *honto*.' The Goose winked at me, since I'd only taught her that word at breakfast, and then, to my horror, they threw their arms around each other. 'Sorry I missed the boat, but gee it's great to be here, and my friend sonny here helped a lot. You should make him a Sir for the way he drove. But ye gods, this moat has got to go!' "

Andreas looked around the table again. What more could he say? "And so they all went into the Emperor's house to have some green tea and live happily ever after. And the moat was fine from then on. Sony didn't make out too badly either."

He raised his glass and took down all the wine again. Maya took a picture of him and Gus and didn't have to ask them to hold it. And then they all spoke to one another as intimates.

Chapter
Nine

The next morning Andreas woke but lay looking. Funny, he thought, how Gus never used to sleep with her mouth open. That she did, now, accentuated the fact that the rest of her face was shrinking back to barely cover the bones. Her cheeks, now, were no longer those round apples, those shiny Macs, but instead some sheeny synthetic, some clinging nylon slip in "flesh." Only her lips were full as ever, but they were dry from the air being pumped past them out and in, and they weren't the right color anymore, either, now that they were a lavender tone instead of her natural coral beach. Just the hairline remained, that elongated letter *M* that featured the widow's peak pointing like an arrow to that clean white space above the brow where her third eye sat stark open and blue as daylight. He wanted to imagine a tear in that wide blue eye— her center, her ground—but all he could see was utter calm.

Her breath rattled already. It seemed to rattle from deep

within her, and it rattled again coming out over those lips
that looked both freezing and parched. It was very uneven,
too, as if Gus had to rummage through a pulmonary thrift
sale, most of which was junk, in order to find a used breath
that was still in good enough shape to wear.

How was he to reconcile the fact that she was decaying day
by day with—but he interrupted himself—decay? Everyone
has heard that if you put a tooth in Coca-Cola, the tooth will
simply decay away, decay itself into oblivion. Was decay the
word, or what was if it wasn't? What else was happening to
his wife if it weren't that she had been yanked—and the
healthiest tooth in the mouth, she was—and dropped into a
glass of Coke to decay away until nothing was left? Decay was
the word, so then how was he to reconcile the fact that she
was decaying day by day with the fact of that eye—that tele-
scope, that wide-angle lens—which couldn't be brighter or
more serene?

He turned onto his back again (God how it hurt; he must
have pulled something in squash) and realized he'd just seen
Gus. He realized that for the first time he had looked at her
and into the center of her forehead; it was enough to take his
breath. Why hadn't he dared look there before? Was he afraid
that he would find her frantic and have no help for her, or was
he scared he would find her calm? (He must have twisted it
on that nosedive after the shot he didn't get anyway; God it
hurt.) Andreas didn't know the answer and wanted to howl.

But where? If he were to howl where he lay he'd wake her;
he couldn't howl in the street and not get lassoed for playing
coyote and put away. He walked around the bed and into the
bathroom in order to howl in the shower. He wouldn't wake
Gus, since she was gone on drugs, but if he did she really
wouldn't mind, he knew, since she would know why.

Not howl. It was that he wanted to moan and think and

moan. He turned on the electric toothbrush and turned it off. He was looking for Gus in the wide but short mirror, remembering her saying that the mirror was merciful for putting her on display only down to the breastbone, as if it knew as she did that the bottom half of her was goat. That had been on a Sunday, after an afternoon under the covers making—if Gus was half goat, was it sodomy?—love. He turned on the toothbrush again.

He wet the silky shaving brush and lathered his face from the wooden cup of soapy cream. His strokes with the razor were timid ones, since lately he'd cut himself a lot, and he covered the space from his cheekbones to that point on his neck by humming inadvertently the wedding march and trying not to think what that meant about loss. In the shower he moaned. Then he aimed the dryer at his forehead and worked the nozzle around until his whole head was scrambled with curls like some midnight Shirley Temple.

He was reflecting that Gus might have dried her hair and his just as she had done a few weeks, a month, ago, after their shower after having made love for the last time. The last time? Andreas peered at himself in the mirror. He had to admit that yes, it had been for the last time. But how could that be right? It was correct, but how could it be *right?*

Gus was still not awake, and so he went into the kitchen to make oatmeal cookies with honey and brown sugar, thinking he could walk the girls to school before playing squash with Christopher, and buy freesia for Gus, that small waxy trumpet flower perfume is made from. The cookies were more divine than even she could have constructed, Daphni admitted at once. Especially for breakfast, divine for breakfast.

"Oh shut up, Daffy," Maya said, "divine is a Mère word."

"So!"

"You know what I mean."

"And don't call me Daffy!"

"Oh shut up. Thanks for breakfast, Pop, it was sumplee deevahn!" Maya got up to leave.

"Please don't say shut up." Oh well. And so they wouldn't all walk to school together, and so they had argued over his cookies. Oh well.

"Okay. Sorry, Pop, see you tonight. See you, Daph."

"Drop dead, Maya."

Oh well. So much for fantasies. Let Daphni take the bus. "Please don't say drop dead," Andreas told her, and left the kitchen with his coffee.

"Sorry, Papa, you're right of course. I bet she didn't even say goodbye to Mummy, though. When will that one ever act her age, I wonder."

Andreas heard her from the dining room, but since he had the choice, he simply pretended he hadn't and went to the door to retrieve the paper. Maya was reading the headlines while she waited, perhaps, for the elevator. "Oh hi," she said, "here, and would you tell Mom I said goodbye? She's not awake, and I said I'd meet Jenny and Heather for coffee."

"Coffee?"

"Don't tell Daphni, she'll say I'm not old enough."

"Okay."

"Pop, I love you."

Andreas laughed. "Can I ask why you're calling me Pop today?"

"I just feel like it. Do you love me, Pop?"

"I love you, mop. Enjoy your coffee."

"I do already. This is our third meeting."

"Meeting?"

"It's a discussion group. Damn, I forgot to press the button because of the paper." She stepped across the tiny hall and called the elevator.

"Do you discuss the news, you three?"

"Pop, we discuss everything. Right now we're on the topic of families."

"I see, well good luck, sweetie."

Maya smiled from beneath the brim of her purple felt hat. Her teeth were square and even and shiny white, her mother's teeth. "Pop, you understand everything."

He closed the door and hoped that he would find Gus awake, but he was ten feet from their bedroom door when he saw Nicky standing in profile examining Gus at slightly more than arm's-length range. He stopped and admired the funny way Nicky's big head tipped forward to balance the night-diapered seat of his little winter pajamas. Funny the way Nicky's torso didn't amount to much, funny how short his legs were; it was as if he were made of Tinker Toy spools and sticks, a spool for his belly and one for his seat, a spool for his head, sticks all the rest.

Nicky's fingers twitched. He wanted to touch her but, not daring, put his fingers in his mouth instead. Then he rose on his toes and dropped his hands for better balance. Still he didn't dare. He reached out an arm and then took a step forward to get a good look. It was the Cinderella watch he wanted to touch.

Andreas sat in the living room and felt useless. True, he'd give Christopher a good run for his money on the squash court, but Gus was the one he wanted to give to, and Ellen was coming, and then Christopher would have her alone for the whole afternoon while he went to the office, where he would feel useless. He started for the bedroom again, but Nicky lay in the bed next to Gus being stroked while he tried to take off her watch. At last he succeeded. "Nic put on," he suggested. She fastened the watch on Nicky's wrist. He chortled with glee. Should Andreas interrupt to ask if Gus wanted him to punch a new hole and cut the strap? It seemed everyone did better without his interference.

"Hello," he said.

Gus extended her very thin arms and said she was so glad he was still there. Nicky scrambled out of the bed and ran around to show Andreas. "Pitty lady!" he exclaimed, and put the plastic watch to his ear. "Tick," he assured them.

Ellen's stomach hurt. She was afraid that Gus would have the look of a stripped store-window mannequin, bald and overly thin. It gave Ellen the creeps and it gave her those cramps. She had so much gas, she bet she could float.

"Your hair!" she said first off to Gus.

"I cut it," Gus answered, and then saw that, with Ellen's degree of embarrassment, she'd obviously meant it as "You have hair!" and not that it had been cut in half.

"How awful," said Ellen. "Of course I meant to say hi and how are you."

"Hi and I'm fine. Bring the chair up and don't worry about this intravenous. I got hooked up this morning because I have a cold." And now she'd have to make Ellen feel better by chitchatting normally. "How is Simone?"

"Simone finished her dissertation. Per Hansen's wife had twins at Roosevelt. Jesús Diaz's visa finally worked out."

"Good."

"Nothing happens at staff meetings still."

It wasn't important, what had mattered for fifteen years was no longer important. Or was it that foreign student advising was one of those occupations one could only love when doing it? "How is the series?" Gus couldn't think of a thing to ask.

"Gus, you did such a great job ordering those seminars." What could she say? Gus looked so awful, so pale and sucked in.

"No, the order is only the night each speaker was free to come. How was the law?" Gus wished she hadn't asked Ellen to come. Her question was answered.

"The law was great, and medicine! It was brilliant of you to have a psychiatrist talk about medicine. She said that the U.S. contribution to International Women's Year was less than one half of what Senegal and Sweden gave. Isn't that awful?"

"Yes, I knew that." Gus had pretended that she still cared, as if caring might serve the purpose of the simple trinket one wore to enliven the little black dress, a costume-jewelry brooch in "rubies" to make the plain black dress less plain. But in fact she didn't care. Had she once been friendly enough herself to work every day with foreign students?

Ellen fidgeted with the nubby cloth of the suit she wore, picking at the cuff of the leg she crossed and recrossed and recrossed. "Can I get you something, Gus? Any book or something?"

Gus drew in a breath. It was selfish and she admitted it. "I'm sorry, Ellen. I wanted to see if I am still at all interested, but I'm not, not at all. I guess that should have been obvious without dragging you here."

"I wanted to come," Ellen said unnecessarily.

"Oh, forget that. I have made you come so I could reject you, and who would want that?"

"We all miss you." Her eyes spilled.

"I should have known that once I couldn't come back to work it was over, that it isn't a briefcase job."

"Gus, are you angry at me?"

"Of course not. And don't feel guilty."

"How could I not?" The tears were coming out in shudders. "I'd so much rather have you there. I don't want your job, I don't like to sit there knowing that all the students want you. I can't stand to sit at your desk and have you be so sick. How could I not?"

But Gus lay still while Ellen wept. She'd given it up; it was sad, but the fact for most who are dying is that family is everything.

"How could I not, Gus? You taught me everything I know."

"It was selfish of me, too selfish, to make you come here." Nevertheless she wished that Ellen would remember that she had picked her to take over, after.

Ellen forced herself to stay there until she had stopped. She had learned from Gus, after all, to disrespect self-pity. She had to sit there for thirty minutes. "I want to thank you," she said to Gus when it was over, "I think I'll do a better job now. I understand what you want me to know."

"Will you tell me goodbye?"

Ellen took Gus in her arms as if Gus were several dozen precious American beauties. "I'll miss you," she whispered, kissing, "I'll always miss you."

"Goodbye, Ellen." Now she was the one crying. "Go now, please."

"Goodbye, Gus." Ellen let herself out the front door.

In theory, Gus disbelieved death could result from the common cold, and yet as she lay in her bed and waited for Christopher and Andreas to return from their game, she could hear a camp counselor call into a megaphone: "Awright, you kids, I want all the C's right over here for the three-legged relay!" And she could see Cancer and Common Cold, their arms about each other's waist, getting strapped together at the ankle. A more unlikely team she had never seen, but she could see them start and knew there was no stopping them, because they knew how to work together. They complemented one another, as they say about human mismatched couples who have no business in the same bed. Their style was graceless, even laughable, but they were going to be the winners. And she was going to be the prize.

She coughed and felt her guts would explode. The I.V.

was antibiotic and tranquilized glucose or something, and she couldn't turn the page without strangling Virginia Woolf in her yards of transparent synthetic tubing. Which made Gus so *mad,* which was simply ridiculous, since Gus and intravenous were colleagues, and the inconvenience of being trickled into was slight indeed.

But then it was *ridiculous* that in 1938 in *Three Guineas* Virginia Woolf went to all that trouble, the question put to her: "How in your opinion are we to prevent war?" and the answer given in fine declarative sentences amply footnoted. As if she wrote in invisible ink. Gus read the sentences:

> You want to know which are the unreal loyalties which we must despise, which the real loyalties which we must honour? Consider Antigone's distinction between the laws and the Law. That is a far more profound statement of the duties of the individual to society than any our sociologists can offer us. Lame as the English rendering is, Antigone's five words are worth all the sermons of all the archbishops.[40]

Gus fumbled with the board and the tubing for footnote forty:

> 40. The five words of Antigone are: . . . 'Tis not my nature to join in hating, but in loving . . . To which Creon replied: "Pass, then, to the world of the dead, and, if thou must needs love, love them. While I live, no woman shall rule me."

What hurt was that it so mattered and then that it so didn't. Antigone had answered the question for once and for all, and for good measure Virginia Woolf had answered again, only nobody listened either time. "Pass, then, to the world of the dead." So much for Antigone, so much for Virginia Woolf, and Nicky would see it all end in T. S. Eliot's whimper, the world passing then into lovely death and deathly love with nobody the wiser. ". . . if thou must needs

love, love them." It was that kind of thing that made Gus
sick.

Which was ridiculous too. What concerned Gus was not
finally whether or not the world loved or whether, even, war
would be prevented. It was why she had to be reading that
book. It was whether she dared say she wanted to be entertained, which was such a damned suburban notion it made
Gus sick and mad and was ridiculous.

But she wanted to be entertained. She had done her part to
prevent war, if only a bit part, and Andreas wasn't any Creon
but one of those Greek kings who loved and let love: wasn't
it okay for her to be entertained? She had come into this
world a crybaby but had no intention of leaving that way.
Leave the spilt milk to her children, and let them cry over it
a while and then try to clean it up. For her own part Gus
wanted to get going on *Between the Acts* and let the Pageant
play itself out. That it wasn't her nature to join in hating but
in loving went without saying.

Then where was that last book? Breathing in the gasp of it
hurting to get up, Gus coughed, which hurt more, and for the
first time in a week, she spelled: t-h-e-A-n-t-i-g-o-n-e-o-f-
S-o-p-h-o-c-l-e-s, "the Antigone of Sophocles, done into English
verse by Edward Pargiter," which was the book Sara read
through while she was lying straight and still in her bed waiting for Maggie and their mother to get home from the party.
Why, again, was she on her feet and leaning against her I.V.
pole? *Between the Acts* wasn't anywhere near. And why had
everyone left her alone? And when on earth would they start
the morphine? She didn't have the energy to risk the pain of
getting herself back into bed, and so she clung to the I.V.
pole and waited for help.

By the time Andreas and Christopher returned from squash,
Gus had slid down the pole and was screaming from a heap
on the floor, screaming with fright at being there and doing

that. Her eyes were wild and frightened the men, who tried to coax her into their arms. "I can't take it!" she screamed. "Don't make me, I can't! Get it over with!" She pulled on the tubing to try to bring the bottle of liquid down on her, and then tried to bring the board out from beneath her arm. They didn't attempt to restrain her since she couldn't succeed, but they did try to coax her hands into theirs, then propping her up until the screaming reduced itself to a lame-dog whimper. "I can't be alone from now on, I have to have somebody near, can't you understand?" Of course they could, they soothed from either side of her, of course they could. Was she ready to let them lift her up? Gus nodded assent.

Dr. Derby was unavailable, Christopher was told, and so he left an urgent message. His instinct had been to give Gus the shot, and he almost had until he recovered enough to remember one doesn't give shots to another doctor's patient even if she's one's sister. Christopher fumed and stalked around the living room while Andreas fixed a cool washcloth for Gus, whose whimpering had reconstituted itself into sobs. "I'm so frightened," he heard her tell Andreas. "I shouldn't be here, I ought to go back. I'm better there, Dr. Derby was right. Derby doesn't want to see me here, and he won't give me more, he won't give me morphine."

Christopher stalked again to stop listening. It enraged him that home care could be so ill-given, when it was so clear from the day before that Gus was where she ought to be, and that going home to die was incomparably humane if only the medication were handled right. He jumped on the ringing phone and yelled, "Dr. Derby?" It was. His lecture to Derby was as if to a subordinate, and Derby conceded that medication was in order at that time. He would stop by himself to see Augusta on his way home and thanked Christopher for filling him in. In the meantime, he'd try to line up nurses.

Christopher gave her the shot and sat until Gus had relaxed into sleep. They had planned to spend the afternoon alone together, recapitulating, he couldn't help thinking with despair. Now he wouldn't see her, they wouldn't finish. He watched her breathing and wished again that she were anybody but Gus. He'd wanted to tell her how much he dearly loved her, how much he always had, and they'd planned an afternoon for that. If he hadn't played squash all morning, maybe, but what was the use? It was the afternoon they'd planned and not achieved.

He sat on the floor beside her bed and picked at the rug. No recapitulation, he couldn't help thinking again. But hadn't she told him about *The Years?* No peroration; there was no speech. No wrapping up what couldn't be wrapped.

Dr. Derby came in the early evening and sat on Andreas's side of the bed. He asked Gus how comfortable she was, but she didn't know what he meant and so she said what she was used to saying, "I'm feeling okay." She doubted he was speaking psychiatrically anyway. "But I wonder if you could graduate me. Frieda gives injections, as you know, and I felt much better this afternoon from my brother's injection." She was trying hard not to blame the doctor for what had happened, however bitter she felt about having been pushed to hysteria when what she wanted was Christopher's company. She didn't say, for instance, that he had stayed beyond Susanna's return in order to have that last time with her.

"I understand, but I hesitate to do that, Augusta. I'm sure you can appreciate that we want to watch you for a few days, since it may well be that this lung infection is controllable. We wouldn't want to start anything, if you know what I mean. That sort of drug only goes so far, and we don't like to miscalculate, understandably, by beginning prematurely. When you're dealing with infinite pain and a finite control, you can misjudge."

"I know all that, but I want you to know that my pain is increasing."

"Well, as I say—and I'm sorry, by the way—let's keep an eye on it."

"Keep an eye on it! It's *blinding* sometimes!"

"I know."

Gus lowered her voice. "Now listen: please don't be conservative on my account. I promise that if I'm still around when I'm full-tilt morphine, you can just smother me under my pillow or stick a pin in my brain like they do frogs."

The doctor squirmed. "Just hang on, if you can."

"I can, but can't you appreciate how sickening it is that I'm in this pain and you're giving me Vitamin C or whatever?" She indicated the gleaming liquid oval at the top of the pole.

He twisted on his spine because he feared his leg would fall asleep. "This development worries us, that's all I can say."

"But why? Seriously, why? So what if I die of a cold! If I die on a Tuesday instead of a Thursday, so what? You even admit that my liver will go, and so will my kidneys. So you cure the infection so that I don't die of pneumonia, so that I can die the following week because my liver can't keep house any longer, or so that you can fix that by running my blood through a machine, which gets me back in the hospital where I guess you think I belong, in order for my kidneys to surrender, and all the rest until finally some Christian nurse who will get blackballed for it sticks that pin in my brain, so that I can go, completely disgusted with humankind, to my reward. Is that what you call healing, Doctor?"

He twisted back and regarded the wall. "No," he admitted.

"At least you can still tell the truth. It's funny, you know, but here in my environment you are almost nothing. In your environment, up at the hospital, I'm the one who's nothing. No voice ever came to me up there to tell you how stupid you could be: the patient's self-confidence is minimal beyond words, and while I don't accuse you of designing your environment to that end, I will say that you do little to correct the fault. Well that's life, is it? That one can only see for oneself where one is compromised? That one can only look out for oneself? Here, I don't care about you, and there, you don't care about me and, well, that's life? Okay, it may be life, true enough, but you will never convince me that it's healing."

"Healing is a combination of things. And life is cruel, I agree with you."

Shock penetrated Gus's face from the inside out, and her voice again rose. "I never said life was cruel; I don't believe it is cruel. What I said was that what you practice as healing is cruel! And why? For what? Why is it that my husband can accept that, barring miracle, I will die, but that you can't? Why can I accept that I will die, and you can't?"

"I guess I believe in miracle," came the reply, meekly.

"Or in medicine. Do you not confuse the two?"

"You are not the first to ask that question."

Gus gritted her teeth against her exasperation. "I'm honestly not striving for originality at this late date. All I want, I can assure you, is confidence in your desire to heal me. And I mean *heal* not in its other definition, 'to patch up,' but in its first definition, 'to make sound or whole,' because that's what I'm talking about. A whole person has a body and a soul, and that's its integrity. Now if you desire to keep me sound, you mustn't abuse my soul the way you do; you mustn't sacrifice my soul to salvage my body by patching it up. Or where— can't you please look at me as I say this?—where's my in- tegrity? Don't you see that there's only one way to keep me sound?"

Dr. Derby, who had managed to look but was sorry he had, went gazing back to the matter of his shoelace. "They say sounding off is good for the soul," he said lamely.

And Gus had to close her eyes against the sight of him, her puffy-faced healer who spoke fidgety nonsense while twirling between thumb and forefinger the plastic threader of a brown cotton shoelace. She just couldn't look. "I've insulted you," she suggested without apology.

"Well, I don't take things like that personally. One is subject to a lot of abuse in this profession, where patience can be a trying thing."

"But I haven't *been* trying! That's exactly what I've been saying!"

"What?" He involuntarily pulled the lace out of its bow. "Oh my dear no, I meant the other kind. No, I quite agree, you've been awfully good. In fact you're a favorite of many of the nurses. Well. All this chatter isn't getting me home. I'll stop by tomorrow morning to see how you're coming along and stop by again on my way from the hospital. I've asked—" and he gestured.

"Frieda."

"I've asked Frieda to keep track of everything, and I think we'll be okay. How are you sleeping?"

"Not very well last night. Can you up that medication at least?

"Yes, of course. I'll give, uh."

"Frieda."

"I'll give Frieda the prescription. Interesting name."

"German."

"Yes. Well, goodbye."

Gus nodded, passive in her own environment, and stared at the door he closed behind him until everything went as white as it was, until she could imagine something ghostly enough to suffice, which was that she would be allowed to haunt that man into sensibility. And what a wretchedly unsatisfactory revenge, Gut admitted, bringing the room back into focus. She didn't even believe in ghosts.

On his way out, Dr. Derby indicated that he and Andreas might step into a private corner to talk. Frieda joined them uninvited. "I don't have to tell you," the doctor began, "that Augusta is worse. Now she has indicated to me that she prefers to stay home, and I have reluctantly agreed. But you should know that there is far less that we can do for her here, though I have ordered nurses and you can tell her that. I will state again that it's one thing or another at this point, and I will try to see that she gets adequate medication as soon as we can get a nurse on. There is increased fluid, as perhaps you have gathered, in her lungs. I don't feel good about there being a small child around." He stopped.

But Andreas ignored the reference to Nicky. What he wanted to know was if all the food Gus needed was in the intravenous.

"Yes, don't worry that she has no appetite. Give her whatever she wants."

Frieda spoke. "She wants medication." She spoke sharply.

"I am aware of that. There are legal complications outside the controlled environment, and, as I'm sure you know, New York state is rather difficult."

"But did you give her an injection?"

"Not yet. If we can get a nurse for tomorrow, I'll give her something first thing in the morning. Her medication is still quite conservative," he said proudly.

"What are you waiting for?"

"I believe I just told you." The doctor turned to Andreas. "Have you any questions?"

"What shall I tell the girls?" His voice caught.

"That we are not optimistic."

"Do you know how long?"

The doctor sighed. It was always the same question, not that he blamed them. There was never an answer. Always then did he wish he sold linen in some stressless Fifth Avenue shop. "I honestly don't, I'm sorry." He put on his hat.

"Thank you for letting her stay here," Andreas said, "and for coming by."

"Oh well, I only live around the corner, and as for her staying here, her brother and sister-in-law were the arm-twisters. I'm glad to oblige over extramedical considerations," he said nonsensically, shrugging his shoulders into his coat. "Perhaps there's peace of mind here." He put his left hand into a pocket. "If not, why don't you give her this, but not before nine and only if she gets really desperate." He handed Frieda a tiny glass vial and a disposable syringe. "Just don't report me for letting you administer this."

While Andreas closed the door behind the doctor, Frieda went in to Gus, to whom Andreas could hear her saying, "We got a little juice out of him after all. I thought I'd lost it for you, but Andreas sweetened him up again."

Tears came into Gus's eyes. "How soon?"

"Three hours from now."

"Frieda, wait with me. All my energy went into Derby, and I have none left to deal with the pain. Will you sit?"

"Of course." She sat.

"Or over here? No, stay. But could you hold my hand? Oh God, I'm so confused. Don't sit on the bed, better back there where you were." Her eyes went wild.

"Hold on to my hand."

Gus grasped at her hand with the parts of the fingers that extended beyond the board's end and took a grip on one of her fingers, which nearly hurt Frieda. Imagine, then, how much pain Gus took in. "Fright-ning," Gus gasped. "Oh God!" She hung on for dear life. "Oh!" Still she hung on. "Oh! There!" The terror drained from her eyes, and the fingers let go. "There I made it," she whispered, "there I made it, I thought so." Gus closed her eyes and said again, "I thought so."

After several moments, Gus opened her eyes to look for Frieda. "Don't go," she said, and closed them again. "I want to complain. I thought this morning that maybe I should have aborted Daphni and gone back to dancing, that was the first thing. I've got this body that hates surprises, I was thinking. And then again Nicky, I thought I should have aborted him too, especially him. I mean just to be safe. I've got this body that hates surprises." She paused and thought she'd said that already but didn't know.

"What I wish I could know is whether it would have made any difference, or if I'd still be thirty-nine and nearly gone. I wish I could know that either way it made no difference, I wish I could believe like Mother that it had been decided already long before. I would like to know I did the right thing. I mean, why was it never even a consideration not to do it the way I did? I would like to think because it was right, but I don't feel sure."

Gus used the other hand to wipe the tears that fell into her ears in a line from the corners of her eyes. She remembered whichever Sunday it was, and Andreas's song. "How could I have risked it like this to be happy? I've been so happy. Frieda, I was thinking that if I'd been more careful I could have been happier, but that's nonsense. We made love the first day we met, and I was never happier. I try to think why. When I found out, I realized I never would have taken a risk like that if I'd been dancing. So careless that I wondered if dancing wasn't too strict, too much, but you know? It wasn't carelessness or carefreeness. It was only because of Andreas and because of me, and so the first time I met him I got pregnant, me, the famous Goose of world renown." Gus stopped and let the breath explode from her in a volley.

"Should I have tried to rescue myself? And then what about Maya; Maya was planned, and so how could she have been a mistake? And if she was planned, wasn't all of it planned? I don't think my life would have had its value without Andreas, without them all. I try and think how it might have been better and can't succeed. That it might have been different doesn't even seem possible, but still. Frieda? Did I do the right thing?"

Frieda cleared her throat. "Yes," she said.

"I thought so. It's hard to be in such pain, but I thought so. I honestly thought so. The pain has no end, but I thought I was right, and I'm glad. Sometimes I feel I'm burning up, sometimes I feel I'm Icarus against the sun, the pain is so fierce. But I thought it was worth it." A beatific smile replaced the movement of her lips, and Gus lay utterly still.

Frieda held the fingers and watched the lips begin to move over soundless words. Between the words, the breath rasped and rattled until there were no more words, only breath, and Gus was asleep. Finally then, Frieda wept. The pain had no end.

Chapter
Ten

*I*t was Monday morning, and Jackson was in need of a pause. He poured into a bowl the beige dust which was all that was left in the Rice Krispies box, sprinkled powdered milk over the dust, ran the bowl under the tap, and gave the sludge a spin with his spoon. He congratulated himself for having gotten up with the first alarm and for having worked so quickly and well. Gus was clean and ready for her patina. He set down the empty bowl and reheated the surface of the bronze in order to work in the green acid treatment—copper scrap in nitric acid—and then the ferric nitrate which would give Gus an amber-colored skin not unsimilar to the beeswax head he'd made from the clay and burned away to get the bronze. By late morning he felt scrambled, frothy. He was a genius.

He searched in his sleeping bag until he found the cele-brating pipe and the black chip of hashish he had been saving for something like that moment. He pulled in the sweet black hash as if he were hollow from the mouth down and up, the deepest ins and the shallowest outs four times or five, and it was one hot-ass piece of sculpture, dig it, it was one hot-ass head. And dig the dope: what a perfect way to go to school.

But by the end of the afternoon Jackson was exhausted, wanting only to put his head down on his desk as if an elementary child in rest period. The first two classes had gone well but the last one, his usually cheerful eighth-graders, had collapsed and crashed and burned right there in the art room. They hadn't gone for his suggestion that self-portraiture is fascinating, no matter that he had shown them slides (Rembrandt, van Gogh, Picasso, and on through to Alfred Leslie) and begged them as a personal favor to give it a whirl by any means at all, including collage and stick-figure pencil drawing. Not a chance, they had indicated, no way.

"Why not?"

Silence.

"Why the hell not?"

Not a peep.

"My other two classes did it! Look! See?" He had held up the evidence.

"Seniors," someone eventually muttered.

"So?"

"So we're thirteen."

Jackson tried but couldn't understand, so they'd drawn whatever they wanted to until the bell, and their silence had left him depressed and exhausted.

"Jackson?" Maya tapped him on the shoulder.

"Hi, Maya, how's Gus?"

"I'll tell you in a minute, but could I speak to you?"

"Please do." He raised his head from the pile of books it rested on and motioned Maya to have a seat.

"It's nothing personal," she began kindly, "but so you don't make the same mistake again, that's all."

Jackson nodded.

"It's very embarrassing."

"That's okay, go ahead."

Maya blushed. "I mean it's very embarrassing to draw ourselves at this stage."

"But aren't you the ones who spend half your life in front of a mirror?"

"Yes, but it's very embarrassing."

"Still, it seemed to me that if van Gogh can draw his bloody ear stump—I mean, what can be more embarrassing?—you can draw a few lousy pimples."

"I can see your point, but it's not just the pimples."

"Then what?"

"Also braces."

"Not many self-portraits have their mouths open, and that's a fact."

"Maybe, but you showed all those realistic slides."

"Picasso?"

"Maybe not Picasso but the others."

"So what's wrong with reality?"

Maya was silent.

"Okay," Jackson said, "I can dig it."

"Thanks, Jackson."

"Okay, but"—here Jackson began to laugh—"but when you're seniors I won't care if you all weigh three hundred pounds, have fifty thousand more pimples than you do now, and have to wear braces on your legs and arms, not just your teeth."

"And Rembrandt looks quite fat himself, for that matter." Maya grinned. "Daphni's shopping with Mère, but I'm on my way home if you want to come and see Mom."

"How is she?" Jackson grabbed his coat.

"Not optimistic, Daddy says."

He shrugged the coat on and wondered what that meant, *not optimistic,* but neither spoke again until they were on the bus. "Can I ask you something, Maya? Why are you protective of people with braces? You got great teeth."

"Because some of my best friends wear braces, Jenny and Heather," Maya answered earnestly. "Did you ever?"

"Yes."

"Then you should remember. Daphni only got them off last summer, and you should have seen how self-conscious she was for all that time. I was very sympathetic too, in those days. You have to be kind to self-conscious people, that's what my mom says." She stuck her bookbag behind her back to prop her forward enough to rest her feet on the floor. "Also Mimi, Mom says. Mimi's awfully that way, so you have to be kind. She's my aunt, so even adults can have it."

Mimi sat in the bedside chair and announced that it was too awfully sinister, the way the windows were done up to entice Christmas buyers to overspend when it was practically still Thanksgiving. "In L.A.," she argued, "we don't have to take that kind of thing seriously on account of the palm trees, so it doesn't intrude the way it does here, it doesn't make you feel guilty for not doing your shopping. And that's the wonderful thing, the utter guiltlessness of everyday life. I could never live again in the east. Pain, pain, and suffer every minute, no hope for the future. Can I get you something to drink?"

"Please, ice water."

"You see, Gus? A very eastern drink." And out she ran.

Gus debated letting Mimi go or forcing it on her. The truth was: if she wanted to engage herself to the fullest extent, she'd have to force it. She didn't want to change her life by pretending Mimi wasn't there, or by inventing another sister. She wanted Mimi to make the adjustment. Once, years earlier, there had been a one-question quiz brought by a foreign student of psychology, and Gus had answered the question firmly, shocking the student into blurting out that nobody else had answered that way. The question was: if you knew you had six months to live, in what ways would you live differently? Gus's answer: none.

Mimi rushed in explaining that she hadn't meant eastern in the real sense but only to mean the east. An Eastern drink would be more harmonious. "That's why we're not affected by things like Christmas windows. We get our life style from the East, where life doesn't impose and dominate, and so we're more free for harmony." Mimi scratched the backs of both hands, and her bangle bracelets jangled in the stillness. "Gussie? Are you there?"

Gus moved her lips, telling inside jokes. The fluid bubbled down the tube and into her wrist, but neither did it make a sound. "This is the pits," Mimi said to herself, but still she sat for a quarter hour, until it was too obvious that she had no idea what Gus was moving her lips about. And so wouldn't it be better to get up and leave, putting off to evening whatever sign Gus might give her that all was or wasn't forgiven, if that was indeed what she waited for? But still she sat. They had so rarely been alone together.

Finally there was a knock followed by Jackson and a turkey sandwich, which action roused Gus. "Have you two been out for lunch?"

Jackson smiled at Mimi. "We haven't even been introduced —hi, I'm Jackson—and I'm just back from school, me and Maya. You mind if I eat this in here?"

"I'm Mimi."

"Hi."

"How was your Thanksgiving?"

"Fine, Gus, but what's with the bottle of hummingbird food?"

"It's just food. Where's Maya?"

"She'll be in." Would nobody mention the head? "The head is setting; it's finished."

"And I'm dying to see it!" But that was Mimi.

Maya came in and went to kiss Gus. "We're having a turkey sandwich," she said.

"Swell sandwich," Jackson said for Maya, "and I ate a load of them over the weekend while I was working on the head. You remember the head, Gus?"

"She's been napping," Mimi explained.

"Have I?"

Jackson sucked his fingers clean, in a way, and wiped them on his pants. "You want to hear?"

"Oh yes," said Mimi.

"I brought this book, Gus, because I use the same technique and it has pictures I teach with too. *Lost Wax Bronze Casting* ('a photographic essay on this antique and venerable art') by Harry Jackson, no relation. I knew you'd want to see how I turned the clay into this beautiful head you'll see, let me see, I think Thursday since the beeswax layer I put on top of the patina has to set." Gus had closed her eyes. He handed the book to Mimi. "Well, you can look at the pictures another time, Gus. It's very authentic and very dangerous working with gases the way Cellini did."

"Who's Cellini?" Mimi asked.

"A sixteenth-century master sculptor, Italian, and if you read the book you'll see that Harry Jackson got everything from Cellini; me too. Call it plagiarizing"—he chuckled— "but it sure is authentic."

"I love authenticity," said Mimi.

Maya had finished her sandwich and, since she'd read through the book for Jackson's class on lost wax casting, excused herself to go practice piano.

"Well first you've got your clay, as you know, which you need to make a negative of, so you use this latex stuff which is synthetic and durable and you apply it and then make a plaster mother mold, a *couche* you can call it, in order to get your negative impression, after which you're finished with the clay." He had the impression that if he talked quickly, Gus couldn't fall asleep on him. "Then, Gus—this'll only take a minute to get to the part about the pouring—you make your wax that you'll burn away."

Gus was working on her own strategy.

"So, making a very long story short, you hook together the two sides of the mother mold, with, inside, the rubber negative and a thin wax layer, and into it you pour molten wax you slush around and pour out the extra. I'm doing all of this twice, you remember, for yours and then again for your mother's."

"In-law," Mimi reminded him.

"Your mother-in-law's. You correct the wax to get rid of the defects because when it's burned out and bronze goes where it was, you got your mistakes in bronze. Are you with me?"

Gus thought she had figured out how to accomplish it, and she opened her eyes to make sure they were still there.

"Good, I see you're with me. It's tricky but worth it." He looked at her. "But I'll skip the details."

"These pictures tell you everything!" Mimi exclaimed.

"Yes, they do. Just remember you're going to be making a breathing system to vent the gases, also a core, and you've got to drive brass nails and pins to a depth of half into the wax to keep the core I told you about from collapsing against the outer investment I didn't tell you about yet when the wax melts off."

Mimi flipped the pages. "I think I'm getting it."

"Gus?"

She smiled and closed her eyes.

"Here's a little-known fact: the Latin *sincerus* comes out of lost wax bronze casting and means 'without wax,' so something *sincerus* has no imperfections or something, and so does sincere."

"I love the origin of words, myself."

"Please turn to the pouring part, since we're going to skip the investments, the details of the core, and the circulatory system part, no matter how important they are."

"How cute," Mimi said, having found the place, "they look like urns or dwarfs with spouts in the top of their head. So you pour the bronze into the spout?"

"Yes." Jackson sighed, impatient with what remained of his audience. "See the ends of these breathing tubes? When the overflow overflows you'll know that the what was once wax cavity is full of bronze."

"What a good idea!"

What pains in the asses women were, Jackson told himself, what pains in the asses! But once he'd said that to Marty and her answer had been, "Making men the asses."

Gus could hardly wait until she would interrupt and make her request. She had only to decide just how naive she would pretend to be.

"You build the oven to suit the molds and put the chimney over the largest so you can tell when the exhaust is no longer greasy carbon that the wax has been lost." He lost his place, had planned to get on with the pouring but still talked wax. "Find the color page." It was just that he felt entitled to mention having tended a twenty-eight-hour burnout fire! "Make the casting pit, disassemble the oven, check on the coke fire and the molten pig of bronze in the crucible."

"Coke and pig, I do love this terminology!"

"Skim off the slag with blacksmith's tongs. Pack very dry sand around the molds."

"Here it is! My God, that color is glorious! Glowing white, Jackson, weren't you scared?"

"I told you it was dangerous," he answered with pride.

"It looks hellish! Did you wear those goggles?"

"Yes, you must." But now he was happy, wasn't he? He'd impressed someone, even if only Mimi. "You have to pour it until the glowing overflows through the two little breathing holes in the lid, spurting up, falling back. Imagine someone pouring the glowing bronze into your mouth, filling all the tiniest capillaries throughout your body, and then having overflow indicated by bubbles of bronze coming out of your nose."

"Imagine! How perfectly awful! But what an exciting thought, in a way, in a terrible way of course!"

"You're sure you're going to burn up. You ever had that sensation?"

"No," Mimi admitted.

"There's nothing that can equal it anyway. When I pour bronze I'm Icarus, period."

"Are you," asked Gus, "almost finished?"

"That depends," he said, hurt. "I was going to describe what I did this morning to clean the head up, removing the breather tubes, plugging the holes, the patina."

"Fine, we'll skip that."

Mimi closed the book. Jackson's voice cracked when he asked Gus if she'd been listening.

"Off and on, but I told you: the part that interested me was the process. Once the clay's done the head is a decoration, isn't it?"

"I'd say a sculpture," Jackson muttered.

"Same thing."

Mimi's bangle bracelets clattered, her arms in the air. "Well, perhaps we ought to change the subject. Who has an idea?"

"I do. I want to return your book, Jackson." Gus pointed to the blue-leather volume. "I want you to read."

"Good old Maxwell Arnold." Perhaps he'd gone on too long after all. And Gus would have questions once she saw the bronze in person.

"How lovely! Maxwell Arnold wrote 'The Forgotten Mermaid,' a dreamy poem I just read while you were sleeping, Gussie. Oh do read, Jackson. I love leather books of poetry."

"Yeah," Jackson said, and slid the Arnold under his chair.

"I want you to read the poem you said reminded you of your grandfather."

"He wrote lots of good poetry, Arnold, lots about water, didn't he?"

"Do you remember the one I mean?"

"Uh, yes I do. It's not about water."

"I know," said Gus.

Mimi interjected, "But does it matter?"

"It's not too good a reading poem," Jackson suggetsed.

"But please read it anyway," Mimi encouraged. "I love hearing poetry read by a man." She readied herself by quieting her bracelets and knotting her fingers.

"Some other time." Jackson stalled.

"Don't be silly, Gus has asked for it." Mimi bent for the book and made a racket. "Now which one was it?"

"Please," Gus assured him.

But what was the story? "I'm not sure which one it was, come to think of it." Jackson leafed helplessly through the book and shut it firmly.

" 'A Wish,' it was."

"And have you read it?"

"Yes," said Gus.

"And you want me to read it?"

"Yes."

"Now really," Mimi said, "isn't that what Gussie already said?"

Jackson didn't like it to the extent that if Gus were Marty, he would have told her she was a stinking bitch and never mind her reasons. And why weren't they discussing the head? Instead, he read:

> I ask not that my bed of death
> From bands of greedy heirs be free;
> For these besiege the latest breath
> Of fortune's favour'd sons, not me.
>
> I ask not each kind soul to keep
> Tearless, when of my death he hears.
> Let those who will, if any, weep!
> There are worse plagues on earth than tears.
>
> I ask but that my death may find
> The freedom to my life denied;
> Ask but the folly of mankind
> Then, then at last, to quit my side.

Mimi's bracelets sounded. "That's the one," said Gus.

> Spare me the whispering, crowded room,
> The friends who come, and gape, and go;
> The ceremonious air of gloom—
> All, which makes death a hideous show!

Jackson turned the page, looking up for a signal that he might stop, but Gus's eyes were closed. There was a signal only in Mimi's clatter.

Nor bring, to see me cease to live,
Some doctor full of phrase and fame,
To shake his sapient head, and give
The ill he cannot cure a name.

Nor fetch, to take the accustom'd toll
Of the poor sinner bound for death,
His brother-doctor of the soul,
To canvass with official breath

The future and its viewless things—
That undiscover'd mystery
Which one who feels death's winnowing wings
Must needs read clearer, sure, than he!

Jackson scanned ahead to see if he could leave out the next
few. This was killing him, but the next few were central. He'd
had no idea Gus could be so hard. On he went:

Bring none of these; but let me be,
While all around in silence lies,
Moved to the window near, and see
Once more, before my dying eyes,

Bathed in the sacred dews of morn
The wide aerial landscape spread—
The world which was ere I was born,
The world which lasts when I am dead;

Which never was the friend of *one*,
Nor promised love it could not give,
But lit for all its generous sun,
And lived itself, and made us live.

Well, there was one right there he could have left out to
speed things. Boy, was she rough. He had no choice.

There let me gaze, till I become
In soul, with what I gaze on, wed!

> To feel the universe my home;
> To have before my mind—instead
>
> Of the sick room, the mortal strife,
> The turmoil for a little breath—
> The pure eternal course of life,
> Not human combatings with death!

Again he stopped. Now what was he going to say when he finished?

> Thus feeling, gazing, might I grow
> Composed, refresh'd, ennobled, clear;
> Then willing let my spirit go
> To work or wait elsewhere or here!

He hadn't a clue. There was nothing to stare at but his feet.

"Well," Gus said, "I rather liked that poem once I read the whole thing. Mimi, did you?"

Mimi gasped. "No," she blurted out, "how could you?"

"How could I like it?"

"Do that! God, Gussie!" Mimi buried her head.

"I thought it was time."

"And what if it was hard already?"

"Now it's harder, that's all." It did hurt Gus to see Mimi weep, but she said anyway, "You were sapping me. I had to."

Jackson felt he would be sick but didn't dare move for fear Gus would notice him. It was the most pitiful sobbing ever, Mimi's wretched guttural sobbing sounds.

Gus said, "Now, you see, we can talk about it. I've wanted to."

"What can we say?" Mimi coughed and choked.

"Whatever we like. Have some of my water, here."

"Yes." Mimi also helped herself to Kleenex and blew.

Again she drank and then, finally, she looked at Gus, whose smile was as broad as a clown's.

"Just whatever we like." Gus beamed.

Mimi blew her nose again and made such a dreadful honking noise that she had to laugh. "And winner takes all," she said, shrugging, "and isn't Gus a winner, Jackson?"

Jackson took that for acknowledgment that he was a witness, and wasn't Gus something. "Sure is"—he whistled, gaining in relief—"and now"—he held up the blue leather book—"any more requests?"

Chapter Eleven

*A*ndreas had slept poorly on the folding cot in Nicky's room and, waking at five-thirty because Nicky had, he felt for the first time in over two years—not since the time of Gus's colostomy—that he could not possibly attend to the day's business. He had a meeting at nine and a new client conference at eleven, but neither was imaginable in any familiar sense. He could not imagine sitting in chairs at tables without explaining himself to the extent of letting his old and new clients know that he wasn't only a lawyer: that he was the husband of the one person in the world he would never choose to help die; that he was the father of a small child who was having trouble sleeping, of a middle child who was not eating, of an eldest who was growing daily more officious; that his mother was in town.

He felt neither the pleasure of completion nor the pleasure of anticipation and wondered how he would sit through a morning with people who would not know about the round-the-clock nurses. He could not, of course, tell them.

Nicky was selecting a book and would need to get beneath the cot's covers in order to hear Andreas read it. Andreas knew that first, then, he must change Nicky's diapers. Only his secretary knew what was going on, but even she knew not very much. It was as if once he left the apartment, no one knew. Whose fault was that? Everything was wet from Nicky's having sweated through a night of nightmares, and Andreas decided to bathe him, keeping the storybook hostage in order to keep the bath short. Why was it that after nine no one would know he had a baby whose mother was fed intravenously?

The story was the one about trucks that bring fruit and vegetables to the city so Nicky can eat: one day, of course, Nicky stows away and gets to see all the country gardens, and is of course amazed to pick a handful of cherries while perched on the shoulders of the driver who'd called Nicky's mother to say that Nicky was with him but would return just as soon as the trunk was loaded up. Nicky pointed to Nicky in every illustration and said, predictably, "Nicky!" For "Maa!" he pointed to the sweet woman who stood on the doorstep to offer milk and cookies to the gentleman driver. Why was it that at ten o'clock no one would know that he'd slept on a cot? Was that his fault, or the law's, or New York's?

Andreas left Nicky on the cot and went into the living room to ask the nurse, who would be knitting under the reading lamp, how Gus was, to which she would answer briefly that there had been no change. Even this nurse, who knew a lot, didn't know that his mother was in town. He nodded and headed for the bedroom and, because Gus was still sleeping, into the bathroom, where in the shower he decided that possibly when he next flew, he'd tell his seat-mate everything.

As he sat with his coffee at the far end of the dining-room table, he heard Daphni shout, "You get out of my kitchen!" which sent Maya flying, weeping, wailing against his chest. "It's impossible, and I just can't take it; I wish so much it was Daphni dying!" He tried to soothe her with Greek love language that translated ridiculously, but Maya clung and stained his necktie with her sorrow. "I have no friends but you," she wailed, "and I can't take any more of Daphni!"

Daphni responded to her mother's worsened condition by ignoring it and by planning instead the fancy Greek dinner Gus had promised her, something to celebrate Mère and Mimi and, not incidentally, Jackson too. There was no help, in her view, for a nonsurvivor like Maya, who was only good for tears. She firmly shut the door that led from the dining room into the kitchen, which provoked Maya to cling all the tighter and wail some more about having no friends.

"Except Heather and Jenny? And aren't you going to see them for coffee?" He gave Maya his handkerchief and said he had a good idea: "Why don't you take your music to school so that, rather than come back here before your lesson, you can take your two good friends out for ice cream. And then I'll meet you back here not too long after your lesson."

Maya recovered. "Okay, we'll be meeting back here for cocktails to talk things over?"

"Yes. Now did you have some breakfast?"

"Well I was trying!"

"It's all right, sweetie, but will you promise to have hot cereal or an egg?"

"For our group? But we always only have doughnuts!"

"Tell Jenny and Heather you're only doing me a favor."

"I'm sure they wouldn't mind this once, especially since

we'll all be having the same thing later." She took the money from Andreas and slid off his lap to collect her music. He took off his tie.

On a stool at the kitchen table, Daphni sat to concentrate on her lists. She announced to Andreas when she had a minute that the menu was set but he would have to be surprised. He asked only that she try and be nicer to Maya, but Daphni replied that, as he well knew, Maya didn't know a thing about food and so nothing could be done about it. And if Maya wanted to go crying to him, that was her business and not Daphni's, so there was really nothing to talk about. But she would give him a hint, she said, which was that dessert began with a *b* and was his favorite, but then couldn't he please let her finish up? She was running late.

Andreas said he'd think all day about what it might be, beginning with a *b,* and that he hoped Daphni would think of a way to be sweet as baklava to Maya, in order that her fancy dinner not be spoiled. "You guessed! Okay, well the *rest* could be a surprise still, only no more hints!"

"What about the other part?"

"Well I'll try, Papa, but that's all I can promise."

"I want you to try hard."

"Okay, one more hint: a little thing you love with an *o.*"

"With an *o-u?*"

"Not ouzo. No more hints, but try an *r.*"

"So we're both trying, right?"

"We both are. See you later, Papa."

"Orzo?"

"No more hints!"

Why was it that at seven, no one knew at all what was on his mind? No wonder they wouldn't know at eleven that he had a wife who loved him second after morphine.

Dr. Derby was the first to find Gus awake, as if she were saving her energy for hellos and not wasting it on goodbyes.

He sat on the chair and said he was so dreadfully sorry for
having neglected to give Gus her note the night before, but
he hoped she would forgive him since it hadn't been inten-
tional.

Gus took the paper and read the script: "Dear Gus, We
think of you with love, Jean Harding."

And she smiled, filled with the warmth of being remembered. So many people were sending notes or flowers or special
things to eat and drink, making of the apartment a Care
warehouse. But Dr. Harding! "Please tell her how much she
has meant to me all along, and that I thank her for remembering."

"I will," the doctor assured Gus, "and I won't forget. She'll
be glad to hear that."

"Poor doctors," Gus said absently.

"Yes."

"It's a shame—"

"Yes."

"—that they can't express their feelings."

"It is. For example, I would like to say that you have been
a fine patient."

"Thank you, I appreciate that. And you have been patient
with me, and good."

"I appreciate that."

"Isn't it a difficult relationship?"

"Very," he said.

"I'm much more comfortable now."

"Excellent. I hope the nurses are treating you well."

Gus nodded. "They are. I had been afraid being here with
the I.V. and no one to change it when it ran out. My family
is doing so well, don't you think?"

"I do."

"I'm very glad to be here."

"In your environment." At last he knew what she meant,

Dr. Derby realized. He almost thought that if he had to be sick one day, he'd want to be home. "I guess I shouldn't have disapproved, but I didn't fully understand." Yet he didn't know if he would dare die there.

"You didn't know how lucky I am."

"Lucky?" She was right that he didn't know.

"To have." She gestured with her free arm, a sweep.

"Family and friends?"

"Everything. Peace."

Dr. Derby watched her close her eyes and smile again. Many patients had taught him many things. "Before you go to sleep, Augusta, there is one thing. I've instructed the day nurse to put you on a catheter, and I thought you'd want warning."

"I don't mind. I've never liked bedpans."

"Some patients feel it's a terrible loss." Many patients, many things.

"I've been voiding into bags for over two years now." Gus was barely moving her lips.

"Yes, of course you have. I thought I'd mention it, is all."

"Is there anything else?"

"That's all. I'll be back again tonight." He paused to figure out how to say it. "And sleep well."

Gus looked up, surprised. It was nice to see a doctor rest. "Thank you," she said. She fell asleep with her hand on the note.

Mère had been put on her honor to speak only Greek because, Daphni insisted, it was important for the total effect that it all be as wonderfully authentic as Mère in person picking out the feta cheese in Greek, also the grape leaves and the squid. No end of protest as to her inadequacy had been raised by the delighted Mère, but the decision was, as she herself put it, a fait accompli, and so off she had gone to fetch the day's feta.

And Frieda had dropped Nicky off at the Armsteads' and gone to International House to see Ellen—Ellen called every day—and to sit in on a seminar about racism on the part of the oil-producing nations.

The nurse had given Gus a sponge bath and had then retired to the living room feeling satisfaction that Gus had accepted the catheter and not protested. This was certainly one of the very most peaceful jobs she'd ever been on: how pleasant it was to sit in front of the tall south windows instead of in a dim little box, and how nice it was to overhear the patient and her sister talking unselfconsciously. The sister at that moment was reading the opening of *Between the Acts:*

> It was a summer's night and they were talking, in the big room with the windows open to the garden, about the cesspool....
>
> She came in like a swan swimming its way; then was checked and stopped; was surprised to find people there; and lights burning. She had been sitting with her little boy who wasn't well, she apologized. What had they been saying? ...
>
> What had *he* said about the cesspool; or indeed about anything? Isa wondered, inclining her head towards the gentleman farmer, Rupert Haines. She had met him at a Bazaar; and at a tennis party. He had handed her a cup and a racquet—that was all. But in his ravaged face she always felt mystery; and in his silence, passion. At the tennis party she had felt this, and at the Bazaar. Now a third time, if anything more strongly, she felt it again.
>
> "I remember," the old man interrupted, "my mother...." Of his mother he remembered that she was very stout; kept her tea-caddy locked; yet had given him in that very room a copy of Byron. It was over sixty years ago, he told them, that his mother had given him the works of Byron in that very room. He paused.
>
> "She walks in beauty like the night," he quoted. Then again:

"So we'll go no more a-roving by the light of the moon."

Isa raised her head. The words made two rings, perfect rings, that floated them, herself and Haines, like two swans down stream. But his snow-white breast was circled with a tangle of dirty duckweed; and she too, in her webbed feet was entangled, by her husband, the stockbroker. Sitting on her three-cornered chair she swayed, with her dark pigtails hanging, and her body like a bolster in its faded dressing-gown.

Mimi removed the bracelets that broke the mood when she turned the pages. She hadn't heard her own voice for years and was bothered by the bangles' metallic interruptions. She could have gone on reading forever that restful prose; she could go on forever listening to the softness in her voice, the softness she wouldn't have thought herself capable of.

"These people remind me," Gus was saying, "of the Whomevers, do you remember, those English people?"

Mimi smiled and stretched out her legs. "Yes, with their little twin children Forever and Never. We always had them showing up for our plays in those outfits; Never's ugly little stockings, and Mrs. Whomever's huge and horrid hats that Mother and Father couldn't see around."

"Poor Forever in her woolen bloomers in the middle of summer."

"And she was forever wetting her pants, and remember? The Luftenant was allergic to that wet wool smell, so we'd always have to stop the play while Forever changed. And Mrs. Whomever would always say, 'Nevie, I say, don't tease your sister!' But then we'd serve them tea again and Forever would wet." There was no tension in Mimi's legs, or anywhere. *Between the Acts* slid from her lap down her legs to the ankles and onto the floor. "Remember the horse?"

Gus smiled, and her eyes dropped shut and then opened. They'd thought of every excuse there was to cover missed cues and unremembered crucial lines. When there was that

silence and their giggling from the wings, one of their parents
would say "Oh, dear!" and one of the children would come out
and say "Not again!" and call to the others, "Come help with
the Luftenant's horse!" Luftenant Whomever would always
insist on reviewing English history from astride his horse, and
the horse would always try to lie down. Gus said to Mimi,
"The horse that drank tea and ate crumpets."

"Yes, and Mother would say that for a horse, he drank extremely well from a cup. She was generous with the sugar
lumps. Gussie, remember when we did Henry? I was Henry
and you were all of Henry's wives? And you kept complaining,
and I kept explaining, 'But each one's a *queen,* Gussie, look at
it that way!' And Christo loved being the tower guard and
hatchet man. What was it he said?"

" 'Soddy, milady.' "

Mimi laughed quietly at their cleverness. "Each time he had
to lock you up or cut off your head, he said, 'Soddy, milady,' and
you would say, 'I should rawtha think *sew!*' "

"Father said he'd heard the Luftenant complain that the
wives weren't in their proper order, and that we'd killed the
same one twice by accident."

"The Luftenant was always complaining that way, and I
always wished we could have invited just the twins and Mrs.
Whomever. I kept suggesting that I'd heard the Luftenant
had gone to India, but Father always said the Luftenant had
just gotten back and would of course be delighted to come."
Mimi lifted the hair off the back of her neck by way of thinking. She held it in a twist and pulled her elbows around to
rest on each side against the temple. "Come to think of it,"
she said, "I was always avoiding criticism, and Father was always providing it, and somehow I always took personally
whatever remarks the Luftenant made about what was off in
our productions. Remember how I'd cry and say the director

shouldn't have to be responsible for everything? And you would always stick up for me, Gussie."

"I remember. I thought you were so beautiful and talented. I wonder if those sets you painted are still in the attic." Gus tried to picture the attic of the house at the Cape but couldn't remember last being up there. Last summer she had spent most of her time in a chair in the garden reading Woolf, or reading Woolf in the porch hammock or on the beach. She had known she was slipping out to sea and had stared at the lighthouse on the far point, the lighthouse she'd walked to nearly every day of all the other summers.

"I wonder too. I haven't been up to the attic in years. It's odd that neither your kids nor mine were interested in doing plays, and that porch was so perfect."

"Yes, it was."

"Gussie, what did you and Christo talk about?"

"These same things. He reminded me of the time I snuck out to go to that teen-age party when I was only twelve and Mother'd said no."

"I remember," said Mimi, "how mean we were! Mother told us after you said good night with all your clothes on under your bathrobe that you would do it, but we decided not to warn you. It's one of the few times he and I were on the same side, and we laughed all night and listened to the radio."

"When I saw the light was on in my room!"

"You must have been terrified. We were hoping you'd try to climb back up the porch column and in your window the way you left. Did you know that we left you brownies on a plate on the roof?"

"He told me that in the hospital, but the birds must have got them, or the rain. I didn't go onto that roof again for weeks, and I never knew where the plate came from."

"It came from us because we felt guilty hoping you'd try

and sneak back in even though every light in the house was on."

"I went in the front door, and Mother never said a word, just went around turning out the lights with me following her around, up the stairs and into my bedroom, not a word. She closed my door, and I heard her go down the hall to Father. I sat under that organdy canopy on my bed and heard him practically choke with laughter. Next I heard Christo's smothered snorting from across the hall, and next you. You had that cackling laugh then."

"And how was the party?" Mimi's shoulders jiggled, and she put her hand across her mouth and crossed her legs.

"It was terrible." Gus laughed, and then Mimi let it go as if a bird she'd held in her hands, and she cackled her adolescent laugh, the one she'd trained away and replaced with a tinny California laugh. "I love you, Mimi," Gus said before closing her eyes to sleep.

Everyone, but not including Gus and the four-to-twelve nurse, sat at the table to enjoy Daphni's meal, of which there was too much. Daphni asked to have her pronunciation corrected, adding each time that she definitely wished she spoke Greek, and would then translate for Mimi, detailing the ingredients for Jackson and Frieda, and then letting Mère give her anecdotal viewpoint on what it was like to have shopped for whatever it was they ate. Maya said nothing because there was no room for conversation that did not concern, in one way or another, what was on the table, with one brief exception:

"Jackson, do you realize that three weeks ago all this began?"

"All what, Daphni?"

"Of course I mean the head."

"Yeah, I realize it. I'm bringing it finished tomorrow morning." He looked around the table and picked Mimi to speak to. "You know that book? You remember that picture of the pouring?" Again he looked around the table, including them all. "It felt to me when I poured the heads like I was Icarus."

Frieda's disgust showed in her mouth. If Gus's pain made her Icarus, then wasn't Jackson being presumptuous? Daphni asked, "Who's Icarus?" and Frieda wished to spit the food back onto her plate.

"This Greek guy—I'm surprised you don't know—who made wax wings but flew into the sun. I believe he drowned."

"How awful," Daphni interpreted, "did this happen recently?"

Maya hissed, "Boy, are you a jerk!"

"It happens to be an extremely tragic story, Maya! How awful, Jackson, that you were in such danger last weekend!"

"My fault, I should have said it's a legend."

"Oh," said Daphni, with a frantic look to Andreas. "Papa, perhaps you could give us one of your nice toasts?"

"Not tonight, Daphni, but shall we drink to the *garides me saltsa?*" He raised his glass.

"Shrimp in tomato, wine and feta sauce," Daphni told Mimi, and then sat back to welcome their praise, while Mère began telling of the intrigue surrounding the purchase of the cheeses.

Andreas rebuked himself for having let this happen. Jackson should have come for supper, yes of course, but not like this, not to some Byzantine Easter feast that based itself in the belief that it was resurrection day, and let's therefore feast and drink and be merry. He should have better listened to Maya.

"Have some fried squid, Mère; you promised you'd try at least everything! It's very Mediterranean," she confided to Mimi, giving Nicky a little more. "Do you like it, Jackson?" Daphni was a one-person orchestra. "Papa, here's your orzo and, Frieda, would you please pass the retsina to me? Who else wants some wine?"

Andreas excused himself to go and sit with Gus. He told Daphni that he wanted the nurse to have her dinner and that she would take his place at the table. "Be back for dessert, Papa! It's the thing that begins with *b!*" Then, seeming to remember the bargain she hadn't in fact remembered all day, Daphni turned to her sister. "Maya, dear, may I get you more of anything? I'm concerned about how little you're eating."

Gus was awake and said how pleased she was that he'd come. She had so much to say, but it sounded like too much fun in there.

"Too much noise," he assured her, "and Daphni's drunk."

"She's been asking to have Jackson for dinner ever since I came home from the hospital. I only hope he's eating; is he?"

"He's eating."

"Then she probably is drunk from feeding her starving artist hero." Gus laughed shallowly. "Tell me how it went today."

"I couldn't concentrate, but it went well. I." He stopped himself. "I want to bring the cot back in here."

"And I want you to. Maybe you should put Nicky to bed with it there so he'll get to sleep. And then bring it in here." She smiled again, wanly. "I want you here. I feel so content, and everything is working out well, isn't that lucky? Being ready is so restful, it's okay to be weak in energy, isn't that nice?"

Andreas couldn't imagine his father having been so content, if he could imagine his father at all giving in to the weakness of his body and not feeling betrayed until the last possible moment. And of course it was better to be actively content rather than resentful, but still. He might have wished Gus would fight it as she had until this last month, he might have wished to have her resisting it as he himself did. Certainly that would have made him feel better, in a way. "I'm glad it's restful," he replied. "I love you so much."

"I know, and we have been so happy. I feel nothing new will happen now, and that's restful too. I'll simply keep floating and one minute stop, and it's not going to hurt. The pain is over, and everything's finally right again. Andreas, I love you. I only wish I'd always known you." Gus stopped to think. "Would you tell me about meeting the Goose?"

"Which version?"

"The one you told my parents after our wedding." Her eyes brimmed with water but were calm, and Andreas realized the drug's power to deceive. His own eyes brimmed with water and anxiety, and he began:

"The first time I met the Goose I think I asked what her field was and why did she have a man's name on her name tag. We were standing around in the room with the murals painted on the walls, and I said that reminded me of home, also the piano, but then if she wasn't a student, what was she? She said an adviser, and I asked did she mean a peace-keeping force? I don't remember her answer.

"We were drinking a punch that was reddish, and I answered law when she asked what I would be studying. What her reaction was, I don't remember. I don't think she had one. In this fashion we were very boring for a few moments longer, and then she excused herself to ask what another foreign student would be studying. The answer was geology.

"Finally she had asked everyone and was back by me at the punch bowl. Have you long been a peace-keeping force? I asked her. No, she said, that was her first day at it. When she laughed, I think I fell in love, and that's exactly what I said to myself. She was wearing a plum-colored sweater and a gray scarf to match her eyes. Her hair was long down her back in a braid. Only the name tag was a mistake. Was she almost through for the day? I asked. And luckily, she was just leaving. I mean luckily because I invited myself along."

"Do you remember how tired I was?" Gus asked.

Andreas laughed. "Of course. I forgot to say how tired she was from having asked all those questions about how do you like New York and what are you studying and where are you from. And how disappointed that there she had gone to school and everything only to ask where are you from and how are you liking New York. But that's what I liked, that she was so tired and disappointed that she didn't even care if I came along. It was just like home, I told her.

"So I asked if she wanted to go dancing, and she said she loved to dance as a matter of fact and that might be just the thing. She'd had this headache all day but did love to dance. As it happened, I didn't know one step from another, but first things first, meaning wine, and who would care? I was like that a lot then, and do you know what happened? So was she like that about who would care.

"So we went to a very bohemian place in the Village, as of course in those days who hadn't heard of the Village and didn't want to go there for a lot of wine and hanging out. And then uptown again to dance, as who didn't know that it was most un-bohemian to dance instead of just sitting there. So we danced, and I think, frankly, that even Captain Ahab would have been swept off his foot."

"I remember your saying that," Gus said. "You had read *Moby Dick* in order to come to the States. Swept off his foot." The tears were funneled by her cheekbones down the sides of her nose and into her mouth.

"Speaking for myself, I was swept off both. And so was the Goose, isn't that right?"

"Yes." Gus wiped her face with her shawl, a frail motion.

"Then we walked from midtown to the upper west side and kept talking as who wouldn't for sixty blocks up and seven over, not counting the Park, which of course made it dawn nearly. Luckily I said I couldn't walk another inch, and especially not six blocks to my wretched little room at International House, and so the Goose said have a seat. Luckily the only chair in the place was her bed."

"We slept for twenty-five minutes."

"The phone rang?" Andreas had lost a detail.

"The alarm."

"Yes, she had set her alarm, how could I forget?"

Gus smiled again. "The Goose," she muttered, beginning to doze.

"Actually, we called her Mother Goose from then on, didn't we?"

"Yes," Gus said, "we did do that."

"And we lived happily ever after too."

"We did." She opened her eyes a peek and then dropped them down again. Never had she known such rest as there was in the echoes of conversation, in the phrases that hummed her back to sleep. "Mother Goose" hummed over and over and over like bay waves lapping, and never had she felt such calm.

Andreas sat and watched and remembered the part he'd left out: the love they had made after sleeping for twenty-five minutes and shutting off the alarm. Touching the body that was so strong and yet so slim and yet so soft, and the legs that wrapped round like the limberest vine, and the hands that flew like moths and coasted like monarch butterflies. Touching the inside of those thighs where there were muscles under the velvet, the velvet blondness down to the soles and up to the crown and down the spine and around and up the breastbone and out. The breasts not round but ellipsoid and matching, and down the waist and holding the hips and pressing, and turning because she tipped him, wanting to be the fountain from that spout, the amaryllis for that stalk, on top. And diving sideways like a pelican, and him coming up but close in down, his knees finding footing, her hands on his buttocks, her legs like antlers for them both, and. Then, following.

He had never before followed a woman into orgasm, followed to join her in that water she said was fine and come on in, and he had loved following that morning and since. Since! For sixteen years. And the last time had been like virgins fearing it would hurt, though they couldn't have known it would be the last, as if that mattered. How unworthy to leave it as virgins fearing, how unworthy of their love for each other.

"Papa?" Daphni touched his shoulder to raise his face, which she held in her arms when she saw its expression, "I wondered if you wanted dessert," she whispered to him after a minute.

Chapter
Twelve

D r. Derby sat and waited for Daphni to stop her wailing. He then repeated himself to say that nothing was imminent; it was better for her and Maya to go to school. Maya had her coat on and stood in the doorway listening to the rattling of her mother's breath. She finally said, "What you don't know is that Daphni only wants to be here when Jackson arrives with that head he made," which sent Daphni into a rage, out of which she screamed, "Tattletale! You *traitor*, Maya, it *isn't* the reason!" Derby said, "Doctor's orders, Daphni," and folded his arms to punctuate. "What do *you* know," challenged Daphni, then, "I'm sorry, okay, I forgot you're supposed to be the doctor."

"And the baby," Derby suggested, "isn't there somewhere?" And wasn't Nicky the reason there were hospital rules? And for good cause? "I don't expect Augusta will wake up again,"

Derby told Andreas, "but still, you see, neither could I have predicted last night."

Frieda hung up the phone and plucked Nicky from his father's arms. "To the Armsteads', Nic," she said cheerfully.

"Then I'm off," Derby stated flatly, draining his coffee cup, "until this evening."

"Cancel today," Andreas told his secretary over the phone, "but anyone who has to may phone. Me? Tired. I don't think so tomorrow either, so try and get that meeting postponed, or else tell Frank he'll be taking it alone and to call. The doctor doesn't know, she's unconscious. They're doing all right, they went to school. Nothing at the moment, thanks. I will." He shuffled past Mère and Mimi and asked the nurse if she would leave him alone with Gus for a time, and shut the door on her way out please. He sat on the edge of the cot on which he'd barely slept the night before, and though he knew he ought to rest he tried to think of what would be more useful, for instance lighting a fire.

And so he balled newspaper and lit a fire he then worried about in case it was taking too much oxygen from Gus. Perhaps he should ask the nurse, he thought, as if she would know how much oxygen a fire took from a room. But she would be in the kitchen, and the kitchen seemed so far, and so perhaps he had better lie down for a nap.

Two nights without sleep, first Nicky and then Nicky and Gus. The promise the first night had been poor, but not last night: hadn't Gus herself said that she was resting and wouldn't stop resting? And why then had she cried, "Let me go!" and not stopped crying it even after the nurse's shot? Nicky had come in with a nightmare, was it Nicky's fault? He'd cried and screamed to be allowed into bed with his mother. And when Andreas said no he had continued to scream while Gus continued to cry "Let me go!" as if she hadn't known that the screaming was only Nicky's and not her own.

Andreas had run with Nicky into Frieda's room and had violently, incoherently commanded her to cover for his impotence and *do something,* which Frieda had done by taking Nicky to the kitchen, as far from Gus as Nicky could get without falling nine stories. And still, "Let me go!"

Her eyes wild with terror had focused, he thought, but how could he know? The nurse had said no, Gus hadn't known him and certainly wasn't accusing him of wishing her to suffer, but who knew? And now, now Gus had been sent to that last stage of abstraction from pain. She was out for the duration, as the saying went.

The helplessness draped itself over him like a flag in flames, and Andreas lunged from under it. None of this was fair! Only the evening had been fair, when he'd sat and they'd talked and the calm had made them both coherent. Again he sat in the chair by the bed and took her hand to wish for a signal that all was as it had been in the evening, and that all wasn't as it had been in the middle of the night, or that she hadn't known him. The hand said nothing until Andreas kissed it and it twitched a little reflex signal he couldn't honestly believe was telling him what he needed to know. And so he put his head on the bed to wait and realized that only the question about the oxygen was resolved, because he hadn't put a log on the newspaper and kindling and the fire had gone out.

Jackson balanced the bronze on his lap so that the other passengers on the bus would see the face and greet it with other than the disinterested stares for which metropolitans are notorious, but it didn't work. The preview run of fifty-six blocks went not only unacclaimed but unacknowledged, causing no end of hard feeling in the artist who ached to make it with the toughest of audiences right there at street level. Only Joe the doorman appeared to notice, but, since he was an empassioned partisan to the extent that if he'd stayed to grow up in Ireland he'd most surely be an I.R.A. dead instead of an elevator attendant, Jackson dismissed Joe's overflowing praise as not being neutral enough. No matter that Joe knew enough to comment on the good likeness it was or wasn't, what did Joe know? What a stinking lot was the artist's, Jackson told himself whiningly.

Inside, the four of them waited: Andreas at the piano he didn't play, Frieda on the couch next to Mimi, Mère in the wing chair. Gus had been still all the morning hours, so still that her breathing seemed to rattle the window shades and the lampshades, as if she were protesting the light. All they could do was wait.

Mimi answered the door and was pained to see her sister's head in Jackson's arms. She hadn't imagined it life-size and hadn't thought it could be lifelike since, as she had imagined it, it would be black. There was Gus as large and blond as she had been in life, if except for her body having been severed. "Oh my God!" Mimi kneeled to look at the face head-on.

"Can I come in?" Jackson needed to unload the weight, which was causing spasms in his arms, and kept going until he found a surface on which he could rest the head, the piano.

Gus in profile was how Andreas had seen her most, lately, from the chair at the hospital, from his side of the bed, lately from the cot; he had never been aware of her profile so much as lately. *Lately!* "Hello," he said to Jackson, not looking up. "Hello," Jackson answered, shaking Mère's hand as she passed on her way from the wing chair to the piano bench to look at the bronze and to comfort Andreas with something in Greek. "You mind if I sit?" Jackson sat anyway.

He could hear Mimi weeping, and Andreas was sobbing. He guessed they liked it. And if he said so himself, it was the finest yet of his career for both looking like the model and for being—how should he put it—art. But shouldn't Gus have kept up her interest? She'd told him at the beginning that the process was what interested her—Gus in process and not Gus in bronze—but mightn't she have changed her mind? And why had his timing been off, all his life?

He thought he'd see if she was awake and had reconsidered. With Mimi in the living room, perhaps she'd be free to discuss the art part. He'd see, and then he'd bring her the head, and then she'd care. Well? Jackson got up from the chair and walked on tiptoe to the bedroom door.

But her lungs were gourds with dozens of dried seeds being shaken, the rhythm section for a dirge! All the moisture had evaporated, and she was a seed pack, an envelope of tiny hibernating grains, dormant, waiting for planting in freshly turned earth!

Jackson was so parched he thought he would go up in flames in Gus's doorway. It was as if the pain of seeing her cauterized his insides, vaporizing every human juice that might have cooled him. He heaved and cried, but they were dry heaves and there were no tears. And since there was nothing to puke up, Jackson knew he was about to faint. He pushed himself out of the doorway and his weight fell forward toward the wing chair. Air, a breath! Mère caught his arm and brought him around to sit in the chair and, though he knew enough to put his head between his knees, she had to press to keep his seat down and out of his impulse to fall forward into a somersault. Blood to the brain and then a flash of brandy, two, and he had gotten back what passed for consciousness.

Mimi went to the piano and turned the bronze to face the room, then pulled up a frame chair to sit and stare at it. Gus had been so vital and so vitalizing. And Mimi had sapped her. She had sapped Gus, Gus had said so, even if she hadn't meant to. Sap her, she meant. She knew that Gus had meant

to say so. Wasn't it awful how late she was learning everything, and how people had to push her to learn, and how Gus
had wanted to be an ally and not a rival? And how she'd
never had the confidence not to show off by introducing something new, some new young alcoholic usually, some new
trendy therapy, some kinky gimmick for living in the here-
and-now without past or future, a refugee from history and an
escapee from promise, and wasn't it perfectly awful? And
wasn't it awful that she had survived? Look at Gus: about to
say something, about to smile, impatient to smile, determined
to say something (look at those eyes), and about to speak.
Two things were good, Gus said to Mimi: that Gus knew
after all that she was beautiful, and that, after all, Mimi had
survived.

Frieda came up behind Mimi to see what Jackson had
made of it; out of curiosity to see whether the bronze had
hardened the expectant quality she had found intriguing in
the clay version; to see whether it had been possible to leave
Gus looking forward instead of down or up or back; et cetera.
It was certainly handsomely crafted, she noted, not messy the
way Jackson himself was, not loose-limbed but clean and sure,
and he surely seemed to know what he was after in her, in the
clay and in the bronze. The shine was wrong, the waxiness
was inappropriate even if the color was right, and the color
was right. She was very glad he hadn't decided to make Gus
green to evoke that ghostly neon light at the hospital, but
gold to evoke, well, gold. It made it more realistic. None of
which meant anything.

It was simply that everyone kept leaving, as if she were a
check-out counter attendant who got paid to say goodbye to
people. "Enjoy the flight!" Frieda wondered if she would ever
be the one to leave but doubted it, and further doubted she'd
ever have a place to leave for. She'd left, of course; she'd left
Germany and her family to the ovens, only that was called

rescue. And what she meant anyway was not being evacuated and readopted by foreigners, but leaving and having another place to go, the way her ex-husband had when he left her. All she knew was where she didn't belong. Others seemed to have a destination. "Enjoy the flight!"

Mimi took the hand that hung near her own elbow but didn't know what to say. She imagined that Frieda, whom she hardly knew and with whom she had in common only divorce, would be insulted if she spoke. After all, it was Frieda who had been here this last month, and where had she been? Doing what?

Mère came to stand alongside Frieda. "Girls," she said, "isn't she lovely?" She'd always been sorry to miss her son's wedding, but wasn't Gus lovely and weren't they happy from all she could tell, in spite of the fact that it had been shocking. She meant when they married. Andreas's father had been furious, unbelieving as he was in things unplanned, believing as he had that Andreas was going to come home to work for him. Wasn't it a shame he couldn't be there to see how lovely Gus was. Perhaps he might have forgiven Andreas.

The nurse was a Penelope sitting knitting, and this eight-to-four Penelope would be followed by the four-to-twelve, then the twelve-to-eight, so that throughout the day and night there was a Penelope to knit her time away waiting for the end of the waiting. Andreas was the one who called them Penelopes waiting for Odysseus to come home from battle. The only difference was that they didn't unravel their knitting and start again, but this was only because it wasn't taking years. Andreas wondered if he would knit to take up the years before his own death, unraveling one year, knitting the next, until at last they would be together. He didn't know what he would do if he and Gus weren't believers in the soul's immortality.

The next Penelope arrived and the hours were knitted and purled away in the gray-colored inches of the sweater she was

making as her husband's Christmas present. Supper was left-
overs, during which interlude Derby arrived to tell Andreas
he thought Gus might live through the night but couldn't be
certain. He also said he guessed it didn't matter that Nicky had
been returned. He guessed nothing was going to wake Gus
now.

Maya sat on her bed with her back to the wall and opened
Minamata ("The story of the poisoning of a city, and of the
people who choose to carry the burden of courage"). The
cover's glossy blackness was fitting for Eugene Smith since his
subject again, or still, was grief. She had borrowed the book
from the library and had kept it all day in her canvas briefcase until just then, when there would be nothing more to do.
Not the text, only the images interested her:

A fishing town, fishing people, their net, a luminous solitary
fish in it; three boats; a million skittering fish this time; no!
a woman holding a deformed person, a daughter or son, and
bathing it; a woman carrying another child; a hand mangled
somehow into a claw; a pipe letting go whatever it was; a
panorama, sparkly lights, a sort of castle back from the sea.
Maya read the white print on the black foreground, "Minamata: the edge of the factory, the dump-way, the bay, and on
to the sea."

She closed the book and clamped it shut, her fingers very
white against the black, and held her breath. She hadn't
known! But did she dare look now that she did? The breath
let itself go and she was dizzy but kept her grip to keep the
pictures inside. She did dare, but just those same pictures
again:

A shore, thin clouds, a bonnet bending over the net, a
luminous solitary fish; a boat at night, a boat in the day, a
squid fisher; millions of skittering fish. Maya took a breath.
The steam from the bath, four panes of light, a scarf on the
woman, a mangled body across her lap; broad daylight, row-

boats, a print on the person arched away from the woman, the mother; a fuzzy face, a spindle forearm, in focus a double-jointed claw frozen wickedly; a diseased bent pipe, pollution; Minamata at night, the castle off-center.

She closed the book and put it under her bed at first, then on the floor of her closet because the door had a key in it. She ran to open the door to the hall and back to get under the covers but leave the light on all night. As she ran her night-gown caught her at the ankle until she picked it up and jumped onto the blanket, hitting herself in the chin with a bony knee. Under the covers head and all, she pulled her knees to touch her chin on purpose and gripped them as hard as she had gripped the book. But her father wouldn't be in again, he'd already been in to say good night.

It was the bath: she had sat on a little stool and supported her mother's back while Andreas bathed her, not Thanks-giving, more recently. She had held her too-thin mother in her lap and helped to wash her face, and Gus had arched up and frightened Maya with her ribs and her mouth gone slack after the pain. The disease was taking her mother away, and Maya didn't even understand what it was or where it had come from. Did it come from a pipe and was cancer factory waste dumped into the water? Then why had she gone on taking baths and making it worse? And why had nobody said a thing and let her drink the ice water at the hospital? Didn't anyone know? Was Eugene Smith the only one in the world who knew about cancer? And why was it Gus and not another person's mother? If only her father would sit on her bed, but she couldn't even hear his voice.

"Daddy," she moaned, "please, Daddy come, please let Daddy come. Daddy!" she screamed. "Please! Daddy! Come!"

"And now Maya's doing it," Daphni wrote into her journal, "and there goes Papa! I honestly think we all should take something for our nerves, only not me so much except on the occasion today of seeing J's art in the flesh when I flipped out after school. I honestly wonder why we had to go to school today, especially me I mean. What a grouch D (Dirty Derby) can be! Waiting three weeks I mean and then having to go to school and not even having *art* today, or seeing him even, God! Or finding if he really loved the dinner or only said so... hmm. But everyone *loves* the head and me most of all (naturally!). I believe it's the best of his entire career! Lucky us! I hope we leave it on the piano always but you never can tell because of Papa's putting the lid up mostly. Oh well! Because it's here and that's what matters most!"

Daphni closed her pen and turned from her side onto her back to think. Immediately she turned back onto her side. "Today, December 5th, is the most important day of my life. THURSDAY, DECEMBER 5TH! ! ! !"

Back she turned to think: if only there weren't so many people cruising around she could sneak in to look at it in the dark, how Romantic! However, she didn't dare even if she didn't sleep a wink all night, in case, which meant in case Andreas caught her. Already once she'd been afraid, and so had he, that he would hit her. And only because she'd said for only about the fifth time how important the head was to her, adding something about Free Speech when he'd asked her to stop saying that.

"Sorry," she wrote, "to ruin a glowing report like this, but Papa is such a big shot sometimes and hurts my feelings I have to admit. But I'm sorry, Mummy gives me the creeps and I can't help it. And if I want to remember her from *last* Thursday and not *this* Thursday what's wrong with that? Frankly her noises are disgusting and not at all like at Thanksgiving. And since that's only a week ago I don't see what's wrong! God, you wouldn't believe the breathing, ugh, and why nobody minds is beyond me for sure. And those filmy eyes that don't even *focus!* What do they expect? Sometimes I don't think I ought to be a doctor anymore but something more like an artist."

By eleven the consensus was to take an hour's rest. Andreas was afraid to sleep, in case, and yet his two sleepless nights had worn him thin. Mère and Mimi refused to leave, in case, but they all agreed to nap until the next nurse came on, when they'd wake and wait together again. Andreas went to the cot in the bedroom and fell dead asleep, and on Gus rattled. At nearly a quarter to midnight the nurse, convinced as she was that it wasn't going to happen on her shift after all, went to prop open the front door of the apartment so the changing of the guard might take place without doorbell fanfare, and so the two of them could go over the charts in the lighted hall-way instead of the dusk of the patient's room. She took a seat on the needlepoint bench underneath the mirror and listened for the elevator. As far as she knew, she was the only one awake.

But Maya was awake, and Maya knew something more even if she didn't know what to think of it. She was lying on her bed and concentrating on the echo of that rattling she couldn't hear except in her mind. The breath rasped in and rattled out irregularly, and Maya tried to put her own breathing in time with it even though the breaths were spaced too far apart for her. After each rattle out there was a pause, a delib-eration, and then the rasp in and the rattle out, the pause again. In one of those pauses Maya heard what sounded like "soon" but she let it go until in the next she heard it again, "soon," and then the breath again being taken in with effort. She'd waited to hear she hadn't known what, and maybe in-deed it hadn't been anything, but "soon" and then "soon" sent her out of her bed to run past the two nurses in the hall, past Mimi and Frieda asleep in the living room, past Andreas on the cot and next to Gus, whose hand she took and held as Gus did her final dance and rattled out.

Maya called out "Mommy!"; the nurses ran in, checked Gus and their watches, and told each other, "A quarter to." Maya called out "Mommy!" another time and woke Andreas. "She's gone!" Maya gasped. "And I felt it happen! She kind of danced and then she just *left!*"

Andreas got up and, moving as if underwater, went to his side of their bed. He picked up the unencumbered arm and put his wife's hand against his face, staring still at Maya, who went on to say, "I tried to say goodbye from all of us, and it was in time I know! Oh but Daddy!" She ran around to his side and knelt on the mattress next to him. "I should have woken you! I couldn't think! It was all in a rush!"

Maya looked to her father but saw instead her mother's arm, which looked to be what was holding him up, a diagonal support for a billboard. She watched him touch the wrist, the forearm, the elbow, the upper arm, and the shoulder as if going down his blind man's cane to see what it had come up against. For the moment she too was afraid to look at her mother's face.

Andreas brought his hand up the arm and down it again before finally, with one hand on her shoulder and the other holding her hand in place against his face, he looked:

Yes, he saw that she had stopped breathing and that her mouth was slack, neither frowning nor smiling, and that there was that deathly silence where her breath had been. And that her eyes were closed, had been closed most likely by the nurses —they *had* been flung open, hadn't they?—and that the forehead in which he'd seen her calm blue center was enhanced by no other such thing, was just skin on bone. And that her hair fell back from her face in unwashed fingers limp as butcher's string, and that it was grayish. And that there was nothing at all to say about her ears, her jaw, her throat, except for that channel down the middle that dropped into the well that was like a brooch at the center of her collar that was piped in bone. And that the sheet came up to her breastbone so the goat part of her, as she had put it, was undercover, what was left of it.

He replaced the arm and straightened the sleeve of her nightgown, a raglan sleeve to accommodate the other arm that was strapped to the board, and then accidently knelt on the arm as he bent to kiss her on the mouth he made by pressing against her cheeks with his hands. Behind his eyes, a thousand images flickered brightly like silent films, and he saw himself kissing Gus and Gus kissing him until there was so much blood in his head he could no longer see the images. Then he put a hand on either shoulder and Gus bore his weight as hadn't been possible for so long, and he spoke to her, whispering in Greek, every word of which she'd have understood.

Maya sat in silence on her knees and stared at the taped and tubed arm of her mother that jutted out from behind her father. Then the background went white, and she looked up above the crouch of her father to see the nurse stopping the fluid from running into the body. That was all: the nurse stepped silently up and stopped the fluid and then took a silent step back. The light caught the bottle so that Maya could see that nothing dripped into the nipple part at the little mouth of the tube; only what was already in the tube would flow into her mother, as if inadvertently to nourish the cancer cells even after death, which made Gus's body the vehicle for such irony that even Maya got it, Maya who didn't know irony from a hole in the wall until that moment.

Andreas sat back on his knees and put his arms around Maya, who had started to cry from her sorrow at not having wakened him. "Shhh, Maya," he soothed, "it's good you were there." He stroked the hair that went down her back as Gus's had and hoped Maya loved him as much as she had loved her mother. She clung and wrapped her legs around him like a vine seeking nourishment. "I love you," she said to answer his question.

He carried her into the living room and placed her in front of the still-live coals in the fireplace. Then he shook Mimi's arm and spoke her name to rouse her from her sleep on the couch, and then did the same with Frieda, who was slumped against the wing of the wing chair as if she'd been trying to listen to someone's late-night theories about life after death, but instead had slipped off with apologies for not comprehending. Frieda's legs were tucked under but had started slipping out of the coil. Her hands were folded in her lap. "Frieda, wake up," he coaxed. "Mimi? Mimi, wake up." When they did, he told them, and both bounded up as if there were an emergency.

Daphni blinked at the harshness of the bedside light and followed her father into the hall to stand baffled as a sleepwalker who's up but doesn't know where or why. He pivoted her toward the living room and gave her a push off, then turned in the other direction to go to Mère, who had accepted Frieda's bed after declining to spend that night at the Pierre, in case Andreas needed her.

He stopped at the door. No—he didn't want to take the chance of being enfolded in her arms for the first time ever, he wouldn't sit on the bed to wake her. And Greek or French? It would be Greek. He offered her his hand and led her into the living room without having to say anything in any language.

Nicky came out from under the piano and whined, "Paa, pick up Nic," which Andreas did. He then carried Nicky, asleep again, while he turned on every light in the apartment and put two big logs on the living-room fire. And so that was what it felt like, was it? It felt like nothing.

Andreas called Chicago to tell Christopher—to whom he'd last spoken two hours before, as he had several times every day since Thanksgiving—but all he got was their answering service. Did he care to leave a message and have the call returned in the morning? The voice took his name. Oh yes, just a minute, the voice thought that his was one of the names to be put through. Yes, it was, would he please hold on a minute? The call was brief, merely to settle on Saturday at the Cape, with Christopher and Susanna renting a car at the Boston airport and driving down to be there by midafternoon, and then they said good night to each other. Andreas pressed the button down.

But what was the order of business next? He let go of the button and put the receiver down on the table, then shifted Nicky to search in the shirt pocket for the paper on which he'd written the names and numbers to call. Or perhaps he ought to consult with the nurses. It was so suddenly unclear, the order. Was it that the doctor had to be notified, or the hospital? And was it that an ambulance or a hearse would take her to be burned? Without asking the nurses, Andreas dialed the funeral home whose man he'd been to see that week, which man had taken his order for the simplest box the law would allow, the law requiring a box for the transporting to the cremation station.

The man expressed his sorrow and asked if the death was pronounced. Was the death pronounced? Andreas said he didn't know but wondered how someone who lived pronounced could die *un*pronounced. What was the meaning of pronounced? Well, was there anyone in attendance? Yes there was: Maya, age thirteen, Maya Kaligas, thirteen years old. The man asked about medical attendants and if there mightn't be one he might talk to. Nurses, Andreas replied, hold on. "Tell him please that she's dead," he asked the nurse, who did and then passed the phone back to him. No, he hadn't called the doctor yet, he said, but would. No, he hadn't called anyone, only her brother. Yes, there was one thing: they'd be driving to Massachusetts on Saturday and would need the ashes.

He hung up after saying that he'd be up all night and the man could come with the box when he liked and yes, there was a service elevator that was, he guessed, not too small. Yes, someone was on the building all night as far as he knew. After that, he hung up. The nurse who should have been gone was going, and so Andreas said good night and thanked her, shifting Nicky again to free his right hand. He really must put Nicky down soon, he observed, shaking hands with the nurse, who was making sincere remarks about Gus.

"Papa? I wish I was there," Daphni whimpered, clutching his hand.

"We all do, Daphni," he said, and gave her Nicky to hold.

Then he walked to the kitchen and back to the living room, back to the kitchen to touch the north window and back to touch the south window in the living room, and back and forth as if to tag up until whenever the nurse would open the bedroom door and say she'd finished removing the tubes. He had picked the dress: a plum-colored cashmere sweater that went to the floor, his present for their fifteenth anniversary, and Gus had agreed, requesting only that they dress her in only that, no shoes and no underwear, no jewelry, and that they remove the plastic flap and tape shut the hole in her side. Back and forth he stalked, touching the windows.

The nurse appeared and motioned to Frieda that if she and Mimi wanted to finish, it was time. It was Mimi's idea to do the bathing and the dressing, and she had asked Frieda to help with the lifting. Her thought was that what had been missing with her parents was that touching, coming to terms with their empty bodies. There being nothing left was the horror she had to avoid by not being able to avoid the fact of the corpse. And she wanted to take care of her sister the way she hadn't been allowed to for her parents.

The nurse had left Gus in her nightgown but pulled back the covers to show her legs, the thinnest version of the same legs Mimi had. Frieda went for a basin of warm water while Mimi pulled the nightgown down—its neck was wide and Gus's shoulders were no longer fleshed out—past the elbows, past the wrists on her hipbones, over those legs. Gus was a stick figure who looked as if she had died from malnutrition: the limbs were twigs, the belly bloated. They started with her face and with two washcloths went down to her feet. Then they dried her and realized she was cold, so they powdered her quickly and pulled the plum sweater's neck over her head, then the bruised and adhesive-tape-marked arm into the sleeve, which came to the wrist, then the other, and then the skirt to her feet. Frieda lifted her so that Mimi could straighten the bed, but should they put on the bedspread? No, said Frieda. Gus was too long for Frieda to support the head and she hated having to let it hang. Finished, Mimi said. Together they straightened her, then last of all Mimi combed her hair and said to Frieda that Gus reminded her of their mother.

Daphni and Maya held hands with Mère and came in to stand on the bed's near side. Andreas had taken Nicky back and stood at the foot; he jiggled Nicky to wake and look, and Nicky did though only briefly, dropping back to his soggy sleep thinking who knew what. As who knew how long the rest of them stood there wishing their various wishes and thinking their various thoughts? The nurse wasn't there to check the time.

Finally Frieda bent to kiss Gus on both cheeks, took Nicky from Andreas, and left the room followed by the four others, leaving Andreas to shut the door and light the candles in their brass reflectors before lying down. First he lay on his back to look at the light and think what to say, and then on his side. What he said was, "I smell your soap and your powder."

He took her left hand and remembered that she'd said no

jewelry and that, besides, she wanted him to keep her ring. Since her fingers had stiffened some, he felt like a thief removing what had gone on so easily when her fingers weren't stiff with cold and swollen from intravenous feedings. And then what? And then what was it he wanted to say? He got up and paced in concentric arcs while he thought, but what hadn't he already said? And a thousand times and in her presence? And which meant more: his having been awake for her life or for her death?

All he could do was what he had promised, to put his weight on top of her and not just at the shoulders but all down her length. With relief he did this and lay there until his fear of hurting her was gone and his muscles began to relax in spite of the fact that she wasn't breathing. And which meant more, his having been awake for her life or for her death?

When he opened the door, the first person he saw was Dr. Derby. The light in the room bit into his eyes, and he felt a shock of anger and relief at having the doctor there at such an hour. "I'd asked whichever nurse it was to call me," Dr. Derby explained. "I thought I might help and, if you don't mind, I wanted to pay my last respects. As you know, Augusta was an inspiration. I'm so dreadfully sorry." He pulled a handkerchief from his back pocket and passed it across his eyes in a motion that was both rapid and exhausted.

Andreas remembered the evening he had come to talk to them about the little boy who died of burns. "You are welcome here," he said more stiffly than he wished to, "and please"—he gestured behind himself to the bedroom door—"you are welcome here."

"These are sleeping pills; very thoughtful," Frieda told Andreas, putting the plastic bottle on the mantelpiece.

"Instead of a useless prescription we can't fill until tomorrow," Mimi added needlessly. "Are you all right?"

Andreas shrugged. "The children?"

Said Mimi, "Nicky I put to bed, but the girls were folding up and went by themselves. Can you tell them good night in case they're awake? I told them you would, and they want their lights left on."

It still felt like nothing, or like fog, something bleary but substanceless. "I need a drink and so does Derby."

"And so do I," Mère said from her corner.

On his way to get the ice, Andreas stopped to kiss first Daphni and then Maya. Both were arranged in sleep like flowers, their arms graceful arches, petal fingers, the softest near-translucent skin, his children, his loves. How grateful he was that they would grow up having known Gus, and were her flowers too. Still it felt, apart from that, like nothing.

Derby was sitting in front of the fire and took his scotch neat and took it gratefully. "I wish to thank you," he said to Andreas. "It's been difficult for me, as you know. I've never had a patient die at home except by accident. I fear I was difficult for you." This he said as a question.

"Yes," Andreas admitted, "but weren't we all for each other?" He pulled the list from his pocket and tossed it into the fireplace. Were they all going to wait with him for that man and the law-abiding box he'd bring? And yes, he himself had been difficult too, especially for Frieda. He doubted that she'd want to stay on.

"That's life," Mimi said, "and look at your mother. I think I'll walk her back to the hotel and sleep in her extra bed. Do they take Californians at the Pierre? And what about jeans?"

"You must say you are a *vedette,* my dear."

"If they ask me to translate?"

"You say you are a movie star." Mère rose from her chair and shook Derby's hand. "I am going to take one red pill, correct?" She smiled and to Andreas said, *"Bonne nuit, mon petit."*

Andreas and Frieda stood for kisses. As long as they were up, said Derby, he'd run along too, and please, if he could be of help don't hesitate.

"May I ask you not to go to bed?" Andreas was pouring another drink. "I don't want to be alone, not so much when he comes as when he leaves."

"Do you want to talk?" Frieda handed him her empty glass.

"I want to play at first. I don't know what to say. And do you mind if it isn't Scarlatti?" He handed it back, a very strong drink.

"Play whatever you like."

"I want to say one thing: I'm glad you're here."

"Me too," Frieda croaked.

But definitely not Scarlatti, not that traitor. He played a base scale and dissonant treble chords, switched to dissonant base chords and a treble scale. None of that tripping Italian madness, none of that Spanish tiptoeing either, nothing contained in its form or content, something German. He warmed up some more and decided what he was warming up to. Beethoven. Something *German,* one of the best machines made in the world that would run forever on warranty, just a little German masterpiece composed late in life by a deaf musician.

Chapter
Thirteen

T he first light straggled in to cause his watch crystal to glint, winking, as he moved his left hand over the keyboard; it showed up the fingerprints on his glass, empty again, countless times emptied, and made the bronze glimmer only a dim sense of purpose, a faint justification for being not an idol to send out divine rays of celestial light, but a discreet idol, whose purpose was to make the most of an early December morning's pale evidence of day.

Frieda sat in the chair across the room from the piano, her head throbbing with chords that were sometimes warm and sometimes disharmonious, depending on what it was that sent Andreas back to the piano after intermissions. Her glass had likewise been countless times emptied, mostly after the arrival and departure of the man with the long wooden box, who was not used to doing business at that hour, he had explained as if to contradict the fact of his perfecto attire, but who well under-

stood the necessity of not having the remains remain, if they
would excuse his pun at that hour of the morning. The children and all.

"No more playing," said Andreas, covering the keyboard,
shoving off as if a little dinghy from a dock. "One more to
the fact that it's finally day?"

Frieda held out her glass.

His hand was heavy pouring the scotch, and again he asked
himself which meant more, his having been there for her
life or for her death. "I don't know," he said to Frieda, "what
I'll do without her, but here: to the day."

"Nor do I." She took the glass; they clinked. "To the day."
She sighed.

"It will probably be as lonely as it was all the time until
we met, those loneliest years in isolation growing up. Mère
has no idea." He sat with his back against the couch and
stretched his legs in Frieda's direction, nudging her dangling
foot with his. "Do you know what I mean?"

"Was it ten years ago that August when we swam at night?
We were standing with water up to our necks and talking
about not having had families, and how important inclusion
was and having siblings and being one. We agreed to be
siblings for life."

"I know, and how at that Cape house we had the feeling,
or didn't have the fear, rather, of being displaced. Is that the
right word?" He sipped, remembering water warmer than the
air.

"It might not be the English, but it was the word."

"It's the word, of course, it's not having to be displaced
persons, exiles, refugees."

"Orphans."

"Yes."

"Andreas? I want to be siblings for life still. Can we make
another covenant?"

"With scotch up to our necks instead of water." He chuckled at that and at trying to get up off the floor, and at pulling Frieda from her chair to stand next to him as if in the sea. "We'd drown if we were trying to swim." He chuckled, holding her arm to keep her from falling over.

"I haven't been on my feet for hours, a drunken promise, God I'm dizzy, eternal, eternal, I wasn't sure I was so loaded, hang on to me, eternal." Frieda burst into laughter.

"Forget the eternal. Do you agree to be my friend?" He held on with both hands.

"Yes," she roared, "do you me?"

"I do you." He let go in order to hug her, but his letting go lost her balance for her and she fell as she knew she would. He tried to catch her but missed as he knew he would, lost his as he thought he might, and fell squarely on top of her. Frieda laughed her crow call until she thought she'd suffocate. "Help!" she crowed, and rolled him off to laugh on his own section of the floor.

They clutched their aching stomachs and their aching heads while sputtering attempted speech and then convulsing. Cackling recklessly, both were flung by the waves of their laughter, shrieking together at the hilarity of solemnity, thinking that what might give the appearance of vulgar burlesque would in fact make them glad for the rest of their lives, was a moment that would make them smile, remembering.

"And I make a living making contracts."

"Does every one end up on the floor?"

Again they contracted with laughter, hands on stomachs, moaning for relief.

"And I make a living making contracts," Andreas bleated, repeating a third time, "and I make a living making contracts!" He rubbed against the grain of what was a forty-eight-hour beard. "You know, I just had a thought. When they made me a partner, I thought it was normal. I thought I'd been raised to think big, and so it was not surprising they made me a partner so quickly, abnormally quickly in fact. But you know what, Frieda? Even though it was certainly true I was raised to think big, I was raised to feel small. Think big, feel small." He buried his fingers in his hair and massaged for the moment it took until his fingers gave out. "So it was amazing I had that confidence, wasn't it? When you think about it."

"No, not when you think about Gus. Did you ever feel small?"

The water was beginning to boil around his eyes. "I never felt small." It bubbled up and over the rims. "No I never felt small, I never did. I felt powerless sometimes but never small. Gus loved me, didn't she?" All the heat in him vented itself in those hottest tears. "And that's why."

"And that's why for all of us."

The tears that had been so close behind the laughter ran then, at last, from both of them, and their language was again sputtered out. It had taken all the long night of numbness and piano noise for the agony to run over, escaping containers, breaking from cages knotted from wire in the isolation chambers of their childhoods. Frieda spoke in German, Andreas in Greek. There was no need to translate one for the other.

The sun made its way across the room and lit them with a ridiculous cheerfulness, spreading yellow as they wept together and apart in deepest darkest inner space, laying gold on the bodies that crept to separate cushioned places to rest, to pass out.

Too few hours later, Mère and Mimi let themselves in. Only Nicky was up and having a slice of bread on his tricycle. "All sleep," he announced gaily, climbing off and running to take Mère's hand to pull her and Mimi past Frieda and Andreas and into the bedroom. "Maa gone," he pointed out, and shrugged his shoulders merrily.

"Yes," said Mère. She then bravely suggested they change the sheets, which Mimi agreed was a good idea and with which Nicky also agreed. And so they peeled the layers off and layer by layer remade the bed in poppy sheets and pillowcases, the blanket blue as the Aegean. "Pretty," Mimi said wistfully. Nicky echoed, "Pitty."

They were in the kitchen making coffee when Daphni appeared and caught the telephone on its first ring. "Hello? Oh hello, Jackson. But didn't Papa call you? But Mummy's —" She handed the phone to Mimi and exploded into her grandmother's arms. Nicky said with confidence, "Daffy cry," and went on with his little bowl of cereal.

The bakery croissants were no longer warm, but the milk was boiling up in its pan and so Mimi pronounced it time for breakfast. Maya had been setting the table, content with the prospect of Mère's kind of breakfast: flaky croissants and café au lait for everyone, the children included. Then she remembered that no one knew, neither Jenny nor Heather, and went to telephone her friends and tell what had happened in the night. Even coffee would have to wait a moment until they knew.

They debated whether or not to wake Andreas and Frieda, but Mère decided one against three that they should all have breakfast together no matter what kind of night it had been. People would be calling and coming by; they must know their plans. She took herself to rouse the two—the others declined—but then changed her mind. After all, hadn't they had to wait up for the authorities? Anyway, what did it matter, having plans or not having plans? And what did it matter, not knowing them? It was certain that whatever they were, they wouldn't be the least bit familiar, not to mention orthodox. She would try to make the best, as usual, of Andreas.

But by midmorning Mère was once more distressed and emphatically disapproving. As if it hadn't been enough to ask her to adjust to a death at home in front of the children! As if she hadn't tried to be helpful by changing the sheets! She took Mimi aside and hissed that it was a disgrace that her son was sleeping on the couch when there should be callers and something else to talk about besides what was perfectly obvious.

Mimi told her to take two yellow pills and forget about it being disgraceful. If she ever wanted to see a disgrace, go to California, Mimi said blandly.

Mère took the pills and managed to pass the time with Daphni, reading aloud to her in French. Maya tried to play with Nicky but ended up taking him upstairs to the Armsteads', explaining that his pealing good cheer was more than too much to be around, then returning to Mimi in the kitchen to help catch the phone before it had a chance to ring.

Finally Frieda appeared to ask Mimi for a remedy she wouldn't try because it involved yet again more scotch. And finally, Andreas padded in. "Not too bad," he lied. Mimi recommended that he greet his mother with an itinerary, and did he want her to take something down and type it up? And how about: "Whither I goest, thou wilt go" or something like that? Andreas said leave it at "Follow me" but, by the way, what was it that everyone wanted to do? Did anyone want to stay on at the Cape for a couple of days? And what was school looking like?

"School's looking bad," said Maya, "wouldn't it be okay to miss some since we haven't missed any? Besides you know Daphni, Daddy, Daphni wouldn't go to school at all if it wasn't for art. I mean, that is, if she didn't have to. Ask her, she'll even tell you that."

"Mimi?"

There was a silence. "I'd love to stay if you wouldn't mind."

"Frieda?"

Frieda was massaging her temples and answered with a weary smile.

"Majority," Andreas announced. "Will someone tell Mère my itinerary calls for a shower at this time? And an overdose of aspirin, tell her. One more thing: volunteers to go up and open the house." He left the three of them to decide.

In the bedroom, Andreas stared at the bed for long confused minutes. The morning Gus had come home from the hospital he had changed their bed and chosen those poppy sheets. It had looked, that wide bed he wasn't used to, like a meadow, an acre at least of tiny gay red poppy flowers on a grassy background. He'd thought of every one of the islands they'd visited that first spring and could hardly bring himself to put on the top sheet even if, with the blanket in place, the poppies would seem to be growing right to the edge of the sea. That night he would sleep in their bed on those sheets Gus might have wished to die on but hadn't. The cot had been folded up, put away.

By midafternoon the apartment was full of *post obitum* callers, all of whom, to Mère's relief, tried to ease the pain by changing the subject. "How marvelous!" everyone kept saying. "What a perfect likeness! Tell me, how do you go about creating such a bronze? I've always wondered."

Jackson answered at length each time, beginning with, "Well, naturally you've heard of Benvenuto Cellini, the sixteenth-century Italian master sculptor? Yes, well I use the same process he did. I have an authentic foundry in the country, you see, where I'm able to re-create the conditions under which Cellini worked."

"How marvelous! How fascinating!"

"Yes, but it's a most risky business, and we take our life in our hands"—oh dear, wasn't that always the way?—"at the crucial stages of the casting process. But as you have so graciously said"—and he pointed modestly to the bronze that still sat on the piano lid—"success is everything."

Ellen said she envied him.

"Well, it's a craft but it's also an art to deal with defects in the metal. The clay's the same: you're crafting something but also you're an artist and dealing with intangibles, things you have to develop a feel for the way Cellini did, for example. Or Michelangelo in marble. Rodin, perhaps you know Rodin." He was glad to matter, to have an excuse not to leave. And he was glad to be so apparently sociable as to shake the devotion he'd always had to his mother's theory about him, which was that he was a total social incompetent. He was glad he'd taken a shower and found an entire set of clean clothes to put on, he was extremely glad he was doing so well and not feeling embarrassed about the fact that some other people who weren't there thought he was an extravagant flop.

"What I meant is that I envy you for all that time you had with Gus."

"Oh. Well me too. That's the best part about being an artist."

Ellen stroked the smooth bronze cheek. "She must have liked you. I frankly doubt she cared all that much about Cellini." She smiled at Jackson wryly. "Not to hurt your feelings, but did Gus matter to you, art aside?"

Did she matter! Gus was only the first in years to find him funny and charming and smart, who took him seriously and made him feel secure so that he hadn't that need to be bullish, who didn't condescend and screw his weaknesses to the wall, blaming him for her ill fortunes, who was the very most wonderful person he had ever known! "If the head is good," he confided to Ellen and all the room, "it's because of Gus. She meant everything."

"As she did to me," said Ellen.

"As she did to us all," Frieda added, "and now can't we speak of Gus?"

And so the *post obitum* became what it had been designed to be: an expression of loss and an affirmation that life, as always, would go on, even if it wouldn't be life as always.

When the man arrived with the ashes, they were twenty or so eating take-out Chinese food and sitting on the floor remembering Gus. Andreas, his fingers greasy from the spareribs, thanked the man at the door and shut it quickly.

"Bronzette!" He carefully placed the urn in the middle of the floor among the cardboard boxes and plastic packs of soy and duck sauces.

"How marvelous, how fascinating!" Frieda mocked good-naturedly.

"Well, naturally you've heard of Benvenuto Cellini?" Jackson responded. "He was a master at bronzette, a sixteenth-century Italian master to be precise."

"God, curly handles," Mimi groaned, "an athletic trophy! You chose this, Andreas?"

"Yes," he admitted "the other choice looked like something they transport plutonium in."

"But she would love it," encouraged Frieda.

"She told me once that something I had, a dress I think or a necklace made of curlicues, or something terrifically ornate and silly-looking, she called it a rococo bonanza." Mimi cackled the laugh she'd abandoned and rediscovered.

Hi, hi, laughed Jackson. "Rococo bonanza. I love the floralette script on the nameplate."

"And look, Mère, it's Greek key design, three bands of it around the base." Andreas turned to look at his mother, then looked away.

Mère was silent. Chinese food was most distasteful to her, as were those flippant people, beginning with her son, who

again had drunk too much. Where were the snows of yester-
year, *les neiges d'antan?* And she'd tried her best to raise him
to be aware of restraints. She motioned to Daphni and asked
her to bring two more yellow pills and a glass of water. God
knew she'd raised him to be restrained. And she never had
liked America, never trusted it from the day he'd decided to
study law at Columbia. Never liked it at all, too reckless a
country. Better France, she had always said.

Maya sighed. "Daddy, wasn't she wonderful? And aren't we
lucky to have all my pictures? I can get them if you like."

"Would you, Maya? I'll help," Daphni offered, astonishing
Maya and the others. "So? I can be nice too, you know, I really
can be sweet!" She fell into her father's arms. "I *can* be nice,
Papa, can't I? And you love me, don't you?" It didn't even
matter that Jackson was in the audience.

"Very much," Andreas told her many times, thinking how
long it had been since Daphni had asked for help, since he
had been allowed to comfort the child in her.

"Good," she murmured, resting there. "But is it *eight?* My
God!" she exclaimed, untangling herself, "I've got to go
pack!"

Mimi rose to her feet, watching Daphni race off to her
excuses. "Unnerving, family resemblances are. But I honestly
do have to go and pack since Frieda and I are your volunteers
to open the house. We're driving up in a rented Ventura,
whatever that is. Shall I walk you home, Mère?"

"I'd like to do that," Andreas said. "I haven't been outside
for two days."

"*C'est vrai,*" said Mère sadly, attempting kindness, "and
then we must give Grise her little walk. I have a horror of
trust in those dog-walking services even if they promised.
Poor Grise, what a sad little visit she's had!" Mère stood
and straightened the center pleat of her suit skirt, buttoned

the jacket and tugged it into place. She was the only one in the room to have dressed herself in black that day.

"I wouldn't mind that." Sure, he'd walk her little bit of canine fluff around the block on a spangled leash. He'd pretend the contemptible perfumed yapper was a yo-yo.

"*Bonne nuit!*" Mère blew kisses to everyone.

"I'm writing in black as you can see," Daphni wrote in her journal, "because I shouldn't have written in turquoise yesterday only how was I to know? Mummy looked so pretty in that dress you can't imagine, but pale. Papa, too, he's exhausted. I never saw someone dead as you know but believe me it's better than earlier in the day. There's something about how still it is that seems like you will be scared but really you're not. Frieda kissed her and then we all did but very softly speaking for myself. I touched her dress because I just needed to and nobody yelled at me. And her shoulder was under there thank goodness because for a sec I thought maybe she was only her face and her hands and feet on account of that dress. It's just I wish I knew ahead of time to tell a million things to Mummy like Maya did. I wish I had a true friend I could say stuff to also."

Jackson left reluctantly after there was nothing more to clean up and he was the lone outsider, the single loose end. He had wished to say something to the urn but couldn't think what it ought to be, except thanks for everything.

Now where? It was the kind of cold that should have brought snow, but there was nothing. He headed for Fifth Avenue to look at the windows while he decided where to go, to look in on F. A. O. Schwarz, on Gucci, on Bonwit's Christmas windows, which all seemed to pretend the economy wasn't as bad as all that. Silver was the season's color, he noted, from the glittery jackets on the Schwarz all-bear band, to the Gucci buckles, to the tinsely dresses on the bleached Bonwit mannequins, silver was the season's color, preposterously.

Only at Steuben did his spirits rise, because crystal was in every season silvery cool and exotic, especially on black velvet. He thanked Steuben for appearing not to be of the moment, for not pulling out silver velveteen for that evening that might have brought snow but hadn't, when he was needing something reliable, someone crystal cool but reliable.

He stood and stared, and as he examined the crystal figurines poised in the showcase, steady, fixed for infinitude, Jackson found himself longing for the olden coachlike days of the early sixties when an art major and an English major could find happiness in a world that was one big humanities department.

What on earth had happened? He spoke out loud as if telling someone, as if telling Gus. I don't know what happened, he admitted, because all I know is that we were so happy for years and years. All I know is we laughed when she was at Smith and I was at Amherst, and throughout two terms in the Peace Corps, and during most of the year we took to come back from Uganda by way of the world. I mean cheerful laughter, spirited innocence, fun and loving, and I don't get it, I don't get what happened.

A crystal carousel was the showpiece. Magnificent transparent creatures followed one another in silent glittery circles, beasts that were winged but content to skate on the crystal ice of the carousel base in the Steuben window, fanciful animals manufactured out of the collective unconscious. I know we were happy, Jackson told Gus, and yet things began happening, mysteries, bickering, my demanding of Marty the one thing I truly hoped never would happen, ever. "Leave me alone!" I said it as if commanding her to doom me, as if daring her to destroy it all. And she did.

He watched his breath for a moment. Steam, he said, as if Gus wouldn't have known for herself, but was I ridiculous to have hoped? Why would Marty have come back when even

Uganda is irretrievable? Masterminded now by a madman field marshal and his terminally syphilitic buddies, gone, a terrifying joke now, gone, a terrifying joke. And why should Marty have spared me terror and why should she not have played that joke on me? She took me literally that day, but who wouldn't have? Except, and yet, and yet weren't we supposed to be in love with one another?

You know, I honestly didn't know. She said it was the last straw, my saying leave me alone, but Gus, I honestly didn't know. I had no idea I was even close to breaking the camel's back, she'd never said a thing. It was almost as if Marty didn't trust me with information about herself. As if, once those early romantic days and years were gone with the wind, she took a vow of silence.

I wish. He was staring at the fragile balanced world, the magical crystal equilibrium, and wished to shatter it, splinter the beautiful cool control of a molten substance fixed forever. And Max, Gus. Marty took Max away too! If I could have been another person. He put his forehead against the glass and thought that if he were dumb he would try to break Steuben's window. He wished he were dumb enough.

Christ, Gus, I'm sorry, you've got enough problems. It's not as if I didn't know you were an adviser; you've probably got hundreds of people already depending on you. I can figure it out, and there's always Lib. He turned to face Fifth Avenue. And maybe she'll spend the night with me. We could always slither around together and do some stunts. She's almost never without a new technique to try, it's amazing; and it's amazing how she offers each as a child offers a drawing or a flower. She says, "Here, this is for you, how do you like it?" And you know I always love it, but. Well it's funny, Gus, because Lib offers sex as if she were a child but as if sex were the same thing as a flower or a drawing, as if it didn't matter who had given her the paper and the crayon, or as if it weren't important that the flower comes from someone else's garden. As if I don't know or don't care or as if it doesn't matter that what she offers me as a gift was given her by some other child.

But what can I say since I always love it?

He shook the cold from his arms and legs as if indeed it had managed to snow. I'll give it a try, trying's better than not. Who knows that better than you, Gus? I'll try. He walked quickly and avoided more windows, managing a flurry of optimism that lasted long enough to get him through revolving doors of a big hotel, where he asked to be directed to the phone booths and if by chance he could have one of the deskman's Luckies. And by any chance did he have a match? And was it okay to look around and smoke his Lucky in the lobby?

Dreary, dreary! Gus, will you look at these vacant people in their synthetic Friday-night duds and hairdo confections fluffed electrically into Caucasian Afros? What a wilderness! What a dreary, dumpy, small-minded man from the provinces are these men and women! Expelling the delicious smoke, Jackson felt relief for being able only to afford the outskirts neighborhood he lived in, where the cars were dismantled free of charge if you didn't inhabit the block, but where no one had hair spun to look Afro without being black or Puerto Rican in real life.

"It's me," he said into the phone, "and before you say no, let me tell you that Gus's ashes were delivered tonight."

"No to what?"

"To spending the night."

A silence.

Jackson quickly repeated that Gus's ashes had just been delivered.

"I heard you. In what way do you mean?"

"On the couch, only so I can be there in the morning, please, when Max wakes up."

"Okay, you can come over."

"I can? Marty, thanks!"

"You're welcome."

He hung up immediately in order that she not recover and tell him to go to hell instead. I can! he told Gus.

If he brought a bottle of wine perhaps she'd have a little, perhaps remember once having cared. If he brought a nice cheese she might possibly let him talk again. If he took her a pineapple maybe she'd even listen to him tell about Gus. And Max would be there in the morning, his son and the only person in the world—Gus had been the other—who knew how to take his self-pity away.

Chapter
Fourteen

T he station wagon was loaded and Grise had been moderately tranquilized into lying, instead of on Mère's lap, with the suitcases and the urn in the back. Andreas was finding himself content with the seating arrangement and with the fact that they were ready to start on their way for the house at the Cape, even with the way being one gray thruway on to another for nearly five hours.

But by two tolls out, at Greenwich, Andreas began having second and third thoughts. Nicky was insisting that he pay the tolls, obliging Andreas to creep along in the Manual lane. And each toll collector seemed obliged to call "Thank you, sonny!" causing Nicky to squeal delightedly and requiring Andreas each time to pick him off his lap and place him determinedly on the seat between himself and Mère. Worse, it took Nicky many minutes to recover from the exaltation there seemed to be in handing out change. Given the nature of the road, he was therefore constantly agitated either in recovery or in anticipation.

Andreas wondered why they had never gotten one of those hold-tight arrangements, one of those fiberglass capsules into which a child could be strapped tight as an astronaut. He guessed it was because that sort of thing had not yet been invented when Maya and Daphni were little, or else because Nicky'd always sat in the back between the girls, who kept him down where he couldn't see a thing. For this ride Andreas had thought it too great an imposition on them, and believed Mère could do it as well, mistakenly, Mère who had never chaperoned a child in her life.

By Stratford, Andreas feared the car would self-destruct, as a barnful of hay will manufacture its own spark if not properly vented. Nicky paid the Stratford toll and was squealing over the "Thank you, sonny!" when Maya reached over the seat and whacked him on the head. She had hit him in a way that dropped his top teeth onto his bottoms with his tongue in the middle, and blood was coming out of his mouth, Mère anxiously announced over the din of Nicky's hysteria. Andreas pulled the car onto the shoulder and screamed, "All of you! Get out!" He had been right: the station wagon had self-destructed.

"All right! Line up against the car!" he yelled. "And Nicky, you shut up!" Thank God he was truly angry enough so he wouldn't simply burst into tears. "Now all of you listen!" he shrieked. "I've had *enough!*" Never had he heard his own voice so shrill with incompetent rage. "If I hear another peep between here and Hartford, you'll get out and walk! At Hartford you may talk quietly for ten minutes, and you will either keep quiet or keep talking from that point on, depending on what I tell you to do! Nicky will not pay another toll as long as I live! Is that understood? We will make one stop, and you will go to the bathroom whether you have to or not because that will be it!" He caught his breath. Between Maya's and Daphni's heads he could see the bronzette container. "I want you to remember where we are going!" he screamed. "Now, Maya! You will sit in the front! Daphni and Nicky in the back!" Oh Christ, and Mère? "No! Mère in the front! The rest of you in the back! Now get in!"

Miraculously, Nicky went to sleep and missed the Milford and New Haven tolls. Andreas was aware that Maya was sobbing quietly to herself, but other than that there was no peeping, as he had commanded. Before long, they were entering Massachusetts, with no one having taken advantage of the ten-minute chatter allotment. The trouble was, enraged commandments were like lies: you could never keep track of what you had said. He knew he'd said something about the bathroom, but was it that they would or wouldn't be allowed to stop? "Does anyone need a bathroom?" No one answered.

It was only when he was about to get on the Mass Pike at Sturbridge that he realized something was very wrong. He pulled over again and got out to walk. What the hell was he doing on the Mass Pike? He was in the God damn center of God damn Massachusetts! And as any fool knew, you got to the Cape by staying *on* 95 to Providence! He was stalking up and back along the shoulder. Was it the tolls? Was he so anxious to get off the toll road that he'd gone to *Hartford?* And was that why Maya sobbed to herself? What the Jesus Christ was he thinking of! What the God damn Jesus Christ had he been *thinking of!*

He went back to the car, got in, closed the door, and stared at the steering wheel. "I apologize, I'm sorry and I apologize." Mère patted his knee and said, "We understand." Andreas cleared his throat. "No, we're not where we should be, we should be in Providence." Said Mère, "Oh, well I wouldn't know about that."

Andreas twisted in his seat and said to the girls, "I'm very sorry," but they only nodded in silence.

Eventually, because all roads in America are interconnecting, they were on the right road again. But Andreas was in misery: was it fair that as his children bury their mother's ashes they be filled with dread? Was it fair that they dread having lost their mother because of having been thereby cast only on the terrible mercy of their father? Was it fair that they might hate him as they bury her, hate him perhaps for having to bury her, blame him for their mother's death?

They pulled up to the house and Daphni and Maya dove from the car to run in mad circles on the side lawn and disappear down the bank to the water. Andreas had no idea what series of thoughts possessed them as he got sadly from the car and shuffled toward the house. Mimi met him on the porch with a spicy, jarring Bloody Mary. Christopher had called and they were on their way from the airport, she said. And how was the trip?

Surprisingly, his recounting the tale made him feel better not worse, especially when Mimi laughed outright and said that she would love him forever, that she'd thought all along that *she* was the only dope the family had. They'd be friends for life, she said triumphantly, and he would have to learn never minding, as had she, never minding being the family fool because there were other things in life; for instance, she knew how to make a dynamite Bloody Mary, right? And he could learn too.

If it wasn't exactly consolation it functioned as such, and Andreas ran down the bank to the beach, where his girls were skipping stones across the water that went to Nantucket and the rest of the world. "Hey," he called to them, "your father's a dope!"

They fell onto the sand with laughter. *"Dope!"* they shrieked in unison, flying up off the sand to race each other to tackle him, to smother him with kisses and sand.

Since the fall had been warm and many were just then getting their bulbs in, it might not be too late to plant a dogwood tree on December 7th, so the minister had told Andreas over the phone. In any event, he would check with the nursery and buy a dogwood that would bloom white, like the one Gus herself had picked out for her parents only three years earlier, exactly, which was an understatement by one month. Andreas came up from the beach by way of the garden and saw that two holes had been dug, and that a leafless tree stood with its feet in a bag beside the bigger of the two. He hoped Frieda had chosen the spot and guessed she had because it was perfect, just where Gus had sat to read. Strange how the dead had been such readers, Andreas reflected. Gus was distressed not to have finished *Between the Acts,* not to know the ending even if it was hinted that there wouldn't really be an end. She had always wanted to know what then, then what; she had always been so curious to know then what, and *then* what, what *then,* all her life. He felt sure that if anyone did, Gus was at that moment knowing what, then. At that moment she had probably finished all the guidebooks, for she was a relentlessly indefatigable traveler and curious, like her parents, about the remotest outreaches known and unknown. Of all of them, Gus was the one most likely to take advantage of being dead, which led Andreas to wonder if that weren't perhaps why she had, as they say, been taken.

He walked toward the house. The minister's car was in the driveway, and so was another one, Christopher's rental. Perhaps he ought to fetch the urn. Fetch, he sounded the word to himself again. Even he knew the story of Jack and Jill ran up the hill to fetch—and then that Jack fell down and broke his crown and Jill came tumbling after. He raised the hatch and reached for the urn, but Gus simply wasn't in that stupid bronzette lidded mug, they must be crazy, they must be crazy! He leaned against the car and pressed the urn to his chest. What if Jack and Jill went up the hill to fetch a pail of water. And *Jill* fell down and broke her crown and *Jack* came tumbling after? He nearly squeezed his own life into the urn he held, wished only that he could go tumbling after.

They met him on the porch and were right, yes, it would begin to get dark and so yes, perhaps they should, perhaps they must. Around the front of the house they walked and down the other set of porch steps that led to the garden. Perhaps they must. And around they stood, as around the plum-dressed body of Gus, so perhaps they must. The words were stunning (beautiful, striking, dazing) and Andreas was dizzy from leaning into the ground to set the ashes down, how far down. "I am the resurrection and the life, saith the Lord; the God of the spirits of all flesh."

The air was cold but the earth was colder. Andreas felt his hand cramp around the clot of earth he was to put on top of the urn to do his part in the return of earth to earth as ashes to ashes. He remembered Gus's telling him that her hand had cramped around the earth three years earlier, as his had not.

He remembered something else he had meant to listen for in the service, and hadn't, something that had made Gus smile during the identical service for her parents. Then, he had heard it too, and it had made him smile as well. This time he hadn't heard it. Oh how he wished someone else had died.

He watched the others putting their bits of earth around the dogwood's roots, watched Christopher tamping them with his foot and Nicky, in imitation, helping. Who knew what Nicky was getting out of all of this, who could tell? Nicky had no concept of death that he could fit this into, not a goldfish or a guinea pig had died as far as Nicky knew, and flowers, though he'd seen dead flowers, flowers always came back. Andreas guessed he knew now why most families kept pets: it was to raise one's children on dead turtles and goldfish and dogs and cats in the event that when the mother dies, the child can say, "Oh yeah, like Greenie and Goldie and Spot and Whiskers, oh yeah, I get it." Well?

Susanna was the first to weep, then Christopher, who lay his head against the trunk of the adolescent dogwood and wept boyishly. Then Mimi, then Maya, Frieda, Daphni, Mère. Then the minister. Everyone but himself and Nicky. Then Nicky, but why? Then Nicky perhaps in an effort to be as grown up as the others, Nicky who was just a baby who might in his lifetime have other mothers, as Gus had said, but who wouldn't have her and who would only know secondhand what she'd been like and what he'd missed. Then Andreas wept, and finally too the sky, left purple after the sun, the purple sky wept rain on them, not as if for a cold front having leap-frogged a warm front but as if for Gus.

Inside, where Mimi's chili simmered and the fire leapt high up the chimney, Andreas asked the minister for his Common Prayer. Andreas read through the "Burial of the Dead" to look for that place and found it three-quarters through the service: "I heard a voice from heaven, saying unto me, Write, From henceforth blessed are the dead who die in the Lord: even so saith the Spirit; for they rest from their labours."

Gus had smiled at "I heard a voice from Heaven, saying unto me, Write," and Andreas smiled to read it: yes, Write, tell me all the news, tell me how the children are getting along and whether you have a President yet who was worth having voted for, and whether the house at the Cape is still what it was, and whether you miss me, Write, and tell me what I'm missing.

That would be Gus, but the missing was his to the point of his needing to blabber, jabber. Words and sentences jitterbugged in his head, phrases jammed their cacophonous improvisations in his skull of a ballroom spinning with twirling mirrored globes and hung with multicolored streamers. Bits of speech entertained themselves at a dance in his brain.

"I miss her!" he shouted. "We loved each other!" He spread his arms to take them all in but his face was shut with pain. "And why? Is the Age not right? Listen! Can it be that love has no place in the here-and-now of this Modify Age we're living in? Is it possible that love can't *survive?* Is the Age not right or is love not right? Listen! How can love have nothing to say to modifiers?"

Andreas stood, pulled in his arms, opened his eyes, looked over their heads, yelled, "So! Here in the Modify Age we don't believe in big noses, small breasts, or marriage, correct? Incorrect. We believe in big noses fixed to look small, small breasts fixed to look big, and marriage fixed to look like sleeping around. Isn't that brilliant?" He stalked to the fireplace, punched a fist into a palm. "Look, I don't mean to scare you," he said, softly, "but understand this:

"We all know our grammar, we all know what modifiers do to nouns and verbs. Modifiers say: My! how quaint and old-fashioned! let's do have a look! we modifiers have always wondered what it is we modify! and look! the noun is the same as the verb! they're both called love, isn't that cute! let's do a little maypole dance!

"And look," Andreas continued in his gentlest voice, "see the modifiers skipping around and nodding cheerily to each other: My! isn't this fun! we're having a look at a noun and a verb! and isn't it pretty the way our ribbons are wrapping around each other, wrapping right down the pole! but oh dear! now look what we've gone and done! we've wrapped our specimen up in ribbons! our specimen died! now we'll never know what a noun is like or a verb is like! now we'll never get a look at love! oh darn, this is no fun at all, darn it!"

How had the clatter in his head turned itself into a minuet?

Or hadn't it? He cleared his throat. "All I'm trying to say is that I loved Gus, and that it's nonsense to me that millions of terrible marriages manage a loveless subsistence living when ours wasn't even allowed to survive in this world, that's all." But the clatter indeed was gone.

He squatted before the fire and seemed to seesaw the others onto their feet. They appeared to be raising their glasses, saying something, his name. All he knew was that his declaration had made him calm. He touched his forehead as if to verify. Was his blue? Her two had been gray, his two were dark brown. Was everyone's third eye sky-colored, and was sky the color of peace, and was that why the sky was blue? He laughed. When Nicky asked him, as the other two had, could he get away with saying that the sky is blue because it's orderly? He was being embraced, and had been pulled up off the floor, was laughing and being kissed by people who were weeping. But which was it: order, calm, or peace. Or was it love.

The minister gracefully gave the grace: "Bless this food to our use and us to thy service. Bless our dearly loved Gus. Amen." Bless our dearly loved Gus; the murmuring rippled around the table as if the wish were that stone being skipped to Nantucket and the rest of the world. And then they sat for bread and wine and a chili that brought more tears to their eyes, it was so hot.

"Mimi, is this Californian?"

"Mexican."

"Spicy. Do even their children eat it? I mean, is it okay for Nic?" Daphni blew on a spoonful.

"You know what? I forgot my camera!"

"It's okay, Maya, I realized in the car that I'd forgotten my diary, if you could believe that either. Mimi, is it?"

"Try."

Daphni blew again and stuck the stone-cold tiny spoonful of chili into Nicky's mouth. "I know just what you mean"— she nodded to Maya— "you like it, Nic? I think he does." She gave him the spoon. "How nice to have another gourmet in the family. I mean a good sport. I think I'm going to switch from food to athletics soon, I can feel it coming. I'd rather admire a good sport any day." She looked around the table to make sure it was safe. "And I wouldn't mind being a good sport either."

Susanna wished Gus could see that now when they sat together they made a family, that there had been progress since Thanksgiving, or rather that they'd recovered the ease of years ago before they had gone their separate ways. She wished they might have responded to Gus at the Thanksgiving table the way they had Andreas just then. She felt sorry for Mère, who knew nothing, got none of the inside jokes, wasn't lucky enough to have been a part of it. It? The past reverberated as a piece. The little movements from roommate to old friend to sister-in-law were as variations on a theme.

Mimi felt it when she walked into the house and saw the photograph on the mantel: three blond smiling kids in swimsuits. And the one of their parents in cotton clothes, also from the forties, another summer picture in which the wind blows their hair back from the faces that squint and grin into the sun. She had come from somewhere, she realized. All the years of undoing, remaking, dismantling, constructing, collapsing, running and hiding; and all that time she had a history. She'd had a root system all that time.

"Mimi, do you remember the night Gus sneaked out? We listened to the radio in my room."

"She never found the brownies we left on the porch roof. Remember? And Christo, you let me spin the globe that night for the first time. Do you have it still?"

"I do; I can't seem to get a new one even though all the boundaries have changed. I told you that night my deepest secret and made you swear that you wouldn't tell them."

"That you were going to be an explorer?"

"Did you?"

"Yes. I promised myself I wouldn't, but I told them the very next day when you didn't let me fish with you. Did you tell them what I told you, Christo?"

"Yes, the next day."

"Don't you wonder what they thought about having three kids who were going to be an explorer, an actress, and a jail-bird when they grew up?"

Andreas had been going to be a pilot most of the time. Or was it a pirate?

Frieda began to clear the dishes, glad for the lemon sherbet she had bought for dessert while Mimi was plotting to fire-bomb their digestive tracts. It was funny that she'd always known she would be a dentist. But no, it wasn't. She'd stood in the hallway all these times to overhear her foster parents whispering about the war and saying to each other the things the child mustn't hear. "They're extracting the gold from the teeth of the Jews!" She'd barely heard it. "Put it back!" She remembered the horrifying pressure in her chest, and the fierce voice in her, the outrage of a terrified innocent jailed mistakenly, screaming, but unendurably silently screaming at them, "Put it back!"

The minister excused himself and said he would love to join them for a walk if it weren't for the sermon he must write for the morning. He then asked Andreas if he mightn't tell the congregation about the maypole ribbons doing in the major parts of speech and doing away with love, if Andreas would let his sermon be used for another. Andreas said he would be there to hear what it was he had said, and with pleasure. And thank you for marrying us, he wanted to add to goodbye, good night.

The rain had stopped but had packed down the sand to make it an easier night walk than it might have been, and the moon was so full one could see one's own hangnails. Andreas carried Nicky; it had been so important to walk all together that even the poor and nonwalkers had been dragged along, the limp, the faint, those with heartburn and heartache.

"It's very cold," Maya understated.

"Not easy to balance," Mère explained timidly.

"Creepy," Daphni offered.

"Nonsense," chirped Susanna, "I could do open-heart surgery with this much light."

"Look at our breath, how pretty," suggested Maya.

"And see how our footsteps look in this light!" Daphni exclaimed.

"How flat the sand is after all," observed Mère.

"See the lighthouse," Christopher said.

"Yes," they all agreed, "yes, see the light."

"I feel I'm walking the deck of a ship," Frieda told them, "coming into a harbor."

"You wouldn't think the light would be visible on the water in this much moon." Andreas shifted Nicky in order to put a cold hand into a pocket.

"You wouldn't, would you," Christopher echoed.

"Let's turn around."

"Let's look at the garden to see how the tree looks."

"And if it got enough rainwater."

They walked more quickly back toward the house, and in silence because they walked into the wind.

"See what a nice thing the moon is doing," Daphni said gently. She turned to the others. "You see how the moon is making the tree have a shadow that lets its branches cover where we put the ashes? A blanket of branches to keep her warm this first cold night."

"Or," Maya suggested, "also like antlers as if a deer was warming the place with her body tonight."

"With his body," Christopher softly said.

"I'm glad we'll be staying for a few days to take care of Mummy."

"It's cold to be out alone at night, Daddy, is she all right?"

"The blanket, the deer," Andreas said quietly.

"And the moon."

"The lighthouse too."

"The loss," Andreas murmured.

"The loss."

They stood in silence to feel the tears, and a cloud left over from the rain dimmed the moon for a moment. Solemn, sentimental, they stood to express their loss in tears that stung, and to say good night to their dearly loved Gus. Then they made their way up the porch steps and around the front of the house. It was good the day was ending sentimentally. There were worse things than sentimentality at such a time: for instance, unsentimentality.

And anyway, as they all stood under the porch light for another look at the water and the lighthouse, Nicky woke up. From his father's chest, in his father's arms, he raised his head and looked into the face of Andreas. Then he put a finger in the sentimental tears that streamed as freely as if poured from a pitcher.

"Juice," said Nicky.